When Chris's stepfather passes away and leaves Chris a house and a wedding ring, it seems like the perfect opportunity to take the next step in his relationship with John.

So, they're both in for a nasty shock when Chris's mother is vehemently opposed to the idea. Despite three years of history to prove otherwise, she insists that John is only a temporary feature in Chris's life, and a man like him can't be expected to stay with someone like Chris in the long run.

Can Chris persuade her that she's wrong in time for the wedding—or will there be an empty space in the photographs?

COFFEE

A Cup of John, Book Two

Matthew J. Metzger

A NineStar Press Publication

Published by NineStar Press
P.O. Box 91792,
Albuquerque, New Mexico, 87199 USA.
www.ninestarpress.com

Coffee

Printed in the USA
First Edition
August, 2019

Print ISBN: 978-1-951057-27-5

Also available in eBook, ISBN: 978-1-951057-26-8

Warning: This book contains sexually explicit content, which may only be suitable for mature readers.

For Laura, with my apologies for making you wait
so long!

Chapter One

RATHER APPROPRIATELY FOR the occasion, it had been raining all day.

Chris took in a deep lungful of smoke and exhaled it smoothly into the chilly afternoon. The memorial garden was blissful after the hustle and bustle of the funeral. The air was open and soothingly cool, not like the stuffy heat of the chapel. He could breathe again. He could gather the shards of grief around himself and try to put them back together, without having to think about his mother's sobbing at his side, or the favourite song that had been played for Jack's last journey, a song now stained with sadness.

The gentle patter of raindrops on the umbrella calmed him, and the far-off chirping of some irate bird provided a gentle counterpoint. Life slowed. From farther off, the chattering of friends and relations had finally died away, and Chris stubbed out the remains of the cigarette as he heard the crunch of gravel.

He'd never been here before, but the footsteps coming down the path were as familiar as his own. Thunderously heavy, an immense weight crushing each step into the ground even as the pace was slow and steady. That slight stress on one step, followed by lightness on the other. That dodgy knee from the rugby accident last year had left its mark in the form of a subtle limp and a tiny scar like a fish hook that made its owner go all shivery when Chris kissed it. Even the speed with which each step followed the other was familiar, like the tower of a body might collapse if the feet were spread too far apart. The hands that clasped Chris's shoulders were as big as spades, and only one person in his life was tall enough to kiss the crown of his head without the use of a box to stand on.

Chris leaned back into the wall of a man who had arrived and lifted the umbrella to let him into the shelter.

"Your mum's gone home with Lauren."

The relief was bittersweet. Mum and Lauren had always gotten along, despite one being Dad's ex-wife and one being Dad's girlfriend. Lauren would look after her—even if it was Chris's job. Even if he was supposed to.

"You did great."

Chris swallowed thickly. "I think it's just sunk in."

It hadn't been real. It had taken so long that it had never quite felt real until this moment.

Jack had died a long, slow, terrible death. Weeks in the hospice. Chris would never forget the gargling way his stepfather had breathed near the end, or the clammy coolness of his skin. The way Mum had cried, soft little sniffles at the corner of the bed on that final day. The gaps between the gurgles, until finally there had been nothing but the eeriest silence. The shaking in his fingertips was over.

Everything was over. The smell of cigar smoke on the tenth of March, the one day of the year Jack lit up. The shuffle of his slippers. The whirr of that deathtrap of a stairlift. The croaking way he'd chuckled, a noise that in a bigger man would have been a belly laugh. The little huff he let out when Mum was in one of her moods, followed up hastily with "*Yes*, dear, of course..." And Chris had never seen it, but he'd known Jack had flashed him little smirks across the table at such moments, conspiratorial understandings between the two men who were most subject to her fussing and flapping, the two men who loved her most. Gone.

"Jack's *gone*."

"I know." The words were soft but firm. The hands on his shoulders rubbed down to his elbows and then back up in a long, smooth stroke. "But so is the pain and the suffering. He's not hurting anymore. And if he was right, then he gets to see his daughter again now."

Chris coughed a shaky laugh. It bubbled out of his ribs like water overflowing. "No such thing as heaven."

"You never know."

Chris sighed and leaned his head back. He closed his eyes and hummed as a kiss was pressed into his temple.

"I should go and see Mum," he said.

But his chest ached. His ribs felt like they were going to cave in, and a red-hot pain followed the scar, as if he'd been wrapped in metal wire, melting against his skin. He *hurt*.

"I want to go home."

The hands pulled. He was turned by the shoulders and drawn into a rain-damp embrace. The arms around his back made the pain worse, but Chris clung and burrowed into the embrace anyway. The kiss on the top of his head slotted two of the jagged edges together and sealed them shut again. The grief ebbed a fraction.

"Come on, then. Let's go home."

"COFFEE?"

"Please."

They'd met over a cup of coffee. Chris had been minding his own business in one of his favourite coffee shops, and along had come this big clumsy oaf and knocked his mug flying. For a split second, Chris had been angry—then the oaf had talked.

He was called John.

And John had a *voice*.

John's voice reminded Chris of swallowing whisky—desert-hot, followed by a deep warmth radiating from the inside and felt in every fibre of the body. Like melting dark chocolate in the mouth on a cold winter's day: smooth, gentle, indefinably rich. He never said anything. He drawled, grumbled, rumbled, growled, snarled, creaked, croaked, coughed, snorted, sniggered, and chuckled, but he never just *said* anything. They'd do the exact same thing in bed, but it became a searingly hot fuck if John growled, or a tantalisingly sweet worship if John whispered. Chris had fallen in love with his voice from the first word, and it was pure dumb luck that the man attached to said voice was just as good.

Chris accepted the cup of coffee, but the heat that soaked into his bones came from John settling down on the sofa next to him, sliding an arm around his waist, and asking what he wanted to watch on the telly.

"Nothing," Chris said. "I don't really feel like doing anything."

"You want to talk about it?"

"The funeral?"

"Or Jack. Or anything, really."

Chris swallowed thickly. "I don't know."

Jack's death had been years in the making. He'd met Chris's mum when Chris was in his teens and he was diagnosed not even a year later. Parkinson's disease. The early stuff wasn't too bad—the stiffness, the shuffling, the shaking. Jack hadn't minded those. "You get old," he'd said. "It's not too different. I'm just getting old, young." But Parkinson's, a brain disease, like Alzheimer's and Huntington's, had eaten away at his head, and if the physical symptoms had taken years to come to a crescendo, the mental ones had taken a bitterly short two years.

In a matter of two years, he'd gone from Chris's affable, elderly stepfather to a ruin. He'd walk into the road at three in the morning, sobbing like a child and crying for his granny. He forgot how to eat. He rang the police a hundred times, swearing blind that Mum was trying to poison him with his medication. Then he forgot how to use a phone, how to talk, how to move. The gentle soul had been torn out and replaced by a man who swore at the nurses who came to help, and slapped Mum for trying to get him to drink a cup of tea.

"I'm glad he's dead," Chris breathed.

There it was. The ugly, awful truth. He was *glad*. He'd been there, holding Jack's hand, and when the silence stretched out and they realised he was finally gone, the only thing Chris had felt was relief. A heartbreakingly awful relief.

"So am I."

He jolted at the words.

"He was suffering," John explained. "Remember last summer, when he still knew it was happening, and he'd just sit and cry for hours that he was losing his mind?"

"Yeah."

"That was—I liked Jack. I wouldn't wish that kind of suffering on my worst enemy, and it was bloody awful watching it happen to someone like Jack."

Chris leaned his cheek against John's shoulder. The guilt eased a fraction.

"In my head, he's been dead for years," he breathed. "He died the summer Mum had to get the social to come and help her get him up in the mornings. I—I think he died then. He just wasn't Jack after that."

"Yeah."

John's soft agreement dissolved into the room. For a long moment, there was only stillness. Poppy's soft weight on Chris's socked feet. John's breathing next to his arm. The steam rising from the coffee cup and stroking Chris's nose. The heat pouring from the gas fireplace, crackling in an attempt to feel real but sounding—to Chris anyway—exactly like every other fake fireplace in the world.

"I'll go and see Mum tomorrow," he whispered.

"She mentioned seeing the solicitor and starting the inheritance process," John remarked. "You know your mum. Ever practical. Do you want to go with her?"

"I don't know. Maybe."

"She, um. She gave me something for you. A letter."

Chris frowned, lowering the cup to his lap. "A letter?"

"Yeah. Apparently, Jack wrote you a letter when he was diagnosed."

A savage lump swelled in Chris's throat. Oh dear God. A letter from Jack. From his diagnosis? That was over ten years ago.

"We can leave—"

"No," Chris whispered. "I—I want to hear it."

There was a long pause, and then John kissed the side of his head and got up from the sofa. Chris took the opportunity to move. The flat was small, the ground floor of a converted house, and perpetually chilly. But he'd turned their bedroom into a den of hedonism, the carpet so thick he took off his socks and buried his naked toes in the fuzz for a long, luxurious moment before stripping and heading for the bed. He was exhausted, hurting, and bound to start crying again. To hell with nightly rituals and dinner. He wanted to go to *bed*.

Poppy, sensing his upset, jumped up onto the end and settled across his legs. Her heavy weight a comfort, he sat up to pet her until John came through. The bed sagged under his immense weight, and Chris rolled into his side to settle against his chest and listen to the gentle beating of his heart.

"Okay?"

"Yeah," he whispered.

The letter was in an envelope. Chris listened to John tearing it open in little tugs, and the crinkle of paper sounded thick. Chris touched the edges—the fancy stuff from the writing desk in the living room, the one Jack had barely touched ever since his hands had started shaking. The desk had gathered dust and ornaments, and now would likely be consigned to the dump or the loft.

"*Dear Chris,*" John read and swallowed. "Erm. Sorry. The handwriting's not so great, so I might struggle a bit."

"That's okay."

"*Yesterday I was diagnosed with Parkinson's disease. I know from both my mother and my late sister what this means for me. I estimate I only have a handful of years before I die, then a handful more before—what's this? Oh—before my body catches up to the fact. I won't burden you with my feelings on the matter because I know you and I have this in common. But it would destroy your mother if I were to take that path, so I will face this, and hope death is not too drawn-out an affair.*"

A lump swelled in Chris's throat. Death had been drawn-out. Death had been long, slow, and viciously cruel. Their worst nightmare.

"What does he mean?" John asked gently.

Chris sniffed. "I—I told Mum and Jack once that if I got another brain injury, and I wasn't going to recover, then I'd rather be dead. I'd rather just die than waste away unable to think or only move my eyeballs or something. If—if I wasn't able to live my life, then—then it wouldn't be worth it. That's what he means. He—he said Parkinson's and dementia were like the brain died, and the body was taking a while to catch up."

John breathed out through his teeth, the shrill whistle piercing in the quiet warmth of the room. They'd talked about it before. John didn't like it, and Chris knew he didn't like it, but it was what it was. Chris believed life was only worth it if you could live it. John believed life was *always* worth it. They had long since agreed to disagree and didn't talk about it much.

"I have written a will, but they are terribly impersonal pieces of paper, so I am writing this as well. I have never tried to be anything but a friend to you. You have always had an excellent and capable father of your own and didn't need my clumsy meddling to complicate matters. You have a wonderful mother who has always done what she feels best for you and could handle you even at your teenaged worst without my assistance. I never felt you needed me—and yet, for all that, I have considered you as a son from the day I met you."

Chris's eyes were hot. He could feel the weight of the tears on his eyelashes.

"I was as proud as any father the day you passed your exams. I worried as much as your mother with every medication change. I, too, was permanently torn

between encouraging you to seize every opportunity and never let yourself lead anything but a normal life, and fretting you would come to harm in your adventures beyond the familial nest and would be safer with us than without— Your stepfather wasn't half posh," John complained.

Chris laughed. The tears spilled over. He nestled into John's side and wiped at his eyes with the heel of his hand.

"He loved reading. Loved learning. Education. That's why I went to sixth form college—he insisted. The only time he was ever angry with me was when I refused to go to university."

John hummed. "That's the first page. He's got rid of the next one; he's started again, I think."

"Just read the new one, then."

"Dear Chris. Things have changed, and so must this. Yesterday, you brought a wonderful young man to dinner, and your mother's worst fears came true. You have fallen in love with someone entirely suitable, and your life will take on new dimensions inaccessible to the dusty old roads your parents have trodden."

"Oh God, he wrote this the day after he met you?" Chris croaked.

John hummed but didn't answer. He just kept reading.

"Much has changed from when I wrote my original letter. You have spread your wings. You have gone into the world on your own, and your independent streak is now felled by the arrival of—by the look on your face and the way you speak of him—the man who opens the next chapter of your story. Forgive me for mixing metaphors, but the facts are quite plain. You love him, and he loves you, and it's not quite how it was done in my day, but that is all for the better, I think.

"Your mother is filled with dread over the whole affair, but I take a perfectly different view. My life was changed when I met Sarah, when we had our daughter, and when I lost them both. I thought I would never recover. All the sound had gone from the world, and I moved through it paralysed from the mind down.

"But love was not gone. My paralysis was because I still loved, and they were no longer here to receive it. To this day, I still love Sarah. I still love Rachel. That will stop only when my heart does, for even as this illness is starting to sap my memories, and I can no longer remember the sound of Sarah's voice, or if Rachel was six or seven when I lost her, I still feel that warmth and aching in my chest when their names are uttered. I still remember someone by that name was here once, and my world was all the richer for it.

"When I met your mother, the sound crept back into the world. Her (terrible) singing of a morning. Your dulcet tones as you tried every day to argue your way out of going to school. Christmases roaring with laughter at the black-and-white films on the TV, and your mother's fury when you came home with blue hair—
You dyed your hair blue?"

"Gina did."

"You totally went along with it, though."

Chris shrugged. "To be honest, I didn't really understand the big deal. Blue, black—what's the difference?"

John snorted with laughter, then carried on.

"—just in time for Hanukkah when you were eighteen years old. (I don't think she ever quite forgave your young friend Gina for that one.)

"Love transformed me once more. I was reborn. I have lived a second life here, with my wife and son. You may not have needed another father, but you are my son as much as Rachel is my daughter, and I have watched you transform in the years I have known you and have been immensely proud and privileged to be here to see it.

"You transformed when you came to love yourself and shed the weight holding you down, and if ever I said or did anything to make you doubt me in those difficult times, then I can only offer my final apologies here. And now you have begun a new transformation and a new chapter in your story. John is a plain, simple man, and you are clearly the sound in his world already. I'm no fortune teller, and you are stubborn as a mule, so who knows? But I would not be at all surprised if when the time comes, it is John reading this letter to you, and you are quite a different man from the one to whom I was writing it."

Chris buried his face in both hands and bawled. It hurt. The emotion tore through his heart and lungs and left ribboned shreds behind. His throat burned, and everything collapsed inwards into a jagged mess, bracketed by the low croon of John's voice, the weight of his arm, the nudge of a damp nose against his elbow, and the thump of a tail beating on his knees. Chris dissolved into pieces, wrapped in the duvet and caught between the hulk and the dog, and let it all happen. What harm would it do? He could come apart all he wanted, and they would stitch him back together.

The crying jag took a long while to ease. When he recovered himself enough to blow his nose into the offered tissue and soothe Poppy's whining, the jagged edges inside were smoother. Jack was gone, but it had been a good life. Jack was gone, but so were the pain and the suffering. Jack was gone, but he was still here. His letters and Chris's memories and the wedding video Chris had put on DVD for Mum last year so she could watch it after the VCR finally bit the dust.

Jack was gone, but only in the sense that he wouldn't come shuffling through the door complaining about the prices in bookshops these days.

"You okay?" John whispered.

"Yeah." It hurt to talk. "Is that it?"

"No."

"The rest, please."

John kissed his forehead and smoothed down his curly hair once more before shifting slightly. Paper crinkled, and his deep, soothing voice started up once more.

"You may be different now, but I imagine some things are the same. You still have your mother's sense, but your father's sense of adventure. You have your irrepressible humour, and, of course, that stubborn streak that has seen you through so much. Perhaps your temper has mellowed with time, age, and happiness—or perhaps you are still explosive. But there is one thing of which I am absolutely certain. You are still loved, completely and utterly, by a great many people. And I assure you they also know, perfectly well, you love them in return.

"You would likely scold me for being overemotional now, and Lord forbid I've made you cry, so I will get down to the practicalities of the thing. I have a will, and your mother knows where it is and its contents. We agreed on it all. I have made arrangements for her to receive my pension and my savings prior to my passing,

in case this disease drags itself out. She will not be in need, and even if she is, I know you will look after her. All I ask is you make the time for her after I am gone. She is spending more and more of her time at home with me, and less with her friends. She will be lonely, and I know the pain of being the one who is left behind. It is a terrible time, and she will need you.

"*But I also leave something to you, in light of this new part of your life. Two things, to be precise. The first is my wedding ring. It is the same one I wore for Sarah and the one I wear for your mother now. It has seen me through the best and worst moments of my life. May it see you through the same and serve as a reminder that no matter what happens, love remains.*"

Chris's heart tightened into an impenetrable ball of rock inside his chest, the pain nothing short of cardiac arrest. It *hurt.*

"*The other is my old home. By the time my mother passed, my dear sister was already very unwell, and so I inherited the house.*"

Chris choked. John stopped dead, and slammed him in the back. Pain exploded over his chest, but it opened up his startled airway again, and he sucked in a shocked breath.

"He's left me the house?!"

"What house?"

"I don't know! You're reading it. Mum owns the house; he can't have left me the house."

John paused, then hummed. "I think he means a different house. He talked about his mum and his sister. Did they live with Ruth?"

"No. They were both in a care home, I think. I don't know; they died years and years ago."

"Maybe he means their house? Hang on, I'll keep going."

Paper rustled once more.

"I still own it. It is a ruin, but I could not bear to part with it. It has been in the family since 1910, when my grandfather bought it with the wages he had painstakingly saved from years in the factory. He bought it to persuade my eminently sensible grandmother he was a good man to marry, and it has been with us ever since. My mother was born, lived, and died in that house. I myself have years of fading but fond memories in its walls and garden. And now I leave it to you and ask you return love to its lonely walls. Be that crafting it into a home for you and John and any future generations you care to gift us with, or be that returning it to its former glory and selling it to some deserving family who will breathe life back into it."

Chris sat up awkwardly, trying to take the pressure off his wound. It ached, but it faded into a dull throbbing under the confusion whirling in his head.

"I didn't even know Jack owned a house," he said stupidly. "Does he say anything else?"

"I dearly hope to have many more years with you and your mother, and to be in a fit state to see you become ever better, but in the event I am not, I know you will be fine. I have been infinitely blessed to be a part of your mother's life and a part of yours.

"Indulge a slowly dying man to impart one last piece of wisdom. Dance. It's good for your heart, good for your soul, and good for your mind. Your loving father, Jack."

"Dance," Chris echoed feebly and laughed a little. "Bloody Jack."

"Well, you dance plenty. Always sashaying around the kitchen, you are."

"Like you can talk, Mr Hug-And-Sway," Chris mumbled, scrubbing at his eyes. He held out his hands and took the letter, rubbing the paper between finger and thumb as if trying to absorb the words. "We need to put this somewhere safe."

"Think we need to go to the solicitor with your mum tomorrow too."

"Why?"

"Well, you've got a house," John replied. "I think maybe we need to figure out what to do with that."

Chris bit his lip but said nothing.

He already had a bit of an idea—but he didn't know if it was going to work.

Chapter Two

CHRIS SLEPT IN late.

He woke up bathed in the telltale warmth of sunlight pouring in through the bedroom window. It was only February, and it would be cold as balls outside, but the sun had some poke in it for the first time in months. He stretched and fumbled for his phone. Gina and Luke had both texted him, and he sent one to Mum asking when she was going to the lawyer's office before sliding out of bed and going to find some coffee.

Thankfully, John was well-trained. He was singing in the shower, but there was a full, fresh pot in the machine. Chris blissfully had a second cup to wash down his pills, then fed Poppy and shoved some bread in the toaster even though he wasn't hungry. No dinner *and* no breakfast was practically laying out the welcome mat for his epilepsy to have a house party in his brain, and he *really* wasn't up for a seizure right now.

"Hug?" he asked when Poppy was done eating and slid down the cabinets to sit on the floor and hug her. She settled her head on his shoulder patiently and let him bury his face in her fur until the toaster popped. "Thank you. Treat?"

She was still young enough to snaffle the treat like a regular dog, and then he draped his toast in a sickeningly deep layer of honey and sat at the little table to eat it. To hell with his diet and whether he'd made a mess.

He felt better than he had yesterday, though. The aftermath of a funeral was a strange limbo, an odd anticlimax. Life moved on, even though it shouldn't. Things were irritatingly normal, even when it seemed like things ought to have changed forever. This was just another morning, listening to John's voice rumbling away in the next room as he dried himself, and shouting, "You put that towel in the wash basket!" when he heard it being hooked over the radiator.

"It's clean!"

"You've dried your arse with it, put it in the basket!" Chris shouted back, and then the door cracked open, and the loud *fwhump* of a towel hitting the basket—then tipping it over—was music to his ears. "Poppy, leave it."

She whined but stayed where she was. She was trained to help him with household chores, as he'd been living alone when they'd started teaching her. John still fought to be allowed to leave his slippers in the bedroom. They kept magically relocating to the rack by the front door.

"Feeling better?" John asked, kissing the top of Chris's head in passing. "That's not enough. Bacon sandwich?"

"Not kosher."

"Since when did you give a damn what's kosher? Since when did you even *know* what's kosher?"

"Excuse me, I know the rules!"

"Fine, but you never cared before."

"And I don't now," Chris said. "But Mum might be in one of her funny moods. And you know she's got a nose like a bloodhound."

"Sausage, then? Got some of the variety packs from the butcher in the freezer."

"Go on, then."

He *really* wasn't hungry, but John was plainly in a fussy mood. Chris left him to it. It was nice to be fussed over sometimes. He just propped his chin on his fist, fed Poppy treats from the half-empty packet on the table, and listened to the far-too-chirpy DJ on the radio.

"Why aren't you at work yet?" he asked as plates crashed out of the wall cabinet. "It's got to be half nine."

"Quarter to ten, and I rang Rhodri last night. Taking the week off, then I'll get back to it. He understands."

Chris grunted.

"How you doing, anyway?" John asked. A chair scraped, and the empty mug was bonked against the table. "Another?"

"Better not, that's my second."

"Orange juice?"

"Please."

"And?"

"And I don't know." Chris scrubbed a hand over his face. "Tired. Weird. It feels like things should be more different than they are."

"Yeah, I know the feeling."

"I'm going to spend most of the day with Mum, I think. You might as well go to work."

"Nah." The fridge door closed. "If you don't want my company today, I can get on with some of the household chores. The bloody light's gone in the living room again."

"Meh, it can wait."

"Not all of us can navigate through our toes," John retorted and plonked the glass of juice down in front of him. "I need to make a start on the van as well, get that rattle sorted. Then this evening, I was thinking you, me, Poppy, and a carvery dinner?"

"See how Mum is."

"How's the chest?"

The abrupt change of subject brought Chris up short. "What?"

"Your chest."

"Um. It's...fine?"

"Just looks a bit—"

Chris rolled his eyes. Of course, he'd forgotten to put a shirt on, and John was like most enormous brick shithouses of men—an absolute wuss when it came to blood and guts.

"Red?"

"Um, yeah."

"It's three weeks old, of course it looks a bit red," Chris said and yawned. "I'll put some lotion on tonight."

The phone started ringing just as John took the pan off the heat, so Chris went to get it. He'd never lived anywhere with a landline before, but it was surprisingly nice. Especially as a ringing phone was usually John's, and for a man who made a living off people calling for help, he did have a tendency to leave his phone in the weirdest places. Chris had even found it in the empty bath, once.

"Bannerman," he said, then shuffled back into the kitchen with it when Mum asked if he'd gotten her text. He nearly dropped the phone and had to pause to let his brain catch up with everything. "Sorry, I left my phone in the bedroom. We're just having breakfast. How are you doing?"

"Oh, I'm all right," she said faintly. "Did you—did you read Jack's letter?"

"Uh, yeah. It was—nice."

"Yes."

There was a long pause.

"Do you have his ring, then?"

"The funeral parlour will. I asked them to take it off him when—well. When."

"Do you want to keep it?" Chris asked.

"What?"

"I'm not going to do anything with it."

"No, no. It's yours now."

"Okay."

There was another pause, and Chris itched for something to say. What was he *supposed* to say? His mother was terrifyingly pragmatic at times, and at others messily emotional. He never knew what response he was going to get.

"So...he's left me a house?" Chris said.

"Oh. Yes. The house."

"Mum, are you all right?"

"Just a little tired," she said. "Are you coming to the office later? It will be quite dull. Just a lot of reading what you already know, I suspect."

"Do you want me to come?"

"It doesn't have to be some family affair."

Chris hesitated. He bit his lip as John put down a plate in front of him.

"I can just come on my own," he said slowly.

"That would be nice."

Chris frowned, a little puzzled. Mum wasn't exactly chatty with John, but she didn't dislike him either. Maybe she was worried she'd cry. Mum didn't like getting emotional in front of people.

"Okay," he said. "I can come round or meet you in town?"

"In town would be best. The house is a bit messy. The cat's been sick again."

"Maybe we should have cremated the cat."

"Christian!"

"Okay, okay," Chris said. "Meet you at the bus station?"

"Yes. For half past eleven. The appointment is at twelve," she said briskly, sounding much more like his mother. Still, he hung up with a sense of trepidation.

"What?" John asked.

"That was weird."

"What was?"

"She didn't want you to come."

"Eh, she's just lost her husband. Give her some slack. I'm just the dumb boyfriend."

Chris snorted.

"Maybe she wants to talk old family stuff with you," John suggested. "You know how private your mum can be. She wasn't too keen on having me round for Hanukkah last year once it was obvious it was going to be Jack's last, was she?"

"Yeah, maybe."

"Doesn't matter," John remarked. "I'll drop you off and get some stuff done around here. Now get that down your neck before Poppy decides to take it."

"She's better trained than you," Chris said snottily, but picked up the hot bap anyway. Warm food woke his body up a little, and the sour nausea from having his medication on just a slice of toast eased.

But the niggling feeling in his gut from Mum's tone didn't.

HE HEARD HER heels clacking on the tiles in the bus station long before she said hello. He smiled, offered her an arm, and got a dry kiss on the cheek. She smelled of perfume and sadness.

"How are you doing?"

"Oh, I'm all right," she said unconvincingly. "This shouldn't take long. I thought we could get lunch?"

He didn't want to, but he said, "That sounds nice."

They meandered into the town centre. Chris hated the bus station and surrounding streets. The pavements were narrow and uneven, the kerbs high and crumbling, and he never completely remembered where to go for which street. And his residual brain damage meant if he walked too quickly, his hands would go numb and he'd drop things, which meant he'd completely lose his sense of direction. There was a reason he never got the bus into town.

But Mum wordlessly led the way, beyond used to his brain and its snags, and Chris let her, chewing over his thoughts in his head.

"Here," she said, and Poppy's harness lifted fractionally. The step was shallower than he'd expected, and he wondered if this solicitor hadn't managed to get one of the fancy old buildings after all. "We're a bit early. I wanted to talk to you about the will, actually."

"What about it?"

"That house really isn't very suitable," she said.

Chris cocked his head. "What do you mean?"

"It's a complete mess. Jack's mother never took care of it, and Jack couldn't bear to step foot in it after she died. It's been left to ruin. I think we ought to auction it off. You'd do better with just the money, especially if you invest it properly. You need to start thinking about your pension."

He snorted. This was definitely like his mother.

"I'm not even thirty! I don't need to think about a pension."

"Of course you do," she said briskly. "Jack didn't have much of one, and it could have been a lot worse. You won't have an employment one at all, you know."

"Yeah, yeah. John's loaded from his business, though. He pays into a private pension plan for the both of us. We'll be fine."

There was a sharp pause.

Then Mum said, "You can't always rely on John, you know."

Chris raised his eyebrows. "What's that supposed to mean?"

"You need to be practical about these things. He might not be around forever."

Chris blew out his cheeks. He didn't like to think about it, but it probably wasn't going to be *him* left behind. John played rugby, went running every weekend, and wanted to buy a bigger flat or a house so he could set up a home gym for pumping iron. He'd lifted the back end of the car to prop it on a stiff jack, once. The worst thing John did was eat like a typical builder, so his arteries were probably a bit fuzzy. That was it.

And Chris had serious epilepsy, took four different drugs just to stay alive, and had been left with permanent brain damage. And he smoked occasionally. Even with the age gap—

"Odds are, John will be around longer than I will."

Mum's grip on his arm tightened fractionally.

But then she said, "That's not what I meant," and Chris's brain paused.

Wait.

"What *do* you mean, then?"

If she meant he couldn't rely on John but wasn't talking about death—

Chris's temper flared. "For fuck's sake, Mum, John's not going—"

A door opened.

"Mrs Rosenberg?"

Chris ground his teeth at the lawyer's interruption, but Mum was already getting to her feet and trotting out greetings. Chris took a moment to get moving, though. Her insinuation was doing the rounds in his head in a confused mess. The flash of temper subsided but didn't die away entirely.

Mum thought John was leaving him. Or he was going to. Mum thought John wouldn't be there when Chris got old, and Chris needed to make contingency plans. After three years of family dinners, John doing odd jobs round the house for them, and Chris's first ever trip abroad when John had won two grand on a scratch card and taken Chris and Mum and Jack to Paris for the weekend, Mum thought John wasn't a permanent thing.

Where in the hell had that come from?

Chapter Three

THE FLAT STANK of paint.

"John!" Chris shouted, even as he opened the back door and let Poppy out into the little garden given over to their flat.

"What?"

"What have you been doing?"

"Painting over that bloody great hole you put in the bathroom door last week. You don't have to punch everything in reach when you go down, you know."

"Ha bloody ha," Chris drawled. "Are you finished?"

"Yeah, just tidying up." Footsteps padded out of the bathroom. "How did it go?"

"I have no idea," Chris confessed, throwing up his hands. "I have the paperwork for this house, anyway. And I'm going to pick up the ring when we collect the ashes. But Mum was really weird."

"Weird how?"

Something—maybe a towel—was dropped on the sofa, then a hand put in each of Chris's back pockets, and a stubbly kiss rasped against the side of his face. Chris sighed and looped his arms around John's neck for another, more on-target offering.

"Mm. Thank you."

The hands squeezed.

"Dinner?"

"Soon," Chris said. "She was going on about how I should auction off the house and invest the money from it so I have a pension—"

"Not a bad move—"

"—because I can't rely on you always being there."

The grip on his bum tightened again. Chris tugged on the T-shirt and realised too late it was paint-stained. He pulled a face and wiped his hands off on John's jeans.

"I—don't take this the wrong way, Chris, but she's right. I eat like shit, and what with Granddad's heart attack last year—"

"Not the scenario she meant."

Another pause.

Then, "Wait, she thinks I'm going to *leave*?"

"I don't know. Maybe. She just kept dropping hints, like nothing's permanent and things only get harder to handle as you get older—"

"She's talking boll—rubbish."

Chris sighed heavily. "John. The word is bollocks. It's not even a swear word, come on."

John snorted and kissed his cheek. Then the hands left his pockets, seized his thighs, and hoisted him up. Chris yelped as the room swung dizzyingly, a board creaked; then he was flat on his back on their bed, bouncing twice on the thick mattress before settling with a startled laugh.

"What was that for?"

"You can stay there and look pretty while I get changed," John ordered. "Then we can go and get dinner, and I'll charm that daft idea out of your head."

Chris lifted his arms and beckoned. The mattress dipped. A hand stroked up his side, and the kiss was firm. Determined. Not quite hungry, but distinctly unfulfilled too. Chris smiled when it broke and nudged his nose into the side of John's contentedly, running his fingers from a paint-spattered shoulder down a bare, bulging bicep. John's biceps were bigger than Chris's thighs, and the best sex was always to be found when they were hard at work keeping John above him. Chris squeezed and grinned at the ripple of muscle as John—very deliberately—flexed.

"I haven't got those ideas," he murmured, earning a stubbly chin rubbing teasingly against his neck. He hummed, curling his toes before carrying on. "You've got a hell of a fight on your hands to get rid of me."

John chuckled. "I hate fighting."

"Well, then, we have a situation here."

"Yes, I'm getting paint all over the sheets, and you're looking unfairly attractive while I'm too hungry to do anything about it."

Chris snorted and pushed at the barrel of a chest hovering over his own. "G'wan, then. Get changed and let's go."

To his credit, John didn't take long to get ready. Obviously, he still had the carvery in mind. He was in an affectionate mood, and Chris soaked it up, the drive-by hugs and snatched kisses not only pleasant surprises— John liked to try sneaking kisses so Chris wouldn't hear them coming—but affirming against Mum's disturbing words.

And yet, Chris still couldn't figure out where she'd gotten the idea.

He'd been with John for three years. They'd moved into the flat together almost bang on the nose of their first anniversary. They'd been on that weekend in Paris, and they had a joint account for the bills. John had taken four different first-aid courses and even qualified to do health and safety assessments on building sites. He'd replaced Dad as next of kin on Chris's medical paperwork—of which there was a *lot*. Chris had signed over power of attorney to John in the event of another brain injury. He'd wriggled into every cranny of Chris's life. Where had Mum magicked this idea of leaving from?

Chris shook it off and picked up the envelope of paperwork from the coffee table as John put his boots on. He turned it over in his hands thoughtfully. Auctioning off the house wasn't a bad idea, exactly. They could always do with the money. Even the whole pension idea wasn't *bad*, and there was always the potential John might lose the business, no matter how successful he'd made it. But—Jack had wanted them to turn it into a home. Their home or someone else's. Not just get rid of it.

"Is it nice outside?"

"Nice enough. Why? Want to walk round to the—"

"I was thinking maybe we'd go look at the house," Chris said, holding up the envelope. "I'm sure the address is in here."

John thumped his foot—presumably to force his boot into place—then the sofa groaned as it was released from his oppressive bulk. He plucked the envelope from Chris's hand. Paper rustled, and then John let out a low whistle.

"Bloody hell, that's a posh area. I've done fittings out there. Your Jack's come from money. You *sure* you don't want to auction it?"

They took the car. John had a work van, but the footwell was on the small side for Poppy, and Chris didn't like her sitting up on the seat. And the suspicious rattle was getting on his tits. The car was on its way out too, clattering up the hill all the way out of Sheffield like some contraption out of a science-fiction film, but at least it didn't lurch with every gear change. Chris tracked their route from memory until John swung off about halfway there and careened down the side of the hill. Gloom flickered over Chris's eyes. He had retained just enough light sensitivity to tell a dark room from a bright one, and from the flickering, he guessed at woods. John laughed and called him spooky.

"Yeah, sixth sense," Chris said.

The road gave way to a bumpier one, and narrower going by the way John suddenly forgot what an accelerator was. The car crawled along, bumping and banging the whole way, and coasted to a stop in a patch of warm sunlight.

"Oh, wow. I think that's it."

"Helpful," Chris drawled. "Anything in my way?"

"Nope."

He popped the door open and got out.

The first thing to strike him was the quiet. It couldn't have been five o'clock yet, but all he heard was the whispering of nearby trees. The air smelled like a snowy winter, crisp and clean. The beep of the central locking on the car sounded obscenely out of place.

"Are we in the middle of nowhere?"

"Well, not quite," John admitted. "But you'd have to shout hello to the neighbours. It's definitely detached."

"What's that?"

"Doesn't join to the house next door. Come on. This might be tricky. The path is overgrown as hell."

Chris took Poppy's harness in one hand and John's arm in the other. He shuffled forward carefully from the cracked pavement to the soft crunch of grass grown over a thick layer of gravel. The walk seemed endless. Plants caught gently at his clothes, and a cold shadow fell over them, yawning forever before they reached a set of stone steps.

"Front door. They've boarded everything up. Want to try round the back?"

"Yeah."

'Round the back' felt more like half a mile. The house might be detached, but the side was overgrown with brambles and bushes—and if John had picked this side, Chris wondered how bad the other one was. It made walking abreast impossible, but at least John's bulk cut a nice path for Chris. As they passed out of the shadow again into the fading sun—the warmth poking Chris in the face as they cleared the bushes—he took a deep breath and smelled the faintest hint of woodsmoke.

"Looks like we're in luck. Somebody's had the back door off."

"You call that luck?" Chris quipped but allowed John to lead him into the cool, damp darkness of the house. "Okay. Talk to me."

"Um."

"What?"

"No kidding his granddad bought it." John laughed nervously. "So—we're in the kitchen. And there's still a brick fireplace."

"I like fireplaces," Chris said serenely.

"The ceiling is going to be black plaster underneath, I can practically smell it. And the original copper boiler is still in. No way the wiring is up—"

"Less builder's patter, more salesman, please."

John snorted loudly. "Okay. Here's your sales pitch. I could spend every day for the next *year* on this place, and *then* we'd have to strip everything back to redecorate. This kitchen is green, and not from mould."

"What's wrong with green?"

"Green shouldn't be anywhere near food."

"So why is the saying 'eat your greens'?"

"People who eat salad by choice don't deserve to live," John snapped, and Chris cackled with laughter. He let go of his arm and went gingerly exploring around the cavernous room and—once he had mapped the damp-ridden walls with his now dirty fingertips—demanded the grand tour.

The grand tour showed the ground floor—for the stairs were rotten—of a large, lonely, and unloved house. Two living rooms, a generous study, a dining room despite the dining room table being in the kitchen, and even the top of a stone flight of stairs vanishing down into a cellar that John flatly refused to investigate. From the outside, John estimated the house went up into the roof space with rooms, making it four storeys in total, albeit the very top one likely a single bedroom jammed into the apex. The garden was an expanse of anarchist greenery, and John speculated about whether there'd ever been a drive or not. There was certainly no garage.

"You can build one," Chris said. "There's lots of room, right?"

"I could build a double. But that sounds suspiciously to me like—"

"I don't want to auction it," Chris said as they reached the car once more. "Just listen."

"To what?"

"Exactly. It was Jack's. And it's gorgeous here out in the woods."

"We're not *in* the woods—"

"But they're close. We could go walking there all the time. And we could plant two cherry trees in the garden, and when they're big enough, when we're nearly old, you can put up a hammock for me and I can nap in the sun."

"You're secretly a cat," John commented.

But then he caught Chris's waist and towed him in, the kiss nudging at Chris's mouth almost shyly.

"You want this place, don't you?" John murmured.

"Jack wanted it to be loved again," Chris whispered. "We can do that."

The arms slid further until they closed in a hug. Chris sagged into it and let himself be rocked for a moment, leaning to the rustling in the trees with one ear and John's heartbeat with the other. This could be home. He could feel it. Naps in the garden in the summer after bad seizures. Winters by the fireplace in the kitchen. They could get that other dog John wanted for himself. Maybe even the aviary Chris had coveted since he'd lost his sight.

They could do anything here.

"It's not habitable right now," John pointed out. "There's probably not even power and electric."

"You can fix that."

"And half the rooms aren't safe for you."

"You can fix that too."

"And—"

"And we could borrow Luke's campervan and live like hippies until you get the bathroom and the kitchen sorted, then we could just expand from there into all the other rooms until it's done," Chris argued. "Summer is coming. We have time. Let's do it."

John laughed—a shallow, almost resigned noise.

"You're mad," he said.

"You love me."

"Yeah."

"*Because* I'm mad."

"Well, not only," John confessed and kissed the top of his head. "All right. You ring Luke; I'll ring a letting agent."

Chapter Four

THEY COLLECTED THE ashes on the Saturday after the funeral.

Mum wanted to go to the synagogue first, and Chris made a habit of avoiding places of worship, so they met at the parlour instead, Mum already waiting outside when John pulled up in the car.

"She's by the door," he said. "Want me to come in, or stay here?"

"Can you just wait here?" Chris asked. "I don't know what she wants to do."

He felt impossibly awkward. She hadn't called him since the meeting with the lawyer and their quiet lunch afterwards, and he'd had to text four times to get the time out of her for the collection. Even as she hugged him at the parlour door, smelling of her favourite rose perfume, her touch was wooden and distant. She didn't say anything, and she didn't take his arm as usual. She just held the door, and he stepped into a sombre silence.

He didn't like the funeral parlour. He'd only been once before, right after Jack's death. It was horribly still. The acoustics were eerie, everything too close and too far away all at once, and the hushed tones of the receptionist asking for their appointment time and if they were one of Mr Abbey's clients or Mr Fox's felt like he was at another funeral. Not even so much as a clock ticked as they waited.

"Ah, Mrs Rosenberg."

The man's voice was the kind of slow and serious Chris had only heard in poorly acted movies. It rang false. He didn't know Jack. He didn't give a shit about Jack. He was paid to look solemn and act sorry for every customer's loss, but that's all they were. Customers.

"This way, please."

Mum said nothing. Chris had to rely on Poppy to follow her. They were led into a little room, or perhaps a large one with more terrible acoustics, and the chair was uncomfortably hard. A bag rustled, and something heavy was placed on something wooden.

"Oh," Mum said quietly.

Something light tapped the wood, too.

"And the ring you requested."

Mum's blouse crinkled, and then a small paper box was pressed into Chris's hand. He popped the lid off, and touched the metal ring lying inside. It was scratched and cold. Heavy. Nothing like the warm weight on Jack's shaking hands whenever Chris had gone home from having dinner with them, and Jack had insisted on a handshake at the door like they were strangers.

He put the lid back on.

"If you would like to make arrangements for a ceremony to scatter the—"

"No."

Mum's voice was wobbly.

"No," she repeated in a harder tone. "No, thank you. I—I want to do that myself."

Chris stiffened. "Mum—"

"Myself, Christian."

He bit his lip. There was an awkward silence, then Mr Whoever said, "Take all the time you need. We'll be in touch about the outstanding payments. There's no rush."

The door opened and closed. Mum sniffled, just once, then the bag creaked once more and the heavy thing thumped onto the floor.

"They've put him in a gift bag," she said. "I suppose—I suppose it's easier to carry."

"Let's go home."

"No," she repeated faintly. "I'm—I'm going to walk back. It's a nice day. It's the perfect day."

"You're going to scatter him today?"

"Yes."

"I'll—"

"Alone."

Her voice was very hard. Chris's throat closed up.

"Mum—"

"He was my husband, Christian. I need to say goodbye on my terms. Not—not at a busy funeral with everybody watching. Just me. Alone."

He opened his mouth. The questions jostled for room. When did he get the time to do the same? Why could he not scatter his stepfather's ashes too? Would she at least tell him where, so he could go later?

But then he closed his mouth, and his fingers around the little box. He pocketed it and stood.

"Call me if you need anything."

She wouldn't. He knew she wouldn't. But something hurt and angry in his chest didn't know how to reach out to her without causing more damage. She was grieving, and she'd put up the spikes around herself like she always did. And Chris had never known what to do with his mother when she did that. He had never known how to get past them.

He let himself out slowly. The bustle of the main road was a welcome relief, and he sank into the passenger seat with a deep sigh, switching the radio stations until he found an upbeat pop song.

"Should I ask?" John sounded wary.

"Probably not," Chris mumbled.

"Does your mum not want a lift?"

"No. She doesn't want any company either. Or anything."

"What happened?"

"She's got the urn."

"Okay—"

"She's going to go and scatter him herself. Alone. Today."

"Oh." A hand landed on his knee and squeezed gently. "You okay?"

"I guess," Chris said miserably. "I just— I want to be understanding and give her space and everything, but—"

He left the sentence hanging in the air. But what? Was it horribly selfish to push his way into her grief? Jack was her husband. That was more than a stepfather. But the grossly self-centred part of him wanted to be a part of the final goodbye, too.

"I get it," John murmured. "Hey, do you want to go and do something? A walk? Lunch?"

"Don't you have rugby practice later?"

"I can skip it."

"Don't do that."

"Okay, how about a light lunch and then you can park yourself in the stands and pretend you're admiring the view while I run around in short shorts?"

Chris fought back the smile, but failed. John chuckled and stretched over to kiss the corner of it. Chris recovered some of his superiority by snottily saying John needed a shave, and then the car grumbled as it was forced into the right gear and crawled away into the traffic.

"You like me with a bit of fuzz."

"You're not fuzzy, you're furry."

"Am not."

"Are too. Why do you think you never get a blowjob anymore? I'd suffocate."

"Jesus Christ—"

"Not gonna help you, Johnny boy."

The humour, fragile and delicate like an old glass ornament, was warm too. It had long been Chris's coping mechanism, and he reached out to touch John's thigh carefully as they climbed back down into the city.

"Thanks."

"For what?"

"Being daft with me."

A great paw squeezed his fingers lightly.

"Tell you what," John whispered. "I've got one of Rhodri's mates coming over to the house tomorrow to give me an assessment. And you'll not be allowed to skip out on another Sunday dinner with Nan and Granddad. But after that, how about we go away to the coast for a couple of days? Just you, me, a beach, and a good stormy spring sea?"

It would be cold as hell. The salt and sand would bite in the wind. And John had asbestos toes and would insist on wading even though the North Sea was unbearable outside of high summer. But—

The crash of the tide, and John's arms around his waist, and the wind in his hair? The elements slicing away at his grief and anger until they were scraped away, like a pumice stone for the soul?

"Yeah," he said. "Sounds good. But first...first, I need to talk to Luke."

HE DIDN'T GO to rugby practice with John. Instead, he went to the gym—despite John's arguments.

"You can't go to the gym yet."

"I can go wherever I want."

"Fine, you can't *do* the gym yet. The doctor said so."

"I'm not doing anything. I'm meeting Luke there. We're going to go for a shake, and I'm going to persuade him to part ways with that campervan."

John offered to drop him off on his way to rugby, but Chris waved him off and shut the front door on his protests with a snap.

It had gotten even colder—and much as Chris liked being ferried anywhere he wanted to go, he wanted a little space too. After Mum's quiet rejection that morning, he wanted to breathe. And much as he'd fallen in love with the house, Jack's words had brought a lump to his throat, and it had only sunk into the middle of his chest to lodge there. He wanted some time to get lost in his thoughts and breathe a little.

So he walked to the gym.

It was the better part of two miles, and the least direct route he could possibly have managed, but Poppy could do with the walk. Chris sifted through his feelings in time with the slow shuffle of his feet and the gentle vibrations as the cane bumped cracks and kerbs, the pavements riddled with tree roots and potholes. Jack's words ghosted along behind him like a trail of smoke, but he had no urge to light up a cigarette and obscure them.

It hadn't been Chris's first funeral, but it was the first parent. He had five—his mother had married Jack, and his father had two girlfriends, Caroline and Lauren—and now there were four. He'd known for a long time Jack would go first, but the mixture of loss and relief was still strange. The suffering was over, but the man had disappeared. The quiet support in the background, almost entirely obscured sometimes by the hustle and bustle of the other people in Chris's life, yet there all the same.

That was all Jack had ever been. Silently supportive. He'd come along at the height of Chris's teenage crises and probably met Chris at his very worst. Belligerent, aggressive, rude, taking out every frustration on everyone else. Chris had reacted violently to the slightest hint of misgendering; he lashed out immediately if he sensed pity for his disabilities, whether the pity had been real or all in his head. He lost people in those years. He regretted things from those years. He probably always would.

But Jack had stayed silent.

When Chris came out, Jack simply asked what happened next. When Chris lost his first guide dog, Jack was the one to ask how he could get another one. When Chris introduced them to John, Jack commented that he seemed nice. When they bought the flat and moved in together, Jack added the new address to the little black book in his jacket without further ado. Even when Chris went at loggerheads with his mother over this thing or that—his hair, his dropping out of sixth form college, his moving out—Jack just said, "Let the lad do what he needs to do."

Jack didn't get it. But he sort of had too.

And now his calming presence was gone.

Chris loved his mum, but she could be difficult sometimes. She worried too much. She'd wanted him to stay at home forever, too afraid of what might happen if he stepped foot out the door. Almost all her arguments with Dad revolved around Dad letting Chris do something Mum didn't want him to do. That trip to the trampoline park when he was thirteen with his best mate from school. Camping for his twenty-first with Gina and Luke and nobody else for ten miles in every direction. And the less said about that sailing trip, the better. No doubt she'd have a fit if he told her they were going to move into the house.

As he reached the gym, the rocky pavements having changed to the sagging tarmac of a decades-old car park, Chris wondered if he hadn't gone for someone a little bit like Jack. John had a similar temperament. Unfailingly calm, unwaveringly kind. They were probably the only two people in existence for whom 'nice' wasn't code for 'boring'. And it made Chris out to be as highly strung as his mother, which, he reflected, wasn't exactly a lie.

"Oi! Dickhead!"

Chris pulled a face at the bellow that echoed clear across the car park. And probably the main road too.

"Try again, fuckface!" he shouted back. "I don't think Barnsley caught that!"

Luke cackled with laughter, and Chris was treated to a hug at the gym doors. As usual, Luke stank of Lynx body spray.

"You smell like a virgin," Chris complained.

"Fuck off," came the casual reply, and then a bag hit the floor. "And how's my girl, huh?"

"Don't pet my dog, barnacle-arse."

"Didn't touch her. What crawled up your backside and died?"

"A footlong dick most mornings, more than you've ever had."

Luke crowed with laughter once more, called him a pervert, and ruffled Chris's hair like an obnoxious older brother. "Come on," he said. "I need a fucking shake. My arms are *killing* me."

Luke was trans, like Chris. He'd finally managed to get onto HRT last year, and in the last couple of months had worked up the courage to use the men's changing rooms on his own for the first time. Until then, they'd never been to the gym without each other. He helped Chris use the weights in exchange for getting to change with Chris in the safety of the single-stall disabled changing room.

But going by the crushing grip of his hug, he wasn't going to need that safety net anymore.

"How you healing up?" Luke asked as they were enveloped by the warmth of the coffee shop next door to the gym.

"Fine. I think John's scared of the scars, though."

"He'll get over it," Luke said. "He'll finally get to bang you topless."

Chris rolled his eyes as Luke—predictably—delivered the line at the top of his lungs. Nothing like a vial of testosterone in the arse to bring out the extrovert in everyone. A cup clinked in alarm nearby, and the babble of voices distinctly dipped.

"He's done that plenty."

"Fine, he'll grope you like mad while he's at it."

Chris shrugged, allowing the assessment. "You decided what you're doing yet?"

"Yeah, I'm going for it. Everything. If I'm gonna get sweet pecs, then I'm gonna get a knob to go with them too."

"Yeah?" Chris was rather surprised. Luke had never been interested in surgery before. He'd been obsessed with getting the HRT—and in desperate need of it, he'd been a complete mess before—but surgery hadn't ever come up. Even when Chris had been battling to find a surgeon willing to operate on him, Luke had just groaned and asked what was wrong with a binder and a strict diet.

"Yeah. You look miles better for it, mate. And if you can do it, so can I. I haven't got other medical shit to worry about."

"*I* wasn't worried."

"I also haven't got your mum."

Chris snorted, smirking. They paused the talk while they ordered, and then Luke kicked some people out of their usual table on the excuse of needing space for the dog. She curled up between the seats, tugging Chris's foot farther into the safe zone before dutifully ignoring the pair of them.

"What changed your mind?"

"Dunno," Luke said. "I reckon since my beard's finally started coming through, I've— I don't know. Noticed the tits a bit more? Did you get that? Something wasn't an issue until some other issue got fixed?"

"Kind of?" Chris hedged. "Other way around though, weirdly. I mean, don't get me wrong, I needed the T, but—" He patted the flat expanse of his chest, a little thrill of euphoria arising when his hand went past where his brain still expected to hit boobs and touched his breastbone instead. "—this was always more important."

"Gonna be all or nothing for me, though," Luke said. "Top and bottom."

"No thanks," Chris said, grimacing.

"Why not?"

"John's got enough dick for the pair of us."

Luke crowed with laughter.

"I just don't need it," Chris said. "Packing is fine when I need the weight. I don't need it to be *my* weight."

"Fair play. How's healing going?"

"Great."

"Even with—"

Luke trailed off. Chris cocked his head.

"What?"

"I'm, uh. I'm sorry about Jack."

Chris bit his lip at the sombre tone.

"Yeah," he said eventually. "It was— It's better this way, though. We picked up the ashes this morning."

Luke touched his wrist lightly on the tabletop. "If you need owt—"

"I know. I'm okay, I think. Thanks." Chris blew out his cheeks. "So he left me his wedding ring. And a house."

"A *house*? Fuck me!"

"No thanks."

"Bitch, you'd love to get with this," Luke said dismissively.

"Yeah, right. Maybe when your voice finishes dropping and you don't sound like the class snitch off *Recess*."

"You still watch that shit?"

"It's not shit, it's glorious. And Spinelli is totally a trans boy waiting to happen. I should have called myself Ashley."

"True, but you're no Ashley," Luke said, and they clinked glasses. "Anyway, house. Why didn't Jack leave it to your mum?"

"Not *that* house. Mum owns that house. Apparently, he inherited *his* mum's house, and he's left it to me."

Luke whistled. "What you going to do with it? Flog it?"

"Live in it," Chris said. "It's out near Ringinglow Road. John's going to renovate it, and we're going to live there. It's *massive*."

"Niiiiiice."

"Be a step up from the flat. And John can stop pestering for his own dog."

A bark of laughter met his ears.

"So when's the housewarming party?"

Chris grinned. "Yeah, well, it's not exactly habitable. It's a complete mess. John doesn't even think we can properly live in it yet."

"Your mum won't like that."

"Nah, she wants me to flog it." Chris rapped his spoon on the plastic cup of Luke's shake. "Can we borrow your campervan?"

"Susie?"

"Yeah."

"Why?"

"So we can live on the drive until the house is ready."

"Depends how long it'll take," Luke said. "Got that European road trip in September with Izzy, haven't I?"

Talk turned to his girlfriend, then morphed into an argument about whether it was too early to ask Izzy to move in, then splintered off to a gossiping session about Gina, her girlfriend Jemma, and the three-year itch.

Somewhere in the middle of it, Luke agreed to loan them the campervan until September. Then he leaned over, rapped Chris on the forehead with his knuckles, and said something Chris hadn't been expecting.

"So—when are you going to put that wedding ring to use?"

Chris opened his mouth to laugh and say never. He formed the words in his head to tell Luke to fuck off and did he look like the marrying kind.

But they didn't come.

Instead, he became very suddenly and very consciously aware of the weight in his pocket and the cool gold under his fingertips in the funeral parlour.

It could be warm again.

Chapter Five

CHRIS HAD A seizure on Sunday morning.

He managed to get laid out on the bed in time and came round to Poppy lying along his back to keep him in the recovery position, and the blanket tucked over him.

"John?" he called muzzily.

Something creaked. Bare feet shuffled on carpet.

"What time is it?"

"Half eleven," John answered, and a heavy hand smoothed his curls. "How you doing?"

Chris grumbled. His back ached, and he'd pissed himself. But the usual pounding headache wasn't there, and he didn't have that horrible surge of anger when John touched him.

"Okay. I think."

"Think you'll have another?"

"No."

The only mercy of Chris's epilepsy was a strong aura. He could feel a seizure coming for miles. The strange vertigo, the ringing in his ears, the stabbing headache around his eyes and temples, the nausea, that weird burning smell—the shortest one he remembered had been three or four minutes leading up to the main event. The only sticking point was if he got absence seizures mixed in as well—then he'd lose time and not quite realise before the main event hit.

"Ready to sit up?"

"Yeah."

He pushed himself up and sighed when John rubbed at exactly the right sore point on his back.

"Okay?"

"Yeah. I'm okay. I'm hungry. I mean, I feel sick as hell, but I think that's the drugs. Mostly hungry."

"Well, if you're up to it, we can always pop up and join Nan and Granddad. I rang when you weren't well this morning."

"Yes. Please."

John's family was messy and busy, and Chris needed messy and busy. The silence from his mum and the nagging grief were loud companions when it was quiet. He wanted John's noisy sisters, his bossy grandma, and John dissolving from his usual calm and steadfast presence to the bratty little boy who constantly lost against his numerous female relatives.

Chris needed to laugh.

He showered and found some clean clothes, the rushing sounds of John changing the soiled bed acting like a timer. John took forever to change a bed. By the time the duvet had been thumped into place, Chris had put his shoes on, and Poppy was whining to have five minutes between the front door and the car.

"Come on," he said impatiently. "Even I can change the sheets faster than that."

"It's hard!"

"You have two working eyes, don't give me this 'it's hard' bullshit."

"*You* never pick matching pillowcases."

"It takes you half an hour to make sure it *matches*?"

Chris let Poppy out and then got caught in the doorway for a kiss. He smiled as the fresh stubble scraped against his cheek, and John chewed playfully on his earlobe.

"Are we going to the sea later?"

"Tomorrow," John replied. "Rhodri texted while I was on my run this morning. I've got to pop over to Rotherham with him this evening and sort out a meter for one of the old ladies who's got him wrapped around her little finger."

"Like you're any different."

"I charge!"

"You let that old fella on Psalter Lane pay in apple jam."

"It was good jam, though," John pointed out as he started the car.

"That's true."

At least two Sundays a month, they went out to Hathersage. John's grandparents owned a little cottage just outside the village, with a garden full of lavender and sweet-smelling jasmine. Chris had only ever been on a Sunday, so imagined the cottage always to be filled with the smell of fresh roast beef and the sunny sound of potatoes bobbing in a boiling pan of water. The drive was familiar as the way home from Dad's house, and Chris knew without being told when they'd left the city, when they'd reached the village, and the split second before the car rushed up onto the driveway and John smashed on the brakes to avoid hitting the pear tree. They were met—as always—by a shriek when John let them in through the never-locked front door, and the slap of slippers on carpet.

"There you are!"

Nan's hug was soft and warm. She smelled of talcum powder, freshly baked scones, and a hint of perfume. *Eau de grandmother*. Chris had never had a grandmother—one dead, one disowned—but Nan Halliday was exactly how he imagined all grandmothers to be. He didn't even know her name. She insisted he call her Nan.

"How are you feeling, dear?" she asked, cupping his face in soft palms. "John said you weren't well."

"I'm all right now," he said. "Had a seizure earlier, but it's done with for the moment."

She clucked her tongue. "We've not seen you since your operation, you daft boy. And it shows—you're wasting away! John, you get back here and explain yourself, young man!"

She scuttled off towards the kitchen, presumably after her only grandson, and Chris chuckled, toeing off his shoes and listening to Poppy tuck them into the corner with all the rest.

"Good girl. Come on, let's sneak a bit of roast beef, eh?"

The kitchen tiles were cool under his socks, and he stood waiting for his routine hugs and handshakes before groping for his usual seat. Two out of three sisters had showed up—Tash had bowed out, but Fran was there arguing the merits of trade unions with John's *deeply* conservative grandfather, and going by the cheer and the tiny hands that seized his jeans, Nora had brought her two-year-old.

"No, darling, you can't climb on Uncle Chris!"

"That's not *fair!*"

Chris settled into his chair and sighed. The warmth, the chatter, the sound of John being smacked with a wooden spoon for starving him—it enveloped Chris like a duvet. Safety. Comfort. Like coming home after a very long time away, and he reached down to pet Poppy's ears in silence as she waited patiently for her sliver of roast beef. Plates clattered. Chairs scraped. Familiar voices crashed into each other in a melee. Nora's husband Raj came in from tending to the garden, a job taken over from Granddad since the heart attack last year. Someone wrestled the highchair for Suresh out of the utility room.

Then Granddad folded up his broadsheet, and the table fell quiet. Almost as if they were waiting for grace.

Almost.

"About bloody time, you lazy bunch of fu—"

The wooden spoon whipped through the air, the crack deafening.

"Oi! Lay off, woman!"

"You mind your language, you drunken old sot!"

Chris laughed and slid his fingers across the tablecloth to find his fork. Poppy's tail thumped his socks as she snapped up her roast beef treat. Fran passed her condolences about Jack, and—that was all. The glimmer of grief had its moment and was wiped away by the busy mess of John's family. Of *Chris's* family.

He paused, a roast potato halfway to his mouth.

Home.

It was home. They were his family. Nora and Fran were his sisters too. Raj was his brother-in-law. Suresh was his nephew, and Nan's suspicious questions about Nora's festively plump physique suggested there'd be another sooner rather than later. Nan, who'd said epilepsy was no excuse when he'd offered to stay out of the way that first Christmas he was supposed to come to dinner and had feared having a seizure in the middle of a grand Halliday celebration. Granddad, who'd said he'd make an ugly girl when John had let slip he was trans. The day Nan had come to sit with him in hospital, when John had been stuck on a job and was going to miss visiting hours, and had sat there with her knitting, clacking away and commenting on all the nurses being far too young and "He doesn't need any more morphine, you silly little girl. He needs a good stiff scotch and a decent pair of socks!"

Slowly, he put down the fork.

What did he need a pension for? What did he need to sell the house for?

What did he need to be self-reliant for?

That had been the goal of moving out of the family home. To be able to do things for himself, by himself. He'd thought, once, he'd never get to be like Mum and Dad. There'd be no Jack, no Lauren, no Caroline. There wasn't going to be someone for Chris. He'd plastered it over with a smile and an attitude, but he'd believed it, deep down.

Then that big clumsy oaf had knocked his coffee flying.

"Chris?"

John's deep, searing voice scraped down his skin and made him shiver. His heart picked up, even as John made a noise of understanding and a chair scraped.

"Come on, sweetheart. Not at the table."

Voices rose gently. Calmly. A family used to him, accepting him, loving him. Chris rose with his shoulders between both of John's hands, even as someone else pulled his chair out of the way. The hall door opened by yet another someone else. Then the hall carpet was soft under his socks, and the clatter of cutlery started up again behind him.

"I'm okay," he said.

"You sure? You froze up. Come on—"

The living room was toasty warm from the fireplace. Chris sank onto the sofa where John put him but caught his wrists and refused to lie down.

"I'm fine," he said. "It's not a seizure."

"You promise?"

"I promise. No aura."

"Then why—"

"It just hit me."

"What did? Absence?"

"No. A realisation. A thought."

John huffed a laugh. "Seriously? You scared the shit out of me. I thought you were going to stab yourself in the face with your fork."

"It had a tatty on it!"

"*Potato*," John corrected severely. "You have no right to say tatty."

"I'm Scottish."

"You're as Scottish as my left nut," John grumbled, and thick fingers carded through his hair. A kiss, warped by a grin, was planted on his forehead. "So what was the big, dangerous thought that got between you and your dinner? You realise Nan's going to kill us both if you don't clean that plate?"

"I needed this," Chris said. John was kneeling in front of him, and Chris leaned forward slowly until their foreheads kissed. "I needed to be here. With your family. With *my* family."

"Yeah?" John whispered. His hands stroked down Chris's arms, and their fingers twisted up together between Chris's knees. Loose. Warm. Comfortable.

"It's busy and it's messy and it's fun. They'll wind me up for this later, but they jump to help when it's happening. They love us. And they're—they're for good. *We're* for good."

"Ye-es—"

It burst out of him in a rush.

"I want to get married."

It spilled out, and Chris squeezed John's fingers tight. His heart swelled. There was too much air inside of him, and he laughed breathlessly.

"I want to get married," he repeated. "You're—you're everything. Your family is mine. And—and we're going to turn that house into somewhere full of love again, and Jack left me his wedding ring so it could see another life of love, and—and you're that life. With me. So let's do it. Let's—let's get married. Marry me."

John said nothing. He let go. Chris heard the creak of his jeans as he sat back on his heels. A hollow, dry cough, almost like a surprised laugh.

Then his head was seized between two enormous hands, and he was kissed like their lives depended on it. Smashed back into the cushions. The breath squeezed out of him, and the kiss, broken by a delirious, deep laugh, shivered right into Chris's very bones. He curled up tight inside the sound and clung to the warm body that delivered it.

"You're serious," John breathed against his mouth, punctuating the gap between the words by biting Chris's lip. "Tell me you're serious, because you have this one single moment to back down before I—"

"I'm serious."

His lip was crushed between hungry teeth and then released with another giddy laugh.

"Your dad will kill us."

"Let him."

"Your mums might too."

"Let them."

"Oh my fucking God, come here."

Chris was so startled by the swearing he couldn't put up a fight as John's arms caught around his back and bum, and the world rocked. The power surge of that enormous frame bowing under him and punching skywards like a superhero taking flight—exciting, terrifying, and dizzying all at once. Chris clung on for dear life as John spun them in the middle of the room, laughing like an excited child—then the indignant terror faded as the grip loosened, and Chris ducked his face to find John's and kiss him all over again.

Close. Quiet. Intimate. The gentle touch of John's nose against his own. His shaved scalp hot and delicate under Chris's hands. The shells of his ears, flooded with thrilled heat. The kiss softened until Chris merely cupped John's lips with his own and felt his smile like they were one.

"You're a jammy bugger, you know that?" John breathed into him, and Chris grinned.

"Why?"

"You beat me to it," John confessed and tipped his head back. It was the only warning Chris got, and he clapped his hands over his ears barely in time to avoid being deafened. "*Nan!*"

"What!"

"Get the good booze out!"

A chair scraped. Slippers slapped. The door opened, and Nan's huffy "*What* are you doing, young man! Put him down this instant!"

"Nope," John refused and twirled again. Chris laughed, the joy bubbling up out of him all too much to contain.

"You'll trip on the rug and do yourself a mischief!" Nan scolded. "Honestly, what's got you so—"

"We're engaged!"

Chris wasn't fast enough, that time.

Nan screamed, and he could hear it ringing in his ears for hours.

Chapter Six

HE WAS DREAMING, but he knew they were dreams. Cherry blossoms catching in his hair, the sea roaring, and salt in the air. People clapping as he was kissed. Then the bed dipped, and the beach dissolved away to the firm warmth of a mattress, and the kiss was not on his mouth, firm and promising, but on his neck, soft and hopeful.

He sighed and stretched.

The gentle edge of teeth met his neck, and the shadows of sleep vanished as the kiss turned hungry and sucked a bruise into being. His blood leapt. The mattress shuddered, the sheets rustled, and heat pinned him down, heavy and dangerous and *desperate*.

"Miss me?" he whispered.

John hummed. A massive hand gripped his jaw and rolled his head. Chris lay placid and allowed it, stroking an enormous bicep in each hand and soaking up the heat as John bruised the other side of his throat and made him symmetrical again.

"What time is it?"

"Half one," John rumbled, his weight entirely driven down onto Chris's hips and legs, his upper body held aloft by those bulging arms. His nose tracked down Chris's neck, and teeth chewed on his collarbone, tickling.

"Is that a screwdriver in your pocket, or are you just pleased to see me?"

"What pocket?"

Chris laughed. He squirmed a leg out and hooked it around John's naked knee. He still had his briefs on, but they weren't doing much to hide what was digging between Chris's thighs.

"I've got a problem," John whispered.

"I know, I can feel it."

"Tart. I *mean*, I want to spend hours making l—"

"Fucking."

"Making l—"

"Fucking."

Meaty fingers wrapped around his wrists. The bed groaned. So did the bones of Chris's arm, and it was only the give of the mattress that saved them from breaking as John pinned them down and locked his own elbows. The heat heaved away—and Chris's blood surged south as he was pinned beneath John's bulk. His throat dried out. John's hips were moving ever so slightly, the head of his cock grazing Chris's hip. Did John's weight shake the bed, or Chris's shivering?

"Oh fuck, that's hot," he whispered.

"I want to make love to you for hours," John stated. "But there is no way I have enough self-control right now. So—"

"So where's the problem?" Chris whispered. "Stick it in and fuck me raw."

He could almost feel the eye roll.

"Then—" Chris pushed, but there was no give whatsoever in John's grip, so he gave up. "Then, once you're done and you've fucked me completely boneless, you can get down there and eat me out until I'm so wrung out and exhausted you'd make your stupid love to me all night, and I'd just lie in your arms and let you, totally drunk on sex."

John never fucked him. He liked it slow, sweet, and sensual. And yeah, it was *nice*. Who didn't like getting worshipped sometimes? But every now and then, Chris had an itch and just wanted to be destroyed. Hot and fast and hard and aching for a week after. Those muscles surging above him, that cock like an iron bar splitting him in half, those teeth holding onto him like they'd bite right through if he put up a fight? That beast of a man unleashing all that glorious power on him in a frenzy—and all because it was *Chris* who drove him into said frenzy?

Yes, *please*.

"Please," he whispered.

The hands around his wrists loosened for a moment.

Then they tightened again, and shivered as John dipped in the world's sexiest press-up. His T-shirt grazed Chris's chest, but his body remained elusively far away. The kiss was the sensual worship Chris had become used to—slow and exploratory, as though learning the contours of his mouth for the first time—but the whisper stoked the fire again.

"Tell me if it hurts too bad?"

"'Course."

He choked on startled arousal when the next kiss went deep, an almost savage bite to the softest part of his neck, and then his bruised wrists were released.

"Keep your shirt on," he said breathlessly as John wrenched the sheet back. Cool air rushed in to take its place. Chris's briefs were torn to his thighs and then torn in *half*, and he laughed giddily. "Oh my God."

John didn't really do the whole alpha male thing. He'd been immense since the age of twelve, so he'd never needed to figure out how to fight and was, in reality, a complete wuss. The perfect combination. The sheer size of him, the strength in his bulk, and that deep, thunderous growl could turn Chris on like crazy—but the nuzzle of a nose against his knee, the soft kisses pressed to his labia, the dogmatic insistence on at least a *bit* of foreplay to loosen him up even as Chris whined for the main event...

They added up.

He'd been told over and over—and mostly by John himself—that his fiancé was a scary-looking motherfucker. But he barely even swore. Chris got all of the thrill, and none of the fear.

A thrill that chased up his spine and left him paralysed with anticipation when John was finally persuaded to get on with it, and huge hands spread Chris's legs like the Red Sea for Moses.

"You ready?"

"If you don't fuck me right now, I'm cancelling the wedding."

John huffed a deep laugh. "You're a masochist."

"*Fuck* me, you anim—*ohhh* my God!"

It hurt.

It had been weeks. John's dick was entirely what one would expect to find between the legs of a six-foot-eight man who could lift the back end of a VW Passat. Lube, two fingers, and being fired up hotter than the inside of an industrial kiln only took things so far, and Chris clenched his fists around the pillows as the pressure built up into pain. Hot sparks of agony began to override the arousal. The pulsing in his cock eased. Dizziness crowded his senses, like he was going to fall. He had to gulp for air when a massive hand stroked the side of his face and a thumb teased his lip from between his teeth.

"Breathe."

He heaved on the too-thin air and whimpered.

"Okay?"

"Y-yeah."

"Chris—"

"M'okay. M'o—*fuck*!"

He jolted like he'd been shot when girth met G spot. Everything dissolved. He shoved his knuckles against his teeth and bit down to ward off the shock, and the danger of an imminent orgasm faded.

"Fuck-fuck-fuck, don't move. Don't move—"

It would hurt to come too soon. He'd tear. John would never do it again. And Chris wanted to feel it, wanted to be fucked and ploughed and moved, wanted to smash the paintwork and the plastering behind the headboard. He needed it. *Needed* it.

He shuddered as John leaned down. An elbow cupped his shoulder. The immense prick rendering him frozen shifted inside, and Chris's blood jumped again. Too close, too close, too close—

Teeth. A hoarse whisper in his ear. Wet fingers on his dick.

"Come."

He shattered. One touch, one growl, one savage spike of lust as teeth worried the shell of his ear—

Like a seizure without the pain. Like a death without the fear. Like being smashed to pieces and put back together all at once. Like-like-like—

Gone.

Drifting.

He was being rocked by a warm tide but held in a firm grip too. No, not a tide. A hammock, swaying in the breeze. No—

He clutched and blinked away the haze clouding his mind. Biceps strained under his fingers. Lips grazed his abused ear with every thrust. The wonderful, mind-blowing, incredible sensation of being fucked, well and truly *fucked*, from the inside out. Hips bowing up into his. The scary hollowness, then the unyielding fill. Again and again and again, so hard it hurt, so hard it couldn't fit again, or the next time, or the next, or the next—

He pulled. Weight eased down onto him. The rough rasp of the cotton T-shirt between them. The flex of muscle as he was driven into. The gasps of mindlessness against his ear. Pinned down, forced to take everything, able to feel every inch inside of him and every pound holding him down. The electricity in their skin. The heat in the air. The *shakes*. John was close, so close, so damn *close*—

"God, I love you."

He clenched. Barely. His muscles fluttered weakly, as if they'd been ripped to shreds but still fought to obey him. The flood of heat a filthy euphoria. The way John smashed into him for it and stayed there, right there, sealed tight like they'd never be separated, groaning his release in the deepest pitch Chris had ever heard, so low he *felt* it—

John pulled out slowly. For a moment, Chris was cold and empty without him, and he whimpered wordlessly.

Then, wide fingers—work-rough, love-gentle—began to massage him in their hot mess, and Chris dissolved all over again. He lay broken open and blissful under the kiss that caressed his mouth and the fingers that explored him from the inside out. He wanted more. Wanted everything. But he lay there and accepted whatever came next, soaked in sensual laziness down to his bones.

"I love you," he whispered, tangling a hand in John's sweat-soaked shirt. "I fucking love you. So, so much—"

"Shh."

He was silenced with a long kiss and poured back into the pillows by a gentle hand and a gentler kiss.

"You had yours, now let me have mine."

Chris chuckled drunkenly as the kisses were laid on a path from his chin to his cunt. Soft presses, now. No teeth. Tiny bursts of affection on his oversensitive skin. The blowjob as gentle as the hands that smoothed their mixed mess into his skin. The pleasure intense, yet not the frantic need of before. Coaxed to another climax rather than driven there, he sighed when it was over, cast adrift yet again in the hazy afterglow.

"C'mere—"

"You okay if I go again?"

"Yes. Please. W'nt you—"

John chuckled. He slid inside easily this time and settled over Chris like the incoming tide. Chris looped both arms around his neck and held on, losing himself in sex-drunk kisses and the rough caress of calluses on his skin.

He didn't know if he came again. He didn't know if John did.

He woke in the morning, bathed in the warm glow of an early spring sun, with the stench of sex filling the air, and complete and utter contentment sunk right into his very soul, so deep it would never truly be dislodged.

"IS IT JUST me," Chris asked as the car bounced and leapt over a rolling country lane, "or is this not our usual seaside spot?"

John laughed. "Er. Well, no. I couldn't get a room there, and the beach up here is *glorious*, so—"

"Where are we?"

"Bamburgh."

"Where?" Chris asked.

"Northumberland."

"Okay. *Where?*"

"North Sea, massive beach with sand dunes, and we can walk about five miles down the beach to the next town to get dinner."

It was windy and cold, wherever the hell Bamburgh was supposed to be. Chris stretched, his spine crackling and bursts of aching pleasure shimmering through his muscles. He felt like a whole new human being. True, everything ached like he'd run a marathon, and he wouldn't be having any sort of sex for a week after being smashed open on John's sledgehammer of a sausage, but it was *good*. It was his first testosterone shot, their first time, and the weekend in Paris all rolled up into one ball of happiness. They could have been taking a trip to Scunthorpe, and he wouldn't have cared.

"All right?" John asked as he slammed the boot.

"Better than all right."

John's hand drifted to the small of Chris's back.

"I really need a shower to sort my backache," he said. "How about we check in, I have my shower, then we go and find the beach and walk down to the next village for dinner?"

Chris grinned. "Deal."

The hotel was a small converted house. Cosy, but it smelled airy and open. They found their room at the top of a flight of stairs—too narrow for Poppy, really, but it would have to do—and the door closed behind them with a satisfyingly heavy thump. Chris lifted his arms.

"Kiss me and tip me into bed."

John laughed and obeyed. The kiss was sharp and playful, then the room dipped dizzyingly and Chris crashed down into a deep, soft mattress, trapped as one of the bruises on his neck was softly sucked.

He grinned. He knew exactly what was coming.

"So—"

Right on time.

"You all right?"

"Yep."

One wrist was lifted in gentle fingers and the bruises kissed. Chris let him without an argument. There was a reason John usually refused to give him a good, hard fucking. John had—issues, sometimes. His size and appearance had been used like a weapon against him before, and he'd been a complete mess when they'd gotten together. Terrified into a paralysis of leaving marks, or people thinking he was threatening or violent. He'd gotten much better after eighteen months of weekly counselling, but he still had his quirks. Like kissing any marks he left behind as though Chris were made of priceless crystal. Like waiting for Chris to initiate contact the first few times after leaving marks in the first place. Like—

"I wasn't too rough last night?"

—outright asking.

Chris smiled and presented his cheek. John chuckled and obediently kissed it.

"This morning. And no. You were perfect," Chris said. "Exactly what I needed."

"Didn't hurt too bad?"

"Hurt exactly the right amount. You couldn't tell from me coming all over the sheets?"

John laughed, and the set of his shoulders eased under Chris's hands. "That was hot as heck."

"Hell. Or fuck. Fuck works good."

"I didn't even know you *could* ejaculate."

"For someone who is so good at sex, your understanding of how it actually works is terrible," Chris complained. "You can ejaculate with a cunt, too, you know."

"In my defence, I never thought I'd *have* to know that," John replied.

"That was *dangerously* close to an ignorant comment."

"Oh come on!"

"You owe me a coffee."

John bitched, Chris insisted, and—of course—Chris won. He was promised a coffee before John heaved himself up off the bed and vanished into the bathroom. Chris propped himself up on his elbows, grinning as he heard the shower start up and John's tuneless humming permeate the room. He'd not closed the door again.

It wasn't *entirely* selfish. Chris had long since learned John's issues were easier to handle if Chris flashed his haughty attitude around. It was pretty difficult to coerce somebody so demanding, after all. He stretched again and worked his phone out of his pocket. Might as well make use of the interlude.

They hadn't broken the news to anyone yet. The Sunday dinner had dissolved into happy shrieking and plenty of boozy toasts, and Chris was woken in the small hours for a fuck after John returned from his emergency appointment in Rotherham. When they'd finally gotten up, they'd just jumped straight in the car and headed north. There'd been no more calls. Neither of them really used social media. They hadn't told anyone else—not Chris's family, not any of their friends, nobody. And with the excitement still thrumming along the edges of Chris's skin, he thumbed through his contacts until he found the first one who'd not be at work. Maybe not the first person he *should* tell. But the first person who would be available—and Chris was too keyed up to wait. Predictably, Luke never answered with a hello.

"What's up, slag?"

"Whoa, you were in our bedroom last night?" Chris asked.

"What! Oh God, I didn't need to know."

"I mean, 'slag' might be appropriate. I was *begging* for his—"

"Shut up!"

"And then when he—"

"Fuck *off*," Luke whined. "Jesus, why do I have you for a friend?"

"Oh, that's nice. After I was going to ask you to be my best man and everything." A long pause.

Then Luke said, "What?"

"Surprise, I'm engaged," Chris said and beamed.

It felt unreal. And in more ways than one. Chris had never really thought about getting married. Wedding bells and monogamy weren't really the default in his family— Dad had two girlfriends and had been very technically engaged to Lauren for about a decade now. Mum was more of a traditionalist, but even then, she'd gone through boyfriends like other people went through hot dinners between divorcing Dad and marrying Jack. Sometimes, more than one boyfriend at a time.

Chris never anticipated proposing. He hadn't planned on it. He'd known he would probably remain monogamous—John was definitely not open to sharing, and Chris wasn't going to jeopardise their relationship for some potential fun with someone else—but he'd never given marriage much thought.

Until yesterday.

So he wasn't entirely offended when Luke said, "Pull the other one."

"I'm serious."

"No fucking way."

"Yep."

"*You?*"

"Me."

"He popped the question, and you said *yes*?"

"*I* popped the question," Chris said.

"Holy fuck."

"So, you gonna come?"

"Fuck yeah," Luke said and laughed. "I better work on my beard. When did this happen?"

"Yesterday."

"So no date set or anything?"

"Not a thing." Chris stretched out into a starfish, occupying the whole bed. "I just— We went to his nan's for Sunday lunch yesterday, and I was just hit with how much they're my family, too, so...yeah. Engaged. Getting married. Best sex of my life last night when he got back from a work emergency."

"Aaaaand that's all I need to know," Luke said. "You told Gina yet?"

"Not yet."

"And your folks?"

"Also not yet."

"Should cheer your mum up, at least."

Chris opened his mouth—and hesitated. *Would* it cheer her up? Her unpredictable mood lately made him uncertain. And her surprise conviction that John was a temporary thing... Would she interpret this as Chris lashing out at her?

"I hope so," he said stupidly.

"Er, will it...not?"

"I don't know," Chris admitted. "She's been funny lately."

"Best tell her in person, then. Don't ring her up. Go for lunch and drop it then. She'll take it better that way."

"Since when did you get to be an expert on mums?"

"Oh, right, haven't seen you since you asked for Susie. Which is a go, by the way. Izzy can't get time off until late September, so you can have Susie until then. Anyway, so my mum rings me up yesterday, fuck knows how she got my number—"

Chris relaxed into the cushions and played counsellor about a family far worse than anything his had ever thrown at him, but the uncertainty played out in the back of his mind, surfacing during Luke's predictable tangents.

Dad wouldn't think anything of it. Lauren and Caroline would just be a bit bemused. John's family was all thrilled and excited, enough for the entire world.

But Mum?

How was Mum going to see it?

Chapter Seven

CHRIS IGNORED IT.

He pushed off the thought of telling family entirely. He rang Gina before John got out of the shower, then abandoned his phone in the hotel room and fought his way up the sandy beach and over slippery rock pools, hand in hand and so irrepressibly happy he could burst. Who the hell cared? Who cared about *any* of it? With salty kisses on a windy, frozen beach and the sea roaring just metres away, locked warm and safe in John's arms, Chris found himself completely incapable of caring what his mother might think. What *anyone* might think.

Their evening was a short meal, a long walk, and—despite the soreness—a long, gentle night of John's lovemaking, one hand playing with Chris's bare ring finger as the world moved both inside him and around him.

But by the next morning, dizzy love had worn off into a more practical excitement.

"I don't even know how to plan a wedding," Chris said as he laced his shoes. "Or being married in general. What about names? I'm not changing my name. And I'll need to change my will. And—"

John chuckled. "Shame. Christian Halliday has a nice ring to it."

"Changed it once, never again. Never change your name when you're on benefits."

John laughed, hauling Chris up by the hand. "I'll be sure not to. Breakfast?"

"Breakfast."

The hotel did a mean bacon sandwich, and the waitress squealed and brought them free seconds when John said they were newly engaged. Chris basked in the warm happiness—and the taste of incredible bacon—and steered John back onto a conversation once the bacon was gone and the coffee in hand.

"We could go abroad. Gina said it's cheaper now."

"You can't fly, Granddad can't fly, I burn like nobody's business the minute there's an inkling of sun, and Rhodri's obnoxious enough when he's in this country."

"But we wouldn't have to invite my great-aunt Greta."

"You *have* a great-aunt Greta?"

"Just because you haven't seen so-and-so in ten years doesn't mean you don't invite them to the wedding," Chris said, mimicking one of Dad's many aunts. He snorted. "That's the only time my dad's family ever get together. Weddings, funerals, and christenings."

"I can't even guarantee Tasha would show up," John admitted ruefully.

"She'd really miss your wedding?"

"I think she still believes the lies Daniel spread about me." John's voice was a little tight, and Chris winced.

"Well, she's an idiot, then. More room for my random aunts and uncles."

"What about your mum's family?"

"They won't come. They've not spoken to us in years. Probably for the best. They were pissy enough about Mum marrying Dad, I think this—" Chris gestured vaguely between them. "—would be a bit much."

"You're a bit much for most people."

"Oh, *charming*."

"Not like that!"

"Too late. You owe me another coffee."

John sighed, and his chair scraped. Chris smirked to himself as he drained his cup and reached for his pills. He was still on the heavy dose after the surgery. At the upper end, his epilepsy *could* be ninety-nine percent controlled—but the drugs left him with awful side effects that just weren't worth it. He'd take a seizure or two every week if it meant not feeling permanently sick, having constant migraines or random bursts of vertigo, and being so tired he napped during the day with or without an aura. Still, the scars were healing nicely, and the pain was gone. He'd get to finish up with them soon.

"Good riddance," he told the pill and washed it down with John's orange juice.

"Hey!"

"You left it unattended, so it's your fault."

John grumbled. Chris ignored him.

"I called Luke while you were in the shower this morning. Izzy can't get time off work until the end of September, so we can borrow the campervan until then."

"You still want to go ahead on the house?" John asked in surprise.

"Well, yeah."

"That'll be fun, organising a wedding *and* a renovation."

Chris just laughed, settling back with his fresh coffee in hand. He tucked his feet between John's under the table. "We can manage."

"We'll revisit this conversation in six months when you're tearing your hair out," John remarked. "Did you tell him about the wedding?"

"Yep. Him and Gina."

"They excited?"

"Mostly surprised."

"Why?"

"Apparently, I'm not the marrying kind."

John chuckled. "Well, lucky for me you changed that tune."

"Lucky for you I *exist*," Chris said snottily. "Anyway, Susie is ready when we are. We could—"

"Who?"

"Luke's campervan."

John snorted with laughter. "He *named* it?"

"You named your van."

"I have not!"

"Yes you have, you call it 'Useless Old Wreck' all the time!"

John groaned. Chris was kicked lightly. He laughed and called John a berk.

"So when can we move?"

"You seriously want to plan a wedding *and* commit to a renovation?"

"Yes," Chris said, then bit his lip. "It just—it'll help."

John's voice softened. "With what?"

"Things being...different now," Chris said. "I can't work up the energy to tell Mum yet, and I can't tell Dad and Caroline and Lauren before Mum because then there'll be an almighty row, and I still— It's still weird. Without Jack. I can still hear his letter."

John's fingers peeled his own away from the cup. Chris set it down and let John cover both of Chris's hands in his own. Warm. Familiar. Rough yet impossibly gentle.

"Being at your nan and granddad's helped. It was just busy and warm and fun. And the house will help, because it'll be you and me, and hard work. By the time I get all the quiet moments back, I'll have figured some of this out." Chris's throat felt scratchy, and he swallowed. "I'll have...I don't know. Come to terms with it, I guess."

John squeezed gently.

"We can do whatever you need," he said, "but I don't want you to run yourself into the ground with all of this."

"I won't. Promise."

"Come on. Let's go out and enjoy the coast. We can call Luke and get the campervan—"

"Susie."

"—when—not a chance—we get back."

"What about the flat?"

"To be honest, I think we'd be best off just selling it," John admitted. "It would free up the cash for renovations. And once I get the water and electric switched on at the house, the van will keep us until the winter."

"September. Luke needs it for a road trip."

"Eh, that's six months. I can get at least a *bit* of the house done by then, even if we end up living in the kitchen for a while."

"And—"

John groaned and squeezed until Chris squeaked.

"Stop with the planning for five minutes," he said. "We'll sort it. But not in some massive, stupid rush. There's no need. Get your posh coffee down you, and let's go out."

Chris licked his lips and tilted his chin up. The table groaned as John leaned over and kissed his throat. The gentle graze of his unshaven cheek was intimately familiar, and Chris sighed, breathing out all of the budding plans and building tension.

"Thursday," he said.

"What?"

"Get Luke's van and set it up at the house with Rhodri on Thursday. And while you're doing that, I'll tell Mum."

CHRIS HAD FALLEN in love more than once, but always with the same man.

Before John, there hadn't been anyone. There'd been one friend with benefits—now long since out of the picture—but never a partner. There'd been friends, but never lovers. There'd been one or two crushes, but kept firmly a secret under the weight of his gender and disability. Chris had been too shy and scared to push for more when he was younger, and by the time John came along, too brashly used to his solitude to bother trying to find someone else.

The simple truth was he'd never really been all that lonely. With a busy family and both Luke and Gina always somewhere to be found, his only lonely moments had been at night and the early mornings, when the rest of the world was shut out by the bedroom door. And it hadn't bothered him. He hadn't thought anything was missing, even after he'd banished the demons saying he'd never find anyone anyway.

John had—literally—just walked into Chris's life without Chris ever trying to find him.

Chris had started it, really. That incredible voice, tempered with an odd shyness and a sweet, surprised response to being flirted with had pushed Chris into ever more outrageous flirting and their first date. There'd been—something. Something there that even now Chris couldn't define. He didn't know exactly what had been lurking beneath the surface, calling to him when they'd first met.

Chris was emotionally cautious with people, and he didn't know if it was wholly a byproduct of his gender or disabilities. Sometimes, he thought they hadn't made much difference. Like Mum, in a way. He didn't like lots of people around. He didn't need crowds. He didn't really bother with most folks and had very little urge to make new friends. Both of his best mates were a product of continual exposure over long periods of time. As with John, he'd never deliberately decided to get to know them. It had just sort of...happened.

John had just happened.

Faster, but still just happened. He'd been attractive from the start. Funny in how he responded to flirting and refused to swear, sweet in his determination to come off like a gentle giant, and completely shaggable for a number of reasons. And slowly, the exciting thrill of being with him had given way to an idle sort of heat. Like basking in the sun. Calm and steady, but still noticeably better than being somewhere else, with someone else. He had become a permanent feature of Chris's life.

But every now and then, he got that thrill again. Falling in love in a rush—like how John fell in love. He'd loved Chris from the beginning, and Chris wondered if this was how it had felt. The sudden breathlessness and the rush of heat. The moment when he caught himself just hearing or touching, without really listening or feeling. As if it were the first time they'd met, but Chris already knew how incredible John really was. As if he *could* fall in love in that very first moment, rather than waiting for the feeling to grow.

He loved those moments.

Sometimes they came for a reason, like their trip to Paris. And sometimes they came out of nowhere, like when John bracketed Chris against the battlements of Bamburgh Castle in a high wind, the kiss on the cheek a hot point on his frozen face.

"Hello," Chris said, beaming and flushed with warmth from head to toe. "What was that for?"

"Just appreciating the view."

"Is it good?"

John dashed his nose against Chris's. "Perfect."

"Sleaze," Chris said, but he was smiling uncontrollably.

"Your face says you think otherwise."

"Yeah, well, *your* face—"

The nipping kiss interrupted him, and Chris leaned against the cold, damp stone to smile as John nuzzled his cheek, rubbed his stubble against Chris's ear, then curled a hand into his windswept hair and tilted his head for another kiss. The benefits of a boyfriend who couldn't fit into the little doorways leading into some of the keeps, dungeons, and towers. Public displays of affection had never been entirely off the table.

"I love you," Chris whispered.

On the edge of a castle, in the warmth of a bed and breakfast hotel, in the wreck of their car, at home—wherever. Chris loved him. John was his future, but he was the past and the present, too. Everything came back to him. The one man Chris wanted, and the one man he'd never gone looking for.

"I *love* you."

John smiled against his mouth and didn't answer.

Chapter Eight

CHRIS...DIDN'T IMMEDIATELY go telling people.

Like Mum. Or Dad. Or...anyone else.

He focused on trying to get the campervan first. But with John busy and Luke working, Chris found it remarkably easy to just continue packing up the flat and...neglecting to mention the news. He put it off. He wasn't ashamed of it, because breaking even moderate news to his bitterly divorced parents could be awkward. Wedding news, when he was doubtful one of them would be entirely happy about it?

He wasn't too keen on the idea.

But eventually, John and Luke touched base, and when letting agents started coming to the flat to make assessments and quote prices, Chris figured it was now or never. The longer he left it, the worse reception it would get. So two weeks after they got back from Bamburgh, he got his nice jeans out of the cupboard.

When Chris was young, Mum had been an ardent atheist. Mostly out of rebellion against her own much more orthodox parents, who'd disowned her for marrying a Scottish Presbyterian. Hell, Chris had chosen his own name as a not-so-subtle fuck you to his maternal grandparents and their refusal to have anything to do with him or Mum. But since Jack had started the long, slow decline to his death, Mum had become a regular at the synagogue again. Chris didn't know if it was just for some community support, or whether she really had found her faith again, and he didn't ask.

Chris didn't go in—he was about as Jewish as he was Presbyterian—but he dressed up a bit nicer than usual, sent her a text when her phone would be on silent in the middle of the service, and waited outside on the wall.

It was mid-March already, and he turned vague wedding ideas over in his head as traffic ghosted past and Poppy nudged her head higher into his hand when he paused in stroking her ears. He'd like an autumn wedding. Crunchy leaves, warm but crisp weather, noisy birds. Maybe they'd get married at John's beloved coast, or stay closer to home for his family. Chris wasn't too keen on the idea of a tuxedo, but he had to admit, from Nora and Raj's wedding, that John had a *very* nice package in a pair of suit trousers. They'd have to dance. He liked a good hug-and-sway with John, so there'd have to be dancing. And—

"Hello, darling."

"Hi, Mum."

He slid off the wall and hugged her. She hugged back, better than she'd been since the funeral. He hadn't seen her since she'd scattered the ashes, and although he'd called, she'd been clipped and short with him. But her hug was warmer, and he hoped she'd recovered a little from the shock.

"How you doing?"

"All right. You?"

"Fine." Okay, a *bit* warmer. Still, she took his arm and suggested a cafe down the road, and they swapped pleasantries at least a little less awkwardly than the day at the funeral parlour. Chris avoided asking where she'd scattered Jack. Mum avoided telling him. The cat had been sick again. Maybe she ought to take it to the vet. Nice weather.

He loved his mum, but they'd never really understood one another. Chris had inherited most of his dad's rebelliousness but with none of the instinct to keep it under wraps. Nobody would guess Dad had two girlfriends and supported his trans son, but nobody would be surprised by photos of Chris with blue hair. Hell, he still wore his lip ring more often than not, and it was only his curly hair that hid his scaffold from the world. He still toyed with the idea of getting a tattoo, just to say he had one.

Mum was more—conservative. Not really politically, but she had a certain properness about her—always controlled and put together. She worried about what the neighbours would think. She *over*thought. And for all that Chris figured he probably should overthink more, he wasn't so good at it. If he'd done so, he'd never have dated John. Never have fallen in love. Never moved out. Never done anything, because everything he'd ever done involved taking a risk. So much of what was normal for Gina and Luke was risky for him.

And he'd be taking another risk in the cafe, when she came back with their coffees. He pulled in a deep breath.

"I have some news."

"Oh?"

"I'm—"

John wasn't permanent, she thought. John was going to leave him, she implied. He needed to plan for the future, she said.

"—engaged."

Her cup hit the table with a sharp clunk.

"What?"

Not 'pardon'. Not 'sorry'.

"I'm engaged."

She said nothing. Chris fidgeted with his cup uncertainly.

"John and I are getting married."

"Yes, thank you, I know what engaged means."

Her voice was tight. Every vowel short, every consonant clipped. It sounded so under control that Chris cringed, the urge to apologise instinctual and insulting. His temper flared, even though she'd barely said a word. He fought to keep his words behind his teeth.

"I didn't expect that," she said eventually. "Congratulations."

Chris drew back, frowning.

"That's it?"

"Sorry?"

"Congratulations? That's it?"

She sighed heavily through her nose. "I'm having a little trouble processing it, Christian. Truth be told—"

"Your son is getting married, what's to process?"

She should be happy. She should scream like Nan had. She should be excited for him. Wasn't that what mums *did* when there was wedding news? If anyone was supposed to grumble and not respond, it should be Dad. Not Mum. Not *any* mum.

"Truth be told, I didn't expect you to agree to such a thing."

"I didn't," Chris snapped. "I proposed."

She coughed. He must have told her mid-sip. The cup clunked again.

"Oh."

He gripped his own tightly, a familiar anger starting to creep up his spine, hot and hurting. Why couldn't he propose? It wasn't the eighteenth century. He could propose to his boyfriend if he wanted. All right, John was the more romantic of them, and it was a bit surprising Chris had beaten him to it, maybe, but—it wasn't *that* shocking. Was it?

Was it?

It felt like he was telling the barista. Hell, the barista would probably be happier for him. He'd at least get a free coffee out of it, and congratulations that sounded sincere.

"I thought you'd be happy for me."

"I am."

"You don't sound it."

"I'm surprised."

"You can be both at once, you know."

John was. His family was. Luke and Gina were.

"Are—"

He bit down on his temper. He wanted to blow up. He wanted to shout and scream and demand her to be happy for him. It took everything he had to think of Jack, and force the room in his anger to make allowances.

"Are you sure it's a good idea?"

He had to put his cup down, his fingers were shaking so badly. Poppy sat up and rested her head on his lap, sensing—something.

"Yes, or I wouldn't have asked," he snapped.

"Christian—"

"Why wouldn't it be a good idea?"

The silence yawned. And Chris wanted an answer, because he couldn't think of one himself.

"I don't get it," he said. "I know you've never exactly been chatty with John, but I didn't think you hated him."

"I don't hate—"

"It's been three years, so it's not like we're not serious about each other. He's—he's supportive, he's kind, he makes me happy, he treats me well, he's good for me and

I'm good for him—what's the problem? We can afford a wedding—I mean, not a really fancy celebrity-style thing, but we can afford a little party and a good photographer for the day. His family are excited, and—and I'm excited, and I want you to be excited."

It felt like a lame finish, but he'd run out of words. He clenched his fists on the table, and even though she was just on the other side of it, she'd never felt so far away.

"I don't understand."

"You don't want to."

"Excuse me?"

"You don't want to understand," Mum said. "You're—you're caught up in the moment, in being in love—"

"Three years is hardly a mome—"

"—And you're not looking at the bigger picture or the long term. He'll— I just worry. I just worry you'll commit too much, too hard, and eventually, the inevitable will happen and John will break your heart. And I worry when it happens, there won't be anyone there to break the fall."

"What are you *talking* about it?" Chris blurted out. "What bigger picture? What, you think John is going to leave me?"

"I know you don't want to hear it, but—well—yes."

"Why?" Chris demanded. "Has he said something to you? Because everything he's said and done to me—*for* me—tells me loud and clear he's got no intention of going anywhere, and—"

"And I think maybe he really believes that, but—"

"Then why would—"

"For goodness' sake, Christian, be reasonable. Your disabilities might be easy enough to handle now, but—"

Chris caught his breath.

His disabilities.

She—

"No way."

"Sorry?"

She couldn't have just said that. She *couldn't* be talking about that. He gaped stupidly at her, stunned beyond words. He had to struggle to find them again, struck dumb with shock and horror.

"This—seriously? This is about—"

His stomach tightened, and it was nothing to do with his medication. His heart hardened into a stone fist inside his chest. It wasn't beating anymore. There was a hollow echo in his ears, like the absence of sound itself.

"You think I'm too—"

Too what?

Too difficult? Too disabled? Too demanding?

"So, one day," he choked out. "One day, you think John's going to leave because I'm too hard to handle."

There was a long, long silence.

"When Jack—"

"No," Chris said. "Don't you dare. Don't you *dare* bring Jack into this. This isn't about Jack; this is about you, and what you think of me."

"It's nothing to do with what I think of you!" she snapped. "You're my son!"

"And I'm too fucking difficult for someone to love!" he shouted back. The coffee shop clattered into silence, and he didn't give a shit. "I shouldn't get married because one day he'll leave, and it's *inevitable*! It's just what happens to people like me, is it, Mum?"

"You have to be—"

Realistic. He knew that would be the next word. He had to be realistic.

"I *am* being realistic," he said, shoving at the table. The chair crashed to the floor. Around them, the whole cafe was silent, and he groped clumsily for Poppy's harness. "I know him better than that. I know *us* better than that. But I wish I'd known *you* better."

He was shaking so hard he thought he might seize, but it was nothing compared to the screaming in his head and the pain in his chest. His mum thought—his mum thought—

He smashed out of the cafe and stopped dead in the street, his chest heaving. He ought to ring John and ask to be picked up. Or Dad, and tell them the news and Mum's reaction. He ought to rant and rage and vent his anger, not his horror or his sadness. He ought to hold onto the indignation and the fury.

But he didn't.

Instead, he rang Gina.

And with the first cheery, "Hello, honey!" he burst into tears.

Chapter Nine

HE STIRRED WHEN a deep, familiar voice sounded in the hall.

He'd cried all over Gina, then ranted, then cried some more, then—because of course his epilepsy had turned up to prove a point—had a seizure on her kitchen floor, then called her an interfering bitch when she'd bullied him onto the sofa to sleep it off. And somewhere between the seizure and now, she must have called John, because he could hear them murmuring in the hall.

Crap.

At least Gina was used to him swearing at her in the aftermath and wouldn't take offence. He sighed and sat up gingerly, rolling his head on a stiff neck. Poppy licked his knuckles, and he stroked her ears.

"I'm okay, sweetheart."

The door cracked open. "Chris?"

"I'm up," he said, holding up both hands. "I'm sorry for whatever I said this time."

"Oh, the usual." Gina hugged him, still standing, and kissed the top of his head. "John's come to take you home."

He hugged right back. "Thanks for letting me vent and crash out."

"It's okay," she said. "Your mum's being a cow. It's going to be the best wedding ever, and—don't tell the thug in my hall because he'll get an ego to match his shoe size—

we both know you're absolutely making the right decision."

Chris held on tighter and buried his face in her chest.

"I'm sorry she's being like that," Gina whispered.

"She's my *mum*."

That was the most unfathomable part. He semi-expected Caroline to be against the idea—marriages were oppressive tools of the patriarchy, blah blah blah—and he could even see Luke being wary of it, given how well his parents' marriage had gone. But *Mum*?

His own mother?

"And she's wrong."

"I know," Chris whispered.

"Damn right you know," Gina said. "Fuck that noise. It's John who doesn't deserve you. Big louts are ten a penny, but diamonds like you are rare."

"Okay, okay, don't overdo it," Chris grumbled and released her.

His knees hurt when he stood, and he staggered to the door rather than walked. John had obviously been listening in, but he didn't say anything. He just helped Chris into his jacket and shoes, kissed his cheek, and complained about Gina's taste in décor.

"Her carpets are nice."

"You would not be saying that if you could see the colour."

"And with that, you can both fuck off," Gina said.

Chris chuckled, though it was weak and feeble, and offered one last hug before stepping out into the chilly stairwell. Her flat was lovely, but the rest of the block left much to be desired.

"So what happened?" John asked as they descended the concrete stairs to the car park.

"Gina didn't say?"

"Just that you'd had a row with your mum, then a seizure on her floor, so could I bring the car because her sofa's not really fit for spending the night on."

"Yeah, no kidding," Chris groused. "My knees are killing me."

The car was a welcome relief, and he dropped the seat back to lie down a little more as John fired up the engine.

"Did the row cause the seizure?"

"Probably, yeah."

"What was the row about?" he asked as he heaved the car around and out into the road.

"Mum thinks it's a bad idea."

"What?"

"Us getting married. *Me* getting married."

"Why?"

To Chris's relief, John's response was bland. Once, the news would have fucked John up. And cruel as it sounded, Chris didn't have the energy for it. He needed to vent and be upset, not guard against John's issues as well. He needed John to be sure of himself, and he could have cried at John's bland question. The lack of surprise, or anger, or agreement. They dug into the weak points, and Chris sniffled like a kid as the reason poured out.

"I'm too hard to handle," he said, tears prickling at the corners of his eyes. "I'm—I'm—one day—"

John's hand squeezed his knee briefly before vanishing again.

"She said it's inevitable that one day you'll leave me."

John snorted.

"My disabilities are only going to get harder to deal with as I get older, and one day it'll be too much, and you'll be gone. *Anybody* would be gone. She—she thinks—she thinks—"

"She thinks a load of old sh—stuff."

The lack of a swear word jerked a wet laugh out of Chris, and he scrubbed furiously at the tears.

"*Shit*, John."

"And that."

"It wasn't even about *you*. It was me. I'm too hard to handle. Anybody would be gone. That's what she was implying. That no matter who I was marrying, it would be a bad idea because I'm too much. I mean, whose *mum* thinks like that? Does—does she even—I mean, would she love me more if I wasn't like this? If—"

"Oh hey, no—"

"But that's what she's saying!" Chris exploded. "It was all that I'm difficult and nobody will want to handle it forever and—"

"You *are* difficult," John interrupted. He'd dropped his voice, the rumble like a train miles underground, and it shook through the anger and the hurt, a purr soothing damaged sinew. "I was at the supermarket when Gina called. You know I have *four* different varieties of coffee in the boot? You're ridiculous. Who needs *four* types of coffee?"

Chris managed a wobbly smile.

"And God forbid I have a hot soak in the bath, because then it's bitch bitch, moan moan; it just steams up the bathroom and makes the tiles slippery; you've lived all your years without one so why can't I manage; I only leave tide marks anyway—"

"You *do*."

"And let's not get started on how damn *cold* your feet are. Never mind your epilepsy; that's going to be the straw that broke the camel's back. One too many cold toes on my balls in the middle of the night and that's it. I'm out."

Chris laughed. It was John's TV tone. The one he used when whining about a TV show he secretly liked but didn't want to admit it. So, most of the things Chris liked to watch.

"You know she's wrong, don't you?"

"Yeah," Chris mumbled. "But—it hurts. And I—I believed it too. For so, so long. You know when you're still young and dumb and you buy into what everyone's telling you?"

"You know I do," John breathed.

"It's like she's just tapped right back into that, and if—if you weren't you, if we didn't have this and you hadn't *proven* her wrong...I might."

"I think maybe you need to listen to my family on this one, not yours."

Chris found a packet of tissues in the glove compartment and started seriously cleaning up his face. "What d'you mean?"

"I know marriage isn't the way your family does things, but it is mine," John pointed out. "Until death do us part. Nora married wrong, then got divorced and had to do it again, and much as Nan and Granddad like Raj, they've not forgiven her for choosing wrong the first time. But you? You saw them. They're excited. They're buzzing. There's no 'wrong one' with you."

Chris warded off more tears at the declaration by noisily blowing his nose.

"They know I've picked right. They know this is it for me. And so do I. Much as I love you, I wouldn't have said yes if I didn't *know*, one hundred percent, that I want to be here for good. I loved all my exes—except Daniel, obviously—but I didn't get close to marrying any of them. They weren't the right ones. And no matter how hard it might get, you are. This is where I want to be, and it might not be you that gets difficult. I might have a heart attack like Granddad one day, and it'll be you doing all the running around."

"Way you go through bacon sandwiches, you're not wrong," Chris mumbled hoarsely.

"Oh, like you can talk."

"Thank you," Chris mumbled, reaching across on a straight stretch to squeeze John's thigh.

"Your mum is too late. If she wanted rid of me, she should have stuck her oar in earlier, because now you've asked, you're not getting out of it."

Chris laughed. "Oh my God."

"Stuck with me."

"Fate worse than death."

"Death's the only way out now, beautiful."

"Aaaand here comes the cheese."

John snorted. "Like my little speech there wasn't cheesy enough..."

Chris's anger dissolved away into the banter and bickering that formed the bedrock of their relationship—and in doing so, soothed a little of the burn his mother had administered. He blew his nose once more and threw the tissue out of the window.

"Chris!"

"It's biodegradable," he said. "What time is it?"

"Half six."

"Are we going home?"

"I'm guessing by the way you're saying that, the answer's no."

"I want to go to Dad's."

"Wh—"

"I'm going to tell them now. And fuck them, fuck *all* of them, if they aren't happy for us."

CHRIS'S PARENTS SPLIT up when he was six years old. To their credit, they were perfectly civil and a united front when he was a child. But the split second he'd turned sixteen—that had been it. All bets—and gloves—were off.

Mum lived just off Ecclesall Road, and Dad up in Greenhill. It wasn't really too far, but it might as well have been a thousand miles. Chris didn't know the route on foot at all and had never gone direct from one house to the other. So he couldn't pick up on where they were until John soared around the weirdly oversized roundabout at the bottom of Dad's road, and the car surged up onto the potholed street.

"Are they in?"

"Lights are on. Want me to come with?"

"Yes, please."

"Urgh."

Chris pulled a face. John was perpetually nervous of Dad. Said ex-Marines were scary. Please. Dad was about as scary as a pile of dumplings.

He had the same build too. He came to the door and offered a brief, back-thumping hug before letting them in. He was short and squat, perpetually scruffy-jawed, and—apparently—looked so unlike Chris *he* had always been taken for the stepfather, not Jack. He grunted a query as to whether they wanted a brew, shot Chris's request for coffee down, and gave them both tea.

Then said, "What do you want?"

"Why can't it just be a social call?" Chris asked.

"Both of you? Bollocks it's a social call. Out with it."

"I can drop in on my dad and stepmums if I want. Where are they?"

"Caroline's meditating and Lauren's—" Long pause. "*Lauren!*"

"What!"

"Where are you, you daft cow?"

"Don't you talk to me like that, you fat git!"

"Watching the telly," Dad decided, and Chris snorted. "Lauren!"

"For fuck's sake, *what*?"

"Come here!"

The chattering in the next room paused, and she stomped out. A glass banged on the table, and Chris surmised they'd interrupted the evening wine and *Real Housewives*. Oops.

"This had better be good."

"Can you get Caroline?"

"This had better be *really* good," she warned but stalked off anyway. John shifted uncomfortably at Chris's side and took his hand.

"Oh fuck me," Dad said.

"Sorry?"

"You're doing it. You're getting fucking hitched."

"*What?*"

The shriek was deafening, even from two rooms away. A door slammed.

"You're *engaged*?" Lauren yelled from the doorway. Another shriek sounded upstairs, and then the master bedroom door was flung open with so much force it bounced off the wall and right back into the frame.

"Yes," he said.

"Oh my *God!*"

The smell of red wine surrounded him, along with a sheet of hair. Lauren's grip was choking. The stairs pounded, and then he was smothered in a wall of frizz as Caroline joined in, squealing in his ear like a kid. A cork popped. John's deep rumble distinctly said, "Driving," and Dad's snort didn't mask the "Spare room," offered in reply.

Chris clung back.

He cried a bit, then. Clung and cried a bit, and didn't give a shit. This was the reaction he'd wanted. This was the reaction his mother should have had. This was what he'd needed her to do. Be excited and deafen him and hug him and *love* him.

In the mess, John's hand found his and squeezed. Chris squeezed right back, despite the tears.

They were going to do this.

Chapter Ten

CHRIS WAS WOKEN by Lauren's car door slamming below the open window.

The spare room had been his once, but Dad had redecorated after Chris moved out. Chris didn't think much of the bed, the mattress too deep and too small and the winter duvet ridiculous given Caroline kept the heating permanently cranked up to twenty-five.

Admittedly, *most* beds were too small when one had a partner nudging at seven feet tall, but *this* bed was too small even for Chris. He grumbled, kicked the duvet off, and made a bid for freedom.

A highly unsuccessful bid.

The arm around his waist contracted. Limbs curled. In a moment, buried again under a body that smelled of sleep and soap, he groaned.

"John."

"Mm."

"Let go."

"No."

Chris huffed a laugh and ghosted his fingers up a tense arm, ruffling the hair. He had to squirm onto his back to get hold of John's shoulder and shake him.

"C'mon. Breakfast."

"L'ter."

The head that planted itself on his collarbone was intensely heavy, and Chris laughed breathlessly. He scratched gently at ears and stubble until a deep growl, not wholly unlike a purr, shivered through the mass holding him down.

"I'm hungry," Chris whispered, but it wasn't quite the same sort of hunger that rippled through him when John slid up his body, heavy and hard, and caught his lips in a biting kiss. "Mm. Okay. That too."

John nosed at his neck and smiled there. "You'll be so lucky."

"Aw, why not?" Chris whined. He squirmed a leg out so John's hips dropped lower onto his. "That's definitely not your need-to-pee wood."

"I'm not having sex in your dad's house," John parried, still kissing his neck in tiny, soft bites.

Chris stretched his head back and sighed breathily. There were biceps under his fingers, hot and hard. Tiny shifts of muscle against his hips. Brain had reservations, but body didn't care.

"I'll be quiet," Chris breathed, rubbing his naked foot up John's leg. John shuddered and growled before biting him again. "*God*, yes."

"No chance," John whispered, even as he slid an arm down Chris's side and began to gently kiss his chest, lips hovering over the scars. The strange interplay of sensation and numbness over the healing scar tissue was intriguing. "This okay? This—"

"Be better if you bit me again."

"I'm not tangling with a Marine."

"*Ex*-Marine and future father-in-law. I'm not his fourteen-year-old daughter. I'm pretty sure he knows we have sex, and if that is *seriously* why you won't do me right here and right now, you're not getting it for a *week!*" Chris hissed.

John laughed. Bit down on a nipple. It hurt like hell, pain lancing through the arousal, and Chris shoved him off with a gasp.

"Shit! Sorry, sorry..."

The apology kiss was better but the kiss on the scar still strange, and Chris didn't like that either. Then John sucked on his breastbone. Hot hands pulled his briefs down. A mouth sealed over his as even hotter fingers worked him open. Chris held on to the strained biceps, preventing their owner from squashing him flat, and lost himself in the heat, the rhythm, the messy kisses trying to catch his every breath.

"Shh—"

They were clumsy and the bed too small. Oppressively warm. His skin was slick with sweat by the time John groaned in his ear and reduced him to a shivering mess, the low roll of thunder sweeping over him like a tsunami. He lay gasping for air as John brought him to climax on his tongue, then pulled on worn tattoos and hot skin to get his kisses back, tasting salt, sex, and morning breath.

"Love you."

Chris just hummed, drunk on the smell of them. He curled into John's arms, freedom be damned. A breeze ghosted in from the window. He'd last.

Eventually, the smell of eggs and toast drove them into the day. Chris liked to sleep after sex, but John needed feeding on a very regular basis, and once he'd gone for a shower, what little the bed had going for it had been lost. Chris changed into some spare clothes that still lived at Dad's house and headed downstairs to let Poppy out into the garden.

"Morning, darling!"

"Morning, Caroline."

A grunt.

"Morning, Dad."

Another grunt.

Chris left the back door open. It was either late, or summer was going to come early. He sat in his usual spot and smiled beatifically when Caroline gave him a coffee and his father called him a lazy shit.

"Oh, stop your nonsense. Hello, John, darling. Eggs?"

"I can get th—"

"Don't be silly, dear. You've already used up all your energy," Caroline said. "That bed isn't the best for sex, though, so do mind your back today."

John spluttered. Chris smirked into his cup and said nothing.

"We—I—"

"Oh, don't be so *embarrassed*!" Caroline sang. "It's perfectly healthy, darling. Ted, that reminds me, we really do need a new mattress on that bed. The last time we had sex in it, I thought I'd put a disc out—"

John sounded like he was trying to drown in his mug of tea. Chris grinned. Lauren, the perfectly average stepmum—wellies, farm fairs, glass of wine on the sofa on Friday evenings. Caroline, a bit more...alternative. While Dad and Lauren had been curious about things like John's name and what he did for a living, Caroline's first question was where he sat on the kink scale. And she'd been bitterly disappointed to discover John was about as kinky as a tub of soft-scoop vanilla.

"If you used a condom, darling, do pop it in the bathroom bin, won't you? The cat takes things out of the basket in that room—"

"He didn't," Chris said.

"For God's sake, boy," Dad grumbled.

"Ted! Don't you take that tone!"

Chris stretched his feet out under the table until he found John's socks and scratched the cotton with his toenails gently. He earned himself a snort, but then a warm hand squeezed his on the table. Chris figured John was probably blushing hard enough to set fire to his T-shirt.

"Oh honestly, darling, you do embarrass so easily," Caroline said, and plates hit the wood. "Do you have any ideas yet?"

"Ideas?" John squeaked.

"For the wedding!"

"Oh." The relief was audible. "Er. Well, no. We just—"

"It wasn't the most planned proposal in the world," Chris said.

Caroline cooed. Dad made a gagging sound and was promptly smacked with a tea towel or a scarf. They broke off into bickering, and Chris drained his cup and got up to make another, turning it all over in his head. They had to move first. Get started on the house. He could ring round places, like registry offices and whatever, while John got the groundwork done. And Gina loved arranging parties. He'd just get her to be their wedding planner, and everything would be sorted.

He hugged himself at the sink, listening to his father's view on love being disparaged by his not-so-secret romantic of a stepmother, and chewed on his lip.

Everything except Mum.

THEY LEFT THE flat the following weekend. Windy and freezing cold, the day smelled like thunder. But Chris had spent a week boxing up their lives while John rushed about at work, and it was a relief on Saturday to lock the flat door behind them and flip off the homophobic old git who lived upstairs on their way to the car.

"Luke's dropped the camper off," John told him as Chris shut the car door. "I've stuck it right down the side so it blocks up the drive, so the van and the car will always be parked behind it. I need to throw a garage up and—"

"I get it," Chris said. "So we're safe. Not that I think we're in particular danger round there."

"Better than your sodding flat in Parson Cross," John agreed.

"I *liked* that flat."

"The flat was fine. It was the neighbourhood."

"Danny upstairs was nice!"

"He burned someone's house down!" John squawked indignantly, then clapped a hand over Chris's mouth. Chris licked him. "Oh, grim."

"Don't try and silence me."

"No point." The car lurched as he dropped it down off the curb and set off. "Anyway, Rhodri and I cleared a bit of the front garden while the surveyors were round. And, uh. You mentioned..."

Chris cocked his head, frowning.

"I mentioned what?"

John cleared his throat awkwardly. "You said you'd, um. You'd want to plant a couple of cherry trees in memory of Jack."

Chris caught his breath.

"So—I went down the garden centre between appointments yesterday."

"You—you didn't."

"Yeah."

"But I wanted to—"

"I haven't planted them yet," John interrupted. "They're sitting in their tubs by the back door. I figured you'd want to do it."

Chris's lip shuddered uncontrollably, and he had to gulp in a breath. The car slowed a little, and he shook his head.

"M'okay."

"You sure?"

"Yeah. Just—go. I want to—I wanna do it. Let's go."

There was a short pause before a hand squeezed his wrist. Chris turned his over and caught at the fingers briefly.

"Thank you."

John didn't answer him for the rest of the trip, but once they'd parked up on the grass-and-gravel crunch of their new driveway, he came around and folded Chris into a tight hug at the passenger door.

"You want to move in, or you want to get the trees planted?"

"Trees," Chris croaked. "Help me."

"'Course."

He made John draw a diagram on his palm of how the gardens were laid out. The front was a large, flat square. The back, a long, gentle slope up to the woods that cupped the cul-de-sac in the bottom of a large bowl of earth, was narrow but pretty and hemmed in by overgrown firs. It could be their haven—a rock garden, a water feature, flowers and bees, a little shed for John to do his DIY in, and a little summerhouse for Chris to bask on summer afternoons. Hidden away from the world, quiet and secret. Just for them.

So Chris opted for the front. It would be their welcome. Open and airy. Flowers in tidy beds. The cherry trees towering either side of the front path when they were old, raining blossoms down on their visitors. A cheerful hello, or a perfumed welcome home.

Chris moved in while John dug the holes, knowing better than to get near the shovel that weighed as much as he did, and he'd just shifted the last of the boxes into the camper when John called him over. They had to move the pots together, Chris trusting John's verbal directions and hoping he'd not catch his feet on anything. The mighty crack of John breaking the ceramic and dropping the sapling into the pit was like lightning followed by rushing water. The leaves shivered. So did Chris's heart.

He knelt down on the bare soil and gathered the earth into his hands.

Cold. Dirty. He began to heap it around the tree by the handful, ignoring the worms wriggling between his fingers. It would take him an age, but who cared? He'd look after the trees. They'd grow here forever, casting longer and longer shadows on the path, filling the air with perfume year after year. Jack's favourite. Jack's mark, forever.

Chris cried a bit, but didn't stop. He could smell cigar smoke from the tenth of March as he smoothed the dirt flat around the base of the first sapling. He could hear that huffing laugh as he crawled over to the second, squishing stray blades of grass between his fingers rather than bothering to get up. The pain in his chest had returned, and nothing to do with surgeries and scars.

It was just—

Loss.

And he felt like he'd lost his mother too. Like Jack had taken part of her with him and left a shadow behind. She didn't want him to get married. She thought him too difficult to be loved the way John loved him. She figured there would be a different end for him and John than the one that had taken Jack away.

Chris sat back on his heels and scrubbed his hand across his eyes.

"John!"

Footsteps crunched. He lifted his arms. Knees hit the dirt, and John's hands were warm and sure around Chris's shoulders. Chris burrowed. John just held on tighter.

"She's wrong," Chris breathed.

"What?"

"Mum. She's wrong. This is it."

John squeezed. "Of course it is."

Under the shadow of the saplings, Chris let out the last tears. He left muddy handprints on John's back and had dirt smeared on his face, but he didn't care.

The breeze was whispering in the leaves of the cherry trees, and it sounded like Jack's laugh.

Chapter Eleven

LIFE IN THE campervan was surprisingly nice.

Chris didn't like moving house. It screwed up his mental map of everything, and the stress always made his seizures worse. But the campervan was so small it made rearranging everything an easy job, and—given their bed was nothing more than a mattress on the floor—he just had to avoid seizures in the tiny box of a bathroom. Plus, he wasn't really alone. John always had a quiet patch at work during the spring, between Christmas emergencies and summer DIY projects gone wrong, so he busied himself with the house and was always within shouting distance. Chris had help with figuring out the new environment, but the space to do it too.

And the space to make phone calls.

Mum had sent him a text or two—he figured Lauren had had words—but he ignored them in favour of sitting on the steps of the campervan and throwing a ball for Poppy while he rang registrars, hotels, and country pubs. Registrars were busy. Hotels were extortionate. Pubs weren't always keen on hosting a party for a gay couple, and two earned themselves sour reviews on TripAdvisor for hanging up on him.

But it kept him busy, and his mind on the positive. Wedding plans. The sound of the wind in the baby cherry trees. John singing pop songs while he worked, and Rhodri joining in when he came over on Mondays to help with odds and ends. Chris didn't like Rhodri very much—the man was a Neanderthal—but his falsetto screeching to cheesy tunes for teenagers was fucking *hilarious*.

By the middle of April, they had a working toilet under the stairs, replaced floorboards in the hall, and a date.

"You're kidding," John gasped.

"Nope. Can you rearrange your Friday appointments? I've booked us to go look at venues over the weekend."

"You got a date *and* a venue?"

"Well, *maybe*," Chris said, flopping backwards into the pillows. It was late. He was tired, but John had also had a shower, and Chris could smell the good aftershave from the bed. He kicked off the sheets and toyed with the waistband of his briefs.

"Oh no you don't." John interrupted the thought. "You can keep those right where they are until you tell me what you've let us in for."

Chris rolled his eyes. "*Fine*. I'm sick of Fran ringing and screaming in my ear for updates. So I've been ringing round, and I found some options depending on what you want, but—FYI—no churches. Or synagogues. I'm not having a religious ceremony."

"S'fine," John replied. "I don't think I can fit in the chapel Nan and Granddad go to anyway."

Chris snorted with laughter.

"So, civil ceremony?"

"Yeah. If you want a registry office ceremony, the only one with spaces left within six months is in Bakewell. They've got three slots in September. The lady was nice and let me pencil it in, but she said she needs confirmation within the next week or she'll have to free it up again. But if you want like a fancy hotel or something, Gina and I made a shortlist of different types, and I've been ringing round, and if we're okay with a weekday wedding, then there's some spots in September and October left."

John squeezed his feet. "So—what do you want?"

"After you," Chris replied.

John crawled up the makeshift bed and settled down at Chris's side, rubbing a warm hand over his stomach. Chris hummed peacefully and rubbed at the tattoo. The one on John's right arm was much easier to see than the one on his left.

"I'm torn," he admitted. "I want to go the traditional route and have the ceremony separate from the reception. But one of my mates down the yard got married at Bakewell, and it's not the prettiest of registries, to be honest. The village is *stunning*, but the town hall...not so much."

"Okay," Chris said. "We don't *have* to have the ceremony there. I'm sure there's some authorised places nearby, or here in Sheffield."

"I like the idea of Bakewell," John admitted. "Did your shortlist find some authorised places there?"

"Yeah, there's a few."

He pulled up the list Gina had saved on his phone and handed it over so John could make his way through the links. Gina had described them, but Chris knew he'd have to go on visits first.

"How big are we thinking?" John asked.

Chris grimaced. "Um. Well. Between your family and mine, the reception's going to be pretty big. But...don't take this the wrong way, but I want a small ceremony."

John's hand paused on his stomach.

"I don't— I'm going to be wound up and anxious and fretting about something going wrong on the day, and I don't want a huge crowd of people staring at me to make that worse. I don't want to have a seizure on our wedding day. I just want—I just want to say my vows like you're the only one in the room, not worry if I look my best or your builders' mates are thinking it's all a bit gay or if your mum is tutting about my hair."

"That was one time!" John defended his mother's honour, but—to Chris's relief—laughed and kissed the side of his head. "I get it. Okay. How about we meet in the middle. I'll put up with a small, intimate ceremony, and then you grit your teeth and smile through a massive reception."

Chris followed the kiss for another one. "M'kay."

"You can ring the registry woman and cancel," John told him. "I can't get out of Friday morning—bathroom refit—but I'll be done by twelve. Is that enough for your shortlist?"

"Yeah. You have any preferences on it?"

"Let me check..."

Chris settled his head on John's shoulder and listened to his mumbled commentary. Three were placed top of the list. One was written off immediately due to a hideous colour scheme. Another was too small. They debated the last one for a while, John in love with the idea of a castle, and Chris less in love with the idea of being flat broke for the next thirty years.

In a way, he felt simultaneously relaxed and wound up. He'd never really given any thought to getting married. He wanted to be married; he wasn't entirely interested in the *how* of it all. What did he care about colour schemes and homemade confetti?

But at the same time, asking John to make a decision was sometimes like asking him to hang the moon. He could dither about what to have for dinner. Chris had a feeling he'd have to develop some opinions about this wedding, just so John could have a finite list of options to work from.

"There's one thing I do want," John commented as he removed an ugly hotel from the list.

"What's that?"

"I'm going to write my own vows."

Chris winced. "Seriously?"

"Yep."

"I have to listen to your cheese on my wedding day?"

"First moment of the rest of your life. It's appropriate."

Chris grumbled. The laugh was deep and warm, gin and molten chocolate, and then his ear was sucked. Then his neck. Then—other things.

Later, half-asleep and basking in the afterglow, Chris felt the kiss to his elbow and the heavy arms that slid around his waist from very far away.

"Chris?"

"Mm?"

"It's going to be perfect."

"M'ybe..."

"It will be," John murmured. His knees tucked up behind Chris's calves. His lips touched the shell of his ear. "No matter what. Because it's you and me, and this is it."

On a mattress on the floor of his best mate's campervan, his dog dozing at his feet, and his brick shithouse of a boyfriend stroking his skin like he was gearing up for another go, Chris couldn't help but agree.

Then his phone started ringing.

"LAUREN SAID YOU were—upset."

Chris stretched his legs out until his feet hit the door and pushed. It creaked faintly. His back pressed up against the cupboard under the sink, and the chill from the growing night outside seeped through the door into the soles of his feet.

At least this way he could pretend the cold in his bones was from the late hour and not his mother's voice.

"How is the house?"

"What's that got to do with whether I'm upset or not?"

She sighed heavily. "Christian—"

He dropped his hand—and the phone—into his lap. Faintly, her voice buzzed away like the adults on a *Peanuts* cartoon. He didn't want to make small talk about the house. He wanted her to apologise.

"Everything all right?" John asked quietly.

Chris shook his head and lifted the phone again.

"—that she's not received a—"

"Mum," he interrupted. "What do you want?"

She paused. He counted his breaths.

"Lauren said you were upset."

"Yeah, you mentioned it."

"I thought I ought to call."

"Why?"

Another pause. Chris exhaled heavily. He rested his head back against the cupboard door and asked the only question which came to mind.

"Are you happy for me?"

"Are you happy?"

"Don't," he said. "Just answer the question. Are you happy for me that I'm getting married to John?"

"I worry—"

"Are you happy for me?"
Silence.
Then: "No."
Chris hung up.

Almost immediately, she rang him back, but he switched the phone off and reached up to put it on the side. It fell in the sink. He let it and crawled back to bed like he was made of lead. Impossibly heavy. Impossibly dark.

"Hey."

John's arms were warm. His neck smelled of the good aftershave. Chris burrowed, dragging the duvet with him, and cocooned himself in the safest place in the world. John didn't say another word. He simply dropped the weight of his arms around Chris's back, locked over the duvet as though holding him prisoner, and held on.

Chris breathed out in time with John, relaxing into his chest as their ribs fell together, and blinked back the few stubborn tears that tried to come. What was the point? She'd made her position clear. She'd made what she thought of him perfectly fucking clear.

"I don't want her to come," he breathed.

John tugged a little on the duvet, pulling it down slightly, and kissed the top of his head.

"Can't hear you under there," John drawled.

"Open your ears, then," Chris mumbled weakly.

"Cheeky shit," came the soft reply.

"I don't want her to come to the wedding. If she can't—if she thinks I'm too sodding difficult to marry, then I don't want her there."

John squeezed until Chris squeaked, and it held all the jagged edges of hurt together. John didn't grab often. Didn't really crush much. Usually, it was a good thing because if John hugged at full strength, it would definitely crack a few vital bones. But Chris soaked it up eagerly for once; he needed the pressure, all of a sudden.

"I'm not getting involved," John murmured. "You know it's a load of rubbish. You know I'm going to be here as long as I'm alive. Difficult or otherwise. Whether she's jumpy because of me or it's some deep-seated thing—"

Chris pressed a kiss to John's chest and smiled faintly. Once, John would have been in pieces. Chris's predecessor had been an abusive, gaslighting shit and had left John ripped apart. Back then, even a hint of someone thinking he was unsuitable would have dissolved John into complete panic. Even a hint that he could hurt someone made him fall apart.

Three years later and a renewed confidence told another story. Why couldn't Mum see that?

"I can't be that hard," Chris said. "Even *your* issues couldn't stop me."

"Nothing bloody stops you."

Chris managed a slightly more genuine laugh.

"My point being, if you don't want her there, I'm not going to argue with you. Whatever you want to do, it's up to you."

"Thanks."

He knew he ought to make allowances. He knew it might not even be about him. Mum hadn't really taken to John from the start, and Chris wouldn't have put money on his perfect partner being an electrician with terrible taste in music and less than three GCSEs to his name either.

But it felt like it was about him.

Even if she didn't like John, it wasn't up to her to like him. She should trust Chris's judgement. He wasn't stupid. He wasn't incapable of knowing a good thing from a bad one. Marrying John changed nothing because their lives were all twisted up around each other anyway. So if it wasn't about him being too disabled to find someone who'd stay with him, then it was about him being too stupid to pick the right partner in the first place.

Chris wasn't entirely sure which option was worse.

"I can feel you overthinking it, you know," John murmured.

"Yeah, well, deal."

A heavy hand stroked down his back, hard enough to wrestle the knots out of his spine.

"Fuuuck."

"Earlier not enough?"

Chris smirked, but in truth, he wasn't interested, his mood too sour. Instead, he wriggled sideways and wedged himself under John's arm.

"Plan a wedding," he said.

"What?"

"Just talk to me about wedding stuff. Take my mind off it."

Off her.

And because John was a bloody saint, he did. He shifted, a hand coming up to card through Chris's curly hair, and let out a long breath.

"Well," he said. "I know you're not going to give a damn about colour schemes, so I was hoping I could get away with blue. Proper rich dark blue, though, none of this sky stuff. It'll bring out your eyes. Maybe offset it with a nice pale grey for suits. You'll look incredible in a waistcoat, you know. And I don't care if it'll give Nan a fit—you're wearing that lip ring. And—"

Chris tucked his nose against John's skin and breathed, listening to the gentle thump of his heart and the deep, soothing roll of his voice. Like the phrase 'still waters run deep' come to life. Barely a movement stirred the nest, and yet John's warmth and sound permeated every inch of him and swept the nagging anger and tight anxiety away.

"Blue sounds nice," he whispered.

He couldn't remember for the life of him what it looked like—but it sounded nice.

Chapter Twelve

"I'LL BE DONE by twelve." John's coat rustled. "Do you want me to get anything for lunch?"

Chris shook his head, already clicking through the contacts on his phone, counting rather than using the annoying voice assistant. "I'm going to see Dad," he said. "Ring me when you're done, 'cause I'll probably still be there."

"Right you are."

He hit call before John had even fired up the engine outside and rolled his eyes when Dad characteristically greeted him with "What do you want?" rather than "Hello."

"Love you too," Chris said dryly. "Are you busy?"

"Depends what you want."

"To come round."

"Why?"

"Chat."

A snort. "What kind of chat? If you need some sodding marriage counsellor, ask your mum."

Chris's stomach twisted. "Mum's the problem."

There was a short pause. Then a heavy sigh.

"You at home?"

"Yeah."

"You can help me with the weekly shop, then. Lazy git."

Dad hung up, but Chris just shrugged and pocketed the phone. Poppy sat by the open door, likely sulking at the rain, and he slid down to sit with her.

"Trip round the big Tesco with Dad?" he asked, ruffling her ears. She nudged her nose into his palm but otherwise didn't answer.

Dad never really said much. But then, he never really had to. How many times had Chris come home from a miserable day at school to find his favourite food for dinner, despite it having been dinner yesterday too? How many times had bills paid themselves out of nowhere when the benefits didn't quite stretch far enough? And even if Dad claimed to have had nothing to do with it, Chris knew full well why Jamie Collins in Year Five had suddenly stopped bullying him out of the blue after Dad *just so happened* to have run into Jamie's dad at a pub. In his army gear. With two of his mates from the shooting range.

So Chris waited, ruffling Poppy's fur and listening to the rain, until a familiar engine rolled into the cul-de-sac and boots crunched on the gravel-cum-grass combination by the campervan. Dad always wore big boots like John's, but he was short and fat. His gait rolled more. His stride was shorter and quicker.

"Get up off the floor, you daft git. You never heard of a chair?"

Chris stuck his tongue out.

"Put it away or lose it."

"Yeah, yeah—"

He locked up to the music of Dad bitching about the state of the house. The Land Rover was warm, but the radio shit. Chris turned it off in protest at some screechy band from the eighties. What was it with Marines and ABBA knock-offs anyway?

"So what's your mum done now?"

Chris's throat scratched. "She—she thinks I shouldn't be getting married."

"You shouldn't. Waste of bloody money. Have a honeymoon instead."

"Different reasons."

"Go on, then."

"She said I'm too difficult."

"You're a fucking nightmare," Dad agreed.

"Either I'm too disabled for anyone to stay with me, or I'm too stupid to pick the right man to marry. That's what it comes down to. That's what she said."

It burst out of him in an angry rush, and he fumed, shaking in the aftermath, as Dad turned the Land Rover round and set off back towards town.

"You want to tell me what she *actually* said?"

Chris swallowed thickly. "She said I couldn't count on John always being there. And not in the, you know, dead sense."

Dad grunted.

"John reckons it's because she doesn't think much of him, which just means she thinks I'm too stupid to make that decision for myself. But—it sounded—it felt more like she was saying I'm not the kind of person who gets to have a happy ever after."

"Oh fuck me, happy ever after? Your John *has* been a bad influence."

"Fuck off," Chris mumbled weakly.

"Language."

"After you."

Dad sighed gustily. Chris chewed on his lip, wondering which father he was about to get. His parents had always been resolute about not slagging each other off in front of him. It was utterly apparent even as a kid that they loathed one another, but he'd very rarely heard them *say* it. It was more of a feeling in the air.

But there'd been the odd time, once he moved out on his own and was semi-independent, that one or the other would let go. Usually Dad after a few beers, but occasionally Mum too. He wondered which version was about to make an appearance—would Dad call her a stupid bitch, or try to mediate?

"She feels guilty."

Chris's thoughts paused.

"What?"

"Ruth. She feels guilty."

"About what?"

"About the way she felt about Jack. About the way she felt about *you*. And she's doing some mental gymnastics to make herself feel better about it."

"So you know how sometimes you open your mouth and nothing makes any sense...?"

"Cheeky shit," Dad grumbled after heaving another creaking sigh. "We never really talked about the divorce, did we?"

Chris flinched. No. They didn't need to. The ghost, the woman with the voice he couldn't remember from the video of his nursery school Nativity play, said plenty.

"Aunt Kelly."

"Yes—and no."

He'd been six years old when he'd had the accident. Dad's sister Kelly had picked him up from school. Young and dumb, and convinced of his invincibility, he wasn't so hot at understanding his auras. To his childish mind, seizures weren't dangerous. They hurt, and he had a nap. Then Mum would give him a cuddle, and Dad would give him a biscuit, and it was all over. He didn't understand why he couldn't go swimming. He didn't know why the teachers wouldn't let him play on the monkey bars with the other kids. He *was* just like all the other kids.

Aunt Kelly had picked him up from school. They'd walked home through the park. He'd run along the top of the wall and waited for her at the end so she could watch him jump down. It was six feet high. It was going to be the best jump *ever*.

So that was when the seizure hit him.

He'd crashed down off the wall head first. Smashed his skull to pieces. Technically, he'd died then and there on the pavement, but Aunt Kelly was a nurse and had kept him going until the ambulance came. He'd spent months in hospital with catastrophic brain damage. Some of it got better. He learned to walk and talk again. He papered over the holes in his memory until they filled themselves in. But some of them didn't. The personality changes were permanent. He'd never be so outgoing again. He'd never see his parents' faces again. He'd always have migraines. He'd never be able to stop the shaking in his arms if he walked too quickly.

Mum blamed Aunt Kelly for letting him run along the wall. Dad didn't. And Aunt Kelly—

Aunt Kelly had blamed herself.

"Kelly was the final straw," Dad said. "But your mum and I started to break apart from the minute it happened."

Chris bit down hard on his lip at the raw edge in his father's voice.

"They told us you'd die," Dad said flatly. "They had you up on life support so your family could say goodbye. That was it. So we sat there all night, saying goodbye. Trying to get ready to let you go. And you—you can't imagine what that's like, kid. Saying goodbye to your child. You *can't*."

"Dad—"

"Ruth said at least you didn't know. There weren't any pain. That was what she clung to; you weren't hurting. For you, it would just be like going to sleep. We were the ones who'd be left with the hurt, but you wouldn't know a thing. It—it helped her. It made her feel better. And I agreed with her. Sort of."

"Sort of?"

"Next morning, you started fighting the ventilator. You wanted to breathe. And that's when it really changed things because now it wasn't a certainty. I figured you must be getting better, and I was selfish. I said I didn't damn well care if you'd be in nappies for the rest of your life and the biggest achievement you'd ever make would be another first word. I wasn't ready to lose you. I only *had* you."

His voice was cracking. The car slowed and weaved to the side of the road, and Chris heard the tears threatening to break through.

"Ruth was—pragmatic. She focused on whether you'd be in pain, whether you'd hurt, whether you'd get to live a good life or spend the rest of it hooked up to machinery. Something I'd always agreed with before. No point in a life if you can't live it. That's what I believed. It's what I still believe. Only this wasn't some chat watching a depressing documentary. It was my six-year-old kid. I didn't want to let go. I wasn't strong enough to let go."

"So you fought it. Her."

"Bitterly. You crashed three more times, and every time, they asked if we ought to let you go. Ruth said yes. And I said no."

Chris knew how it worked, after that. If there wasn't a united front, the hospital would have dithered and fretted and never made the call, especially over a child. And once he'd shown enough signs of survival, the question would have vanished off the table, never to be asked again.

"Don't get me wrong, the first time you squeezed my hand when they were doing those consciousness tests, your mum changed her tune and was shouting herself blue in the face until they'd get all the right specialists. But her first instinct had been to let you go. To spare you the suffering. And I don't think it ever sat easy with her that if we'd done what she wanted, you would have died when you *could* have lived."

"She—she wouldn't have known."

"Of course she wouldn't," Dad said, his voice clearer. A little croaky, but clearer. "If she could have seen the future, she'd never have even thought it. But it was what it was. And I think Jack's death has stirred it all up again. She's relieved he's gone, that it's over, and she feels guilty for it. Same way she felt guilty for saying we ought to let you go."

Chris swallowed. He knew that feeling. Hadn't he had the same twinge of guilt at the relief when Jack's haggard breathing had finally stopped? Hadn't he been relieved when it was over? Hadn't he wanted the end to come sooner, for those endless days in the hospice to be impossibly shorter? Hadn't he and Mum wanted the same thing?

But—

"Even if she feels guilty, she can't say what she doesn't think," he said. "She thinks I'm too—"

"Trusting."

"What?"

"She thinks you trust too easily."

"So it's about John?"

"I'd have thought so. Or other people, at least."

"It's been three years! And—"

"You don't have to convince me, kid. I've seen the way he looks at you. Thinks the sun shines out of your arse."

"It does," Chris said haughtily.

Dad snorted. "Whatever helps you sleep at night. Anyway, it's not *really* about John. It is on the surface, but not underneath."

"No?"

"Nope. It's about her."

"What do you mean?"

"Look at it how her guilt's making her look at it," Dad said. "We all have an ego, and your mum's no different. She was relieved when her husband died. She opted to let her son die all those years ago instead of fighting for him. Why would anyone else be any different? Why would *John* be any different?"

Chris opened his mouth...and slowly closed it again.

"She's judging herself too harshly in her grief, and she's holding everyone else accountable for that," Dad said. "She wasn't good enough, so why would John be better? If she'd been a better mother, you wouldn't have almost died. If she'd been a better wife, she wouldn't have been relieved when Jack died."

"But—but none of that's her fault. None of that's true."

"I know that. You know that. But your mum's a bit slower on the uptake. That's what guilt does, kid. It fucks things up. Add grief to the mix, and it gets ugly."

Chris chewed on his lip. Her disapproval *ached*, like a slow-to-heal burn. It was inescapable, and yet... somehow, he suddenly felt sorry for her, rather than angry with her. Something thawed in his chest.

"I take it you and John *have* talked about what happens if you have another accident?"

"Yeah," Chris murmured. "He doesn't like it, but he knows my wishes."

Because, ultimately, Chris shared Mum's view. If he was just in agony all the time, or unable to move anything but his eyeballs, or destroyed down to a mess of malfunctioning neurons with no relief like the disease had done to Jack, Chris would rather not be here at all. It wasn't a life without the ability to live it.

John hadn't liked it—but he'd promised.

He'd promised to do what Mum had done. He'd promised to let go. If it came to it, to help Chris move on. And John didn't know the future any better than she had. But he'd do it because it was what Chris wanted.

"You think I should talk to her again?" Chris asked.

"I think you should do what you need to do," Dad said. "But remember what she's been through, eh?"

Chris coughed a laugh as the car pulled back into traffic.

"You know a lot about her for a divorced guy."

Dad grunted. "Yeah, well. If you think a marriage teaches you a lot about someone, just try ending one."

Chris smiled, rubbing his finger and thumb around the space where Jack's wedding ring was going to go.

"No thanks," he said. "We're good."

OVER THE COURSE of the morning, Chris...softened.

Not only had Dad nearly bawled talking about the accident, but much as Mum's attitude pissed Chris off, he was being a hypocrite. Stones, glass houses. There'd been a time when he'd been convinced there wasn't anybody out there for him. If he was just trans, maybe. If he was just disabled, maybe. If he was just queer—he'd not one hundred percent figured out anything more precise yet— maybe. All three? Not a cat in hell's chance.

And yeah, maybe he *was* a bit too trusting sometimes. If he thought logically about how he'd met John, and the complete mess the man had been at the time, Chris could see how it could have gone wrong had John been someone, anyone, other than who he was.

And he'd been relieved too. When the silence had crept into that little room in the hospice. When the shaking stopped. When Jack died. But wasn't that out of love? Wasn't he relieved because he loved Jack, and it had been horrible to see him suffering? He wasn't glad Jack was dead; he was glad Jack wasn't in pain.

With Dad's level-headed explanation to counteract his initial anger, Chris could sympathise a little with what Mum was probably going through. The remarks still stung. Her lack of enthusiasm for the wedding still ached. But maybe he could get her excited again by just—being excited himself. Maybe once they picked a venue, he could drag her out to find cakes or clothes. Then she'd get excited, right? She was always so properly turned out that she'd brighten up once she needed to find a suitable mother-of-the-groom look.

He stewed on it as he helped Dad put everything away from the big shop and had just flicked the kettle on when he heard his phone chime from the kitchen table.

"Who is it?"

Dad thumped a cupboard door closed and shuffled over to the table. "Text from John."

"Saying?"

"On his way and needs a shower. What the fuck's he been doing?"

"Had a job."

"Doing what, putting lights down manholes?"

Chris laughed. "Tit. Probably means he's covered in plaster dust again."

He was proven right when John turned up and was told off by Lauren for getting powder on the doorknobs. He laughed, shrugging on his jacket as John was shooed upstairs to the bathroom, and clicked his fingers.

"Come on, Poppy. One last turn round the garden."

To his surprise, Dad came with him and lit up a fag. It was still drizzling lightly, and the smoke smelled acrid in the gentle spring air. Chris waited, knowing full well what was about to happen. Dad never came out for a smoke unless he had something important to say—and away from nosy stepmums.

"Where's these venues, then?"

"Bakewell."

He grunted. "Nice place."

"That's the idea."

"Not going for no religious bollocks, are you?"

"Nope."

Dad grunted again and then cleared his throat. "Well. You, ah. Have fun. Finding somewhere."

"Uh-huh," Chris said sceptically.

"And, ah, when you do, give us a ring."

"Well, yeah—"

"Been saving up, see."

Chris stiffened. They'd been—

"What?"

"Saving up," Dad said. "There's an account. Consider it a wedding present."

"You'd—you'd—for the venue?"

"Yeah."

Chris's mouth worked soundlessly. The sudden shock numbed him. Dad was—practical. He'd pay the electric if the benefits came in late. Chris's last birthday present had been a bulk box of batteries for his various assistance devices, with a bow on top because Caroline had bollocked him for being too much of a man about presents. He didn't do frivolous spending. He didn't do—

Chris swallowed thickly.

"Thank you."

The words were hoarse and creaky. Maybe it wasn't just Dad who was a bit shit at saying things sometimes.

Dad grunted and clapped him on the shoulder.

"Welcome."

But bad as he could be at saying it, Chris knew his dad had heard it all the same.

Chapter Thirteen

BY SATURDAY AFTERNOON, Chris had decided he hated venue shopping.

"Let's not bother," he said to John over fish and chips on a bench in Bakewell town centre. "Let's buy a honeymoon instead."

John just laughed.

They'd seen one hotel on Friday afternoon that had been immediately written off, then stayed in a B&B overnight and started fresh the next morning. And Chris was already annoyed.

It wasn't so much that the venues were bad—on the contrary, Chris had fallen a little bit in love with the old spa hotel. It was that their reps were so *condescending*. They talked over his head to John constantly, and if they deigned to speak to him, it was in a baby voice. One woman had even said they'd need to show John's fiancé round as well. And if he got invited to feel one more curtain, he was going to scream.

And they'd only seen three places so far.

"Our back garden, cheese sandwiches for afters, done," Chris said. "Or a prison wedding, 'cause I'm going to murder the next person who calls me by *anything* except my name."

"So—that'll be me, then?"

"You know what I mean."

John chuckled. The bench groaned in relief as he got up to throw the greasy newspaper away, and then Chris was hauled up by the hand.

"Come on," he said. "You weren't too keen on Haddon Hall—"

"The big manor house?"

"Yeah."

Chris pulled a face. There was pretty, and then there was just ostentatious. Who needed somewhere *that* big?

"So let's skip it and have a look at that country pub."

"Oh, that'll please Caroline. A pub."

"Give over," John muttered as they headed for the car. "Those pictures—that's not a bog-standard boozer. Proper posh joint. Bet a meal costs thirty quid per person."

"You're so *Yorkshire*," Chris complained.

He kept complaining all the way back to the car, mostly because it made John laugh. There was a huge advantage to being blind and having a six-foot-seven boyfriend. Chris could get all the public displays of affection he wanted. There were no closets for men like John, and it took some seriously hardcore homophobia for idiots to pass comments about a blind guy, especially when he was out with his dog and had his cane tucked under one arm.

The country pub had caught Gina's eye, then she'd found a picture of an aviary and Chris added it to the list. He *loved* birds. A cage full of chattering birds was one of the best sounds in the world, and he grinned when John pulled off the bumpy road into a gravel car park, and the chirping was audible even over the engine.

"I see why you wanted this one," John commented.

"You know me so well. Ask for Louise: she said we could drop by for a tour any time after one." The smell of flowers was everywhere. Lavender bushes brushed his legs as they walked up a flat, flagstone path. John grumbled about low, medieval doorways, and Chris felt him stoop, but the warm interior felt much bigger.

"Oh, wow," John breathed.

"Pretty?"

"Very. Proper old man pub but with more space."

"Whatever that means," Chris said.

It was all about the wood. Boards creaked pleasantly under Chris's shoes, and he could smell the faint traces of woodsmoke from a real fireplace. No TVs or music interrupted the ambience, but a low rush of background chatter and the clink of cutlery from somewhere nearby, perhaps a restaurant area separated from the bar.

"Hi." John's fingers drummed absently on the bar. "We're looking at wedding venues, and Louise said she'd give us a tour."

"Oh, sure. I'll go and get her. You guys want a glass of wine? On the house for Louise's little tours."

They swapped wine for lime and lemonade—John was teetotal, and Chris rarely thought it worthwhile to mix his medication with booze—and John described a chandelier in awe, as if he'd never seen one, while they waited for Louise to appear. Chris wound him up by pretending not to know what a chandelier was.

But, quietly, he bumped the pub up the list. John plainly loved it already. And Chris could still just about hear the birds.

"Ah! You must be John and Chris. I'm Louise Carstairs; lovely to meet you."

Louise Carstairs walked with a brisk, firm stride in very high heels, without a hint of wobbling on them. Her grip was firm when she shook Chris's hand, her perfume understated, but her nails were like talons. Chris imagined she looked a bit like a dolled-up Lauren.

"I run events at *The Bell*," she said. "How about we pop into one of the private rooms and have a chat about what you're looking for?"

Chris had supposed the pub would be ordinary-sized, but he was wrong. They abandoned the large bar area for a long corridor in more medieval wood—or modern wood doing a good job of pretending—and they were led into a cosy side room with fat, comfortable chairs and a cool breeze floating through an open window, in spite of the heat rolling out of a fireplace in the corner.

"I take it you're the happy couple?"

"Yep," Chris said.

"Congratulations!" she enthused. "Weddings are my favourite events, I must say. Not so keen on the christening parties. Always terrified some drunk uncle's going to drop the baby in a fire!"

John chuckled, and they talked children while Louise rustled with paperwork and folders. Chris tuned them out, turning his head towards the window. The birds were even louder here. Was the aviary outside?

"Now, depending exactly what time of year you're looking, we have a range of event types. If you're after a summer wedding, we have a gazebo for the garden and can host the whole affair outdoors. If you want a winter wedding, then we can light up all the fires inside and create a wonderful English manor effect. Practically speaking, we can't take more than a hundred and fifty people on the premises at any one time, and, to be honest, that's our legal restriction. It's like lifts. We couldn't *fit* a hundred and fifty, I don't think—over a hundred and twenty starts to get very uncomfortable."

"It won't be *that* big," John laughed.

"I'll give you a very quick broad overview of what we offer. At the basic level, you can rent out the pub for the day and do all the decorating yourself, not use any of the bedrooms, bring your own band, and so on and so forth. You have to use our kitchens if you want to feed your guests, but we can provide a wide range of food packages, and, of course, we can cater to any dietary requirements. Our packages then go steadily upwards with various add-ins, but the favourite—" Paper rustled. John leaned forward to take her brochure. "—is the silver package. In a nutshell, this reserves the whole pub for your wedding party for the day, includes the honeymoon suite for the happy couple for the night, the wedding breakfast..."

Chris tuned her out again. He didn't really care about wedding breakfasts and honeymoon suites. The birds were excited about something, and the sun was pouring in through the window and warming his shoes on the carpet. They could get married in one of the little rooms, then go out into the garden and have the party. With the birds chattering away in the background the whole time, and those boards flexing under their feet as they walked out, married.

"Can we skip what's included and what's not and go straight to the tour?" he asked.

John groaned. "Chris—"

But Louise just laughed and said, "Sure! We can do this in any order you like. Are you more interested in an outdoor wedding, with September?"

"Yes."

"Okay, so I'll show you the conservatory and the garden, as that's where we'd host an outdoor wedding. If it *does* rain, we can easily move it back inside, but we've been pretty successful so far..."

The private room was at the top of the long corridor, and the garden at the bottom of it. Chris imagined walking from their private ceremony into a garden full of friends and family and clutched John's elbow hard as they stepped out into the sunlight.

The garden was buzzing. Literally. A gentle hum of bees followed them as Louise showed them around. Different scents jostled for attention. Trees rustled. The path was all smooth, flat flagstones, punctured periodically by flowerbeds and bushes, small fountains and rockeries. In the dead centre, an enormous circular slab of stone had been left plant-free and home to several picnic benches. The whole area was surprisingly large, spanning the gap between the airy conservatory and the noisy aviary, and—despite the birds—blissfully quiet. Natural. *Gentle.* It was still too chilly to be used, so it was lonely, yet Chris could imagine it spilling over with noise.

He paused in the middle of the garden and took a deep breath.

"I love it," John stated.

"What?"

"I love it," he repeated, and dropped a hand to touch the small of Chris's back. "We could have the ceremony in that private room, just like you wanted. Then have dinner in the conservatory with all the cheesy speeches, then the party here."

Chris squeaked in surprise as he was kissed and prodded John in the breastbone to persuade him to lay off.

"Am I missing the most beautiful garden in the universe?"

"Probably not," John admitted. "But it just—it *feels* right. I can see us getting married here."

He slid behind Chris and looped both arms around his chest. His lips brushed Chris's ear, and Chris shivered when he whispered.

"You with confetti in your hair, in your best suit, listening to those birds. You'd look—"

Whatever Chris would look like was never said. He just had his cheek kissed and all the air crushed out of him.

"What about getting everyone here?" he asked. "Hotels? Cars? I'm not coming all the way down to Bakewell on the morning of my wedding."

"If I may," Louise interrupted gently. "The honeymoon suite can be made available for the night before the wedding as well as after, if you'd prefer. In fact, it's free at the moment. You could always stay a night as a test run."

Chris turned his attention back to the birds as John haggled about price. It was growing on him. No doubt Dad would bitch and moan about having to come all the way out here, and John's nan would complain about them not using the family chapel. But—it was nice. John was so enthusiastic about it, where he'd been so non-committal about the others. Maybe Chris didn't have to fear John's dithering after all.

"What do you reckon?" John asked, squeezing him again. "Spend the night here and go back in the morning?"

"Sure," Chris said and wondered if the birds would sing at night.

THEY DIDN'T.

But the honeymoon suite made up for it.

Chris had been expecting a poky but cosy room in the attic, much like John's favourite holiday cottage by the coast for their traditional New Year holiday. And he'd been dramatically wrong. The room *was* in the attic, but it was the whole attic of the pub, more of a flat than a room. The private bathroom had a tub big enough even for John to lie down in and a vast four-poster bed that could have sheltered the England rugby team. Chris sprawled out in the bed the moment they went up after dinner and didn't move even when John started that hopeful neck-kissing trick of his.

"If you want to, go ahead, but I'm not moving," he'd said.

It worked. John fucked him so slow and gentle it was like floating in a lazy sea, and the next thing Chris knew was the birds waking up in the garden below, and the desert heat of a phenomenally thick duvet, and a thousand pounds of man wrapped about his back.

He curled his fingers into the pillows and smiled.

They could spend their last night engaged here, and their first night married.

Here, with the fluffy rug by the bed, the velvet curtains that hung from the posts, the power shower that had drummed every last bit of tension out of him the night before, and the only cold thing in the room their wedding rings.

Slowly, he levered John's fingers open and slid free.

He dressed quietly and tiptoed downstairs with Poppy, feeling his way along the wall until he reached a door that opened into the quiet garden. It was very cold, but the birds chirped happily, and he ghosted across the paths to their cage while Poppy explored for some good spots. The birds went wild, and he crooned apologetically at them.

"I'm sorry," he said. "I don't have any food."

"I do."

Louise's voice was gentle, but he still jumped.

"Sorry! You're up early. Did you sleep well?"

"Like the dead," Chris admitted. A door squeaked and closed again. The birds went into a frenzy. "Are they yours?"

"My daughter's, but she's off at university now. Didn't fancy taking on the pub after her dad retires, but our son is more interested. He served you at the bar last night."

Chris pretended to remember.

"Do you like birds?"

"Love them," he said. "We're going to get an aviary of our own soon."

"They do attract a lot of attention. And demand it. Needy things, aren't you? Aren't you?"

Her businesslike manner long gone, she sounded more like John's nan, or Lauren at the stables with her beloved horses. Chris wondered if she was in a dressing gown and slippers. He'd have to ask John how she wore her hair because he fondly imagined it to be in rollers.

"Breakfast won't be long," she said. "Harry's already up and about. Do you have any dietary needs?"

"Food's food," he said. "Are you available today?"

"Sure."

"Good. I'd like to book a wedding, please."

Chapter Fourteen

"OH MY GOD, that's so *soon*!" Gina said.

Chris just grinned.

It was pissing it down outside, but the kitchen was warm and dry. Space heaters. God's gift to renovators. The boiler engineer banged away in the utility room, and John was hanging doors upstairs. The whole house stank of sawdust, coffee, and WD40.

What better environment for arts and crafts?

"At least it's a Friday," Gina continued as she unpacked her kit. "Most people should be able to get Fridays off."

"All of John's mates are self-employed like him."

"What about family?"

Chris snorted with laughter. "Have you *met* his family? They'd quit their jobs to go to his wedding."

"So would I," Gina said, rapping his knuckles with a stack of paper. "It sounds so *romantic*! That pub was gorgeous. Have you picked a suit yet? Oh my God, wear a kilt like your dad does! It'll drive John mad!"

"I drive him mad in my jogging bottoms and two-day-old T-shirts. He'll have a coronary if I wear the kilt," Chris said but shook his head. "Anyway, I'm not wearing that. Feels like a skirt. Urgh."

"Don't let your dad hear you say that..."

Chris smirked and ran some ribbon through his fingers. "Right. Show me how to make the little cards, and you write in them. John's left the guest list on the microwave."

Gina had always been good at arts and crafts. She sold jewellery on Etsy and homemade trinkets at various stalls. Chris had never been that interested, but he'd spent many evenings during sixth form college ignoring his homework in favour of learning how to do something artsy with Gina. He could still knit fairly well, even if he didn't bother.

For a while, they worked in relative silence. The boiler engineer kept singing old nineties songs, and John wandered in and out for fresh mugs of tea, dropping off a kiss and stealing a biscuit from their stash with every pass. The stack of finished invites in the basket slowly grew until Gina broke the quiet.

"Has your mum come around to the idea yet?"

Chris blew out his cheeks. "No."

"You did call and tell her about the date, right?"

"Also no."

"Chris!"

He shrugged. "I just—I don't know what to say to her right now. It's awkward. I want to bite her head off and shout, but Dad said some stuff that made me think twice."

"*I* wouldn't think twice," Gina said.

"Yeah, well, your mum's never made it a secret she hates lesbians."

Gina hummed.

"Dad said she's lashing out because she's guilty about how she feels now Jack's died."

"Eh?"

"He said she feels relieved Jack's died. And she initially opted to let me die after my accident and still feels guilty about that too. So she's...I don't know, she's, like, projecting that onto other people? Onto John? So she figures he feels weighed down by my disabilities, too, and one day, it'll be too much, and he'll leave me."

"That's stupid," Gina said.

Chris shrugged.

"She needs to get over herself. If he dumps you, so what?"

Chris paused, ribbon half-tied. "Sorry?"

"So what?" Gina repeated. "Let's say for a minute he does dump you, or he meets someone else, or—whatever. He leaves. So what? You get a divorce, and you move on. It happens."

"In theory," Chris said with a laugh. "You seen my boyfriend? He's not going anywhere."

"Yeah, but let's say she's right, and he does. Big deal. She left your dad, and the world didn't end. It's not like you've not got anywhere to go if this whole thing with John falls through," Gina said flatly. "You've got both your parents, and me, and Luke. So John leaves. More fool him."

"Yeah." A valid point. Maybe he ought to try that approach. Much as he was certain he'd now die married— or widowed—Chris knew Gina spoke the truth too. There was always the council and their flats again. Dad's house. Preferably not her awful sofa, but needs must. He had places to go that didn't involve John, should Mum's paranoia ring true in some parallel universe.

"I don't need a plus one, by the way."

"What?"

"Jemma's my next ex-girlfriend," Gina said, her voice hard, and Chris pushed away the invite he was working on.

"What happened?"

"We're not going in the right direction, and she's not sure she loves me anymore, and maybe we're just friends, and the sex is good but it's not great like it used to be, and blah-de-blah," Gina said. "Oh, and this all came out last week, only a month after she started that new job at Starbucks with the cute assistant manager."

"Oh. *Oh.*"

"Yeah. So, supposedly we're trying, but I'm done trying."

"Shit. I'm sorry—"

"I'm not," Gina said. "I deserve better than that crap. If I'm not enough anymore, then that's her problem. Know any cute girls?"

"No idea. What's a cute girl sound like?"

"Um, like me, arsehole."

"Then no."

She smacked him with one of her fancy pens, then leaned over and hugged him. Chris squeezed back. Her hair was finally starting to grow out, and it tickled his cheek.

"I'm jealous," she admitted.

"Of me and John?"

"Yeah. Does he have a sister?"

"Three."

"Ooh!"

"One's married, one's mad, and...actually, the other one is mad, too, but in a good way. Maybe. I think. But to be honest, they're more like me than John. They bully him."

"Well, he's like a big kitten," she said and let go. The scratching of the pen started up again. "Are they all coming?"

"Nora and Fran will. Not sure about Tasha; she only shows up once in a while. His parents are going to come up from France."

"No cousins?"

"Nah," Chris said. "He's got some uncle in Australia he never hears from. My family's definitely bigger. His side of the party is going to be all his rugby mates and sparkies."

"Any lesbian ones?"

"Doubt it."

"God, you suck. Get more gay friends."

"Luke's not even gay, but he acts gay enough to count for, like, five actual gays."

They cackled meanly over it together and then fell back into an easy silence as the pile grew once more. Slowly, Chris turned his mind to all the other things that needed to be done. Rings, suits, flowers, speeches, seating plans, paperwork, cake, catering, honeymoon—

"John!" he called when he heard heavy footsteps making their way back down for presumably the sixth mug of tea.

"Yeah?"

"What about a honeymoon?"

He was gifted with a kiss on the crown of his head as John passed.

"Somewhere I can make love to you on the hour, every hour, for two weeks," John suggested. "Coffee?"

"Please, no making love *ever*, and you can't even manage three times a day anymore."

"We don't all get a needle of testosterone in the backside on a regular basis," John complained.

"I get a footlong rod of it up the—"

"*Excuse* me, but unless we're going to talk about pussy as well, then this conversation needs to close down," Gina objected in a faux-refined voice.

"We can talk about that too," Chris said. "Mine gets regular exercise with aforementioned rod. Yours?"

"I'm out." John demurred. "What are you two doing?"

The basket scraped a little on the table.

"Invites," Chris said. "It's cheaper than buying fancy ones."

"They're pretty."

"Thanks," Gina said. "Where's my coffee?"

"No tea?"

"Nah. Working the evening shift later."

"Ahh. Coming right up."

"Make that three, pal!" the engineer bellowed from the utility room. "That's all in, so let's try and fire 'er up, eh?"

Chris rolled his eyes and figured he'd have to wait for an answer to his honeymoon question.

THEY WALKED DOWN to the end of the road to post the invitations that evening.

The rain had eased up, but it was bitterly cold. All the same, Chris pushed them into the letterbox one by one, listening to the satisfying thump as they hit the pile of letters inside. Gina. Luke. Rhodri. Thirty-four for the rugby guys, sliding down in a messy clatter. Dad.

Mum.

Once they were all gone, he shoved his hands in his pockets and blew out a breath. Poppy had been dozing when they'd set out, so he'd left her to it, but he regretted it now. He felt adrift—then John read his mind as always and slid both arms around his waist to anchor him.

"What's wrong?"

"Eh?"

"You're quiet and biting your lip again. And sexy as your lip-ring looks when you do that, it's not your flirty face."

Chris hummed, resting his head against John's chest. John was a whole foot taller than him, and while it was a bloody nightmare for trying to sneak a kiss, it was a godsend for hugs.

"What's up?"

"I should ring Mum and tell her the date."

He'd rung Dad and been made to tell Caroline and Lauren by speakerphone. He'd texted Luke and told Gina when she'd arrived to help with making the invitations. But he'd not rung Mum. Or texted her. Or—anything.

She'd just get the invite in the post, like Aunt Glynis and Uncle Tom in Aberdeen. Who he hadn't seen for nearly twenty years, but couldn't *not* invite because they sent a birthday card and twenty pounds every year and used the right name to do it.

He'd invited Mum just like them.

He ought to ring her. But—

"I just don't know that I want to right now," he admitted.

"Then don't."

John's voice was warm and soothing. He'd pitched it very low, in a soft murmur that purred rather than really spoke. Chris pressed a little harder into his chest to feel it and the steady thump of his enormous heart.

"It might make things worse if she finds out I told Dad but just sent her an invite."

"She's only got herself to blame," John murmured. "Look, don't worry about pleasing other people right now, okay? It's our wedding. Not theirs."

"I don't even know if Mum's going to come."

John shifted. A hand raked through Chris's hair, tipping his head back until his cold mouth was warmed with a kiss.

Then John asked, "What if she doesn't?"

Chris swallowed thickly.

Part of him wanted to tell her not to. Part of him didn't want her sour face and long pauses at his wedding. But she was his *mum*. And telling her to stay away was very different than her ignoring the invite. God, what if she didn't come? What if she looked at the invite, put it aside, and never replied? What if she ignored it? What if he walked out of that little room on the first Friday in September, happily married, and his mother wasn't waiting with all the other guests?

What if?

His heart creaked a little. He'd never had designs on getting married, but now he *was*, it would hurt if his own mother didn't show up. It would hurt bad enough that Jack wasn't there to see it, but Mum too?

"It'll hurt."

"It will," John agreed. "Her."

"W-what?"

"It'll hurt her. She'll miss out on seeing her only son have his first dance as a married man. She'll not see me bawl like a baby when I get to kiss you for the first time as my husband. She won't see the confetti in your hair, or how you won't stop smiling all day."

Rough hands, impossibly warm, cupped Chris's face. The kiss was barely there, yet Chris nudged into it as though it was the only way he could breathe.

"It'll hurt her," John promised, "but you won't even notice. And you know why? Because that garden will be overflowing with people who love us for exactly who and what we are."

Chapter Fifteen

CHRIS TRIED TO put it out of his mind by going into town the next day.

"I need pampering," he said, once his breathing had come down out of the rafters from the unexpected blowjob against the campervan door.

"What do you think that was?" John asked from the vicinity of his hips.

Chris laughed. "Very nice, but I meant something a bit more leisurely."

"Well, I already finished, but if you give me half an hour—"

Chris slid down the door into a kiss and cuddle, laughing helplessly as John offered an increasingly bizarre variety of sexual favours, about two of which he was actually willing to do. The man was so vanilla he wouldn't even wrestle most nights, but it didn't mean he was above threatening to go all dominant on Chris's arse these days.

Eventually, though, the kisses turned sweet and affectionate again, and Chris nudged his nose against John's.

"I *meant* that I have an appointment at the salon."

"Urgh."

"Oh, shut your face. Julian does an amazing massage. You should try it, Mr Rocks-For-Arms."

"No thanks," John grumbled.

Chris grinned. "Give me a lift into town?"

"What do I get out of it?"

John was *insanely* jealous of Julian. It was hilariously sweet. He'd been grumpy the first few times he'd seen Julian fuss and flirt, but when he'd found out it wasn't an act and Julian really was as gay as the stereotype, he'd gone from grumpy to downright sulky. It was just as well that John's response to feeling intimidated by other men was to spoil Chris even more rather than shout about it and make demands, or Julian could have caused major trouble.

"You get me back all pliant and happy and sexy," Chris said.

"Um, what the hell do you think you are right now?"

"Well, you've scraped my elbows against the door with that surprise sucking."

John snorted.

"*And* my hair will look all beautiful."

"See previous answer."

"You're biased."

"And you're blind," John deadpanned.

"*Duh.*"

John agreed to take him, though. Chris was semi-convinced he just lurked outside the shop looking scary and trying to intimidate Julian out of flirting with him. Which, of course, didn't work. Mainly because Julian didn't fancy Chris whatsoever but carried a torch the size of the Olympic Flame for John. He *liked* the big and belligerent act.

"When's the appointment?" John asked as Chris got dressed.

"Half one."

"It's ten now."

"So we go shopping and get lunch."

"Tell you what. I'll take you to your other boyfriend, *and* I'll go get my hair cut at a normal barber's while you're busy—if you come ring shopping with me."

Chris blinked. "What?"

"Ring shopping."

"As in wedding rings?"

"What else?"

Chris didn't bother to offer an alternative. Instead, he opened the kitchen drawer where they stashed their odds and ends and found the box with Jack's ring inside.

"I—I wanted to wear this," he said.

John's fingers closed around his own on the box and lifted them. The kiss pressed to the backs of Chris's knuckles was raspy with stubble, but soft where his lips touched.

"Then wear it," he said. "Just like Jack intended."

"So—"

"Granddad called me when I was at work yesterday," John whispered.

"Yeah?"

"He's excited."

Chris's heart melted a little.

"Wanted to know if I knew of a trustworthy dry cleaner. He's getting his dress uniform out of the wardrobe and is going to wear it. Nan said he's been polishing his medals already."

"Oh my God..."

"And he said he wants me to wear his wedding ring too."

Chris's breath caught. Granddad's ring? Him with Jack's, and John with Granddad's? The molten edges of his heart dissolved entirely, and his knees shivered.

"But—but your nan—"

John coughed thickly. "He, um. He knows—we all—"

Chris lifted his other hand and took John's in both of his own. John squeezed. For a moment, Chris listened to him work at the words before he spoke again.

"We all know he's starting to run down," he said thickly. "He's not— The heart attack took a lot out of him. He's tired. And he's had—it's been a good innings. He'll be ninety at Christmas, but I don't think he's expecting to make ninety-one. And he said he'd like to see his ring go to some good use. Said he—said he wanted to see it start its new life with us before—well. Before."

"Oh, John..."

"So—so I'm going to wear his ring. And you'll wear Jack's. And they'll hopefully bring us a bit of luck on making it in the long term."

Chris chuckled. "We don't need luck."

"Can't hurt."

"Guess not."

"But I wanted to get rings of our own too. Something new, uniquely for us. So I was hoping you'd agree to an engagement ring as well."

Chris rubbed his thumb against his left ring finger. He'd never worn jewellery of any kind. The weight of a ring was going to feel odd, and Jack's was heavy enough. But the idea appealed a little.

A lot, if he was honest with himself.

"Nothing fancy."

"You can pick it out."

Chris cackled. "Oh, and how am I supposed to do that? Newsflash, metal loops just feel like metal loops, no matter what they look like."

John snorted. "Yeah, yeah. Tart. I'll tell you if it's nice."

"Er, as discussed previously? You're biased. You think I look good in a bin bag."

"You do."

"Bullshit," Chris said.

"Well, you're entitled to your opinions," John drawled, dropping his hands and clasping his bum instead. Chris laughed as he was towed in and his neck kissed. "Even if they're utterly wrong."

"Get off, you horny fuck."

"Maybe tonight. So, is it a deal? Come ring shopping with me, then we grab lunch, and I'll drop you off for your pampering session without complaining?"

"With*out* complaining? Oh, deal!"

Chris teased him all the way to the car but quieted when John turned the key in the ignition.

"Wait."

"What?"

"C'mere."

Chris kissed him like his life depended on it. Hard, powerful, purposeful. The kind of kiss meant to replace a speech—and when it broke, he knew he'd been heard.

"Yeah," John murmured, stroking his cheek and kissing it lightly before sitting back. "I know. And me too."

"THAT'S IT," JOHN whispered. "That's the one."

Chris closed his fingers and began to twist the ring around with his thumb.

"It's thin," he said.

It *was* thin. Much thinner than Jack's wedding ring. It felt almost delicate, but for the single stone jutting up from one side. It felt quiet and understated, and not at all what he'd expected John to choose.

"It's blue and silver."

"Of course it is," Chris said dryly, and the sales assistant giggled.

"The stone's like your eyes. That really dark, rich blue. It draws the eye. It's captivating. Hypnotic. Like—"

"If you say like me, wedding's off."

"Like the man I'm marrying," John replied without missing a beat.

"Jesus."

The sales assistant cooed. Which was a little disturbing, as she sounded about nineteen years old.

"I don't know," Chris said. "It feels flimsy."

"It's not at all fragile," the sales assistant chirped. "That whole range can be worn in everyday situations without scratching."

"Try it with the wedding ring," John suggested. "That's how you'll be wearing it."

Jack's ring was heavy and solid, almost old-fashioned. Chris slid it into place and flexed his fingers once more, the added weight dragging slightly. The difference was immense.

"Huh," he said.

"Better?"

"Yeah."

"They look perfect," John insisted. "The contrast is great. They both need resizing, obviously, but once they fit properly—"

Chris chuckled. "You're in love with them, aren't you?"

"Yep."

"Go on, then."

The hand that had strayed to his waist and stayed there from the second they'd walked into the shop slid further around his side and tugged him in for a sideways hug.

"Seriously?" John asked.

"Sure." Chris worked them off and dropped them into John's palm. "They feel fine. But if I get this, you have to get the titanium one."

If John liked the colour scheme on the silver ring, Chris loved the weight and coolness of a thick titanium band that John had tried to talk him into earlier. He could imagine it already. The smooth, cold contrast when John cupped his face, or stroked his side, or gripped his thigh. He even wanted to be finger-fucked with it. He'd have to try to persuade John to try fisting again at some point once they'd got married. Maybe on the honeymoon.

"Hey," he said as the assistant boxed up the rings and measured his fingers for the right size. "Honeymoon."

"You want one?"

"Yep."

"Where?"

"I don't know. A nice beach somewhere, but nothing to do so we can just bask and enjoy it."

"And somewhere we don't have to fly," John added dryly.

Chris pulled a face.

"Could always go to France again," John offered, his thumb stroking Chris's hip gently. "Paris hasn't got any beaches, but Brittany does. And a pretty wild sea, most of the time."

"Deal," Chris said.

"I'll have a look," John agreed. His wallet slapped the table. "All right. Let me pay up for this lot, then you get lunch?"

"Sure. It's getting too hot in here. I'll wait outside."

The street was busy, so Chris just waited by the window. He rubbed the empty space on his ring finger with his thumb as he waited. It had felt odd to wear the rings, but one day, it would feel odd not to, much like when he'd first got his medical bracelet. He'd have to make sure John didn't get some stupid tattoo, though. The man was almost totally covered, but Chris wouldn't put it past him to have their wedding date stamped somewhere. Or Chris's name.

"Christian!"

He stiffened. Poppy shifted at his feet in response, then settled when she recognised the newcomer. Chris felt less inclined to relax, though.

"Mum."

Her hand touched his elbow lightly. She clicked her tongue at Poppy but didn't pet her like she would have done at home.

"How are you?" she asked.

"Fine." He chewed over the thought briefly, then decided to go with it and see what she said. "We sent out the wedding invitations yesterday."

There was a short pause.

"You..."

Another pause.

"You have a date?"

"Yes. The first Friday in September."

"Oh. That's—not long."

"We wanted a summer wedding," Chris said. "And the venue's nice. It's a country pub out near Bakewell."

He expected some comment. Mum had always been particular. Instead, she made another non-committal noise and fell quiet.

"We've just been ring shopping. Engagement rings. I'm still going to wear Jack's wedding ring."

Her hand drifted from his arm at the mention of Jack, and Chris sighed.

"Mum, we're happy. We're excited. Can't you be?"

She said nothing.

"Are you—"

He didn't want to ask, but—

"Your invitation's in the post. Should we have bothered making it?"

"Christian..."

He waited.

Then the door clinked, and John's enormous hand was warm under his elbow.

"Ruth! How've you been?"

"John."

She didn't answer him either, and Chris's temper flared.

"Fine," he spat. "If you can't be happy for me, then don't bother coming."

Then without a care as to where he was going or whether he crashed into people, he tugged on Poppy's harness and walked off.

If he'd wanted Julian before, now he *needed* him.

Chapter Sixteen

"OH HONEY," JULIAN said the minute Chris walked into the salon. "Why do you do this to me?"

Usually, Chris would rise to the bait. This time, still simmering with hurt and anger, he just stalked off to Julian's little room at the back of the shop. Low murmurs sounded behind him. The main door clinked shut—then the door to Julian's room.

"Get yourself in that chair, sweetie."

Second only to John, Julian had been the greatest find of Chris's life. He worked in a salon in the city centre, renting one of their back rooms out to offer pedicures, manicures, facial spa treatments, and massages. And despite John's grumbling, no happy endings. He'd recently finished his training as a hairdresser as well, and Chris had immediately dumped his usual barber in favour of Julian.

And regretted not a second of it as those clever hands began to work through his curls.

"What's happened, sweetie?"

He sighed as Julian ignored the scissors and began to massage his temples.

"We're getting married, and my mum's against the idea."

God, it sounded so deceptively simple when he said it like that. Like the shitty plot on a daytime TV show. Chris could hardly believe it was happening to him. Usually, he'd be throwing crisps at the telly and shouting at the hero—or more likely heroine, in that scenario—to grow a pair and tell their mother to go fuck herself.

And now here he was, ready to punch the shampoo bottle in Julian's salon because his mum didn't think he was fit to get married.

"Well, pardon my French, but fuck your mother," Julian said. "Now let's get you settled, and Auntie Julian will make it all better. Those poor feet first. You *never* look after those..."

Chris slowly relaxed as Julian fussed about. Once he was submerged to the ankle in a bubbling footbath, and some gritty substance had been smeared over his face for a mask, complete with cucumber eyes, he let out a deep sigh that expelled most of his tension.

"That's better," Julian crooned, resuming the head massage. "Now let's be sensible, shall we, sweetie? You're still gorgeous. Say it!"

Chris cracked a smile and was told off for it. He didn't really care. It was why he loved Julian in the first place. He'd found the salon when he was still being taken for a girl, and barely recovering from a savage bout of depression in his late teens that had left him in a mess. And Julian had flirted with him.

It sounded silly now, but at the time, Chris had clung to that flirting with utter desperation. A flamboyantly gay man flirting with him, giving him massages, calling him gorgeous, calling him *him*? It had been something he'd needed. Someone who didn't have to love him like his family did. Someone who didn't have anything to lose but a single customer in a long line of them if he said the wrong thing. Someone who'd chosen to flirt with him, to call him attractive, to boost his shattered ego. Someone who'd never acted like he was anything other than what he was right now.

John didn't get it, and Chris had never bothered to tell him. John hadn't seen how bad Chris had been back then. By the time John came along, Chris had managed to rebuild his confidence and his self-esteem, through a mix of transition, friends, and Julian. In a way, Chris hadn't needed Julian for years.

But he had, once.

And it was still so *easy* with Julian. He couldn't deny just how easy it was to check his problems at the door and succumb to the lure of the chair. To relax, even as his temper was still simmering. To feel as utterly safe under Julian's dextrous hands as he did in the warm circle of John's hugs.

"I'm still gorgeous," Chris echoed.

"You have that bear of yours wrapped around your little finger, growling at any attractive hairdressers in a ten-mile radius. Say it!"

Chris laughed, was scolded, and offered an abridged version.

"John loves me."

"You're getting *married*, and I better have an invite, honey."

"I'm getting married, and it's in the post."

"And I have a world-class expert to make me the most handsome groom in the known world."

Chris snorted.

"I already am."

"*Much* better," Julian enthused. "So what does your mother know?"

"She thinks—"

"Ah-ah! What does she *know*?"

Chris sighed. What *did* she know? She thought this, and she said that, but she didn't know shit. She should know better, but she didn't.

"Nothing."

"There. You see? Nothing. Let her disapprove. You don't let a beast like him go! Who knows when you'll find another stud like that."

Chris hummed as Julian's clever fingers began to work at the knots in his neck. He zoned out as Julian chattered away about everything under the sun, lost between the hot water slowly boiling his toes and the tingle of tea tree oil and peppermint destroying the HRT's latest attempts at giving him teenage acne. Julian was right. Let Mum have her opinions. They would have a nice party anyway; everyone else would be there, and thanks to Julian, Chris would look his best.

"Now, this hair," Julian said, fluffing it out.

"It needs cutting."

"No, no, no, sweetie! You should grow it out some more."

Chris snorted. "Yeah, okay. It'll go wild."

"And so will your man," Julian promised. "I've seen how handsy he gets when you've had it loosened. Imagine him when you have to scoop it up in a nice little rubber? *Don't* laugh at me, mister, I'm talking! Let's try growing it out a little before the wedding, hmm? And if you don't like it, I'll cut it for free before the big day. How's that?"

"Fine, but you'll need to loosen it anyway, or it'll be a nest."

"Of course!" Julian said as he sifted through it. "You need to use conditioner more, you know. Shower gel is *not* shampoo, honey, I don't care what they taught you in man school."

Chris argued back half-heartedly but wondered about having longer hair. He'd always cut it long enough to ruffle the curls, to let them fall a little, to drive John a little crazy about them. But never long enough to have to tie up or need conditioner. Never to touch the collar of a shirt. *Certainly* not shoulder length. It was unthinkable, after all that effort to transition.

But—

What did he need the security of short hair for now? He'd not been mistaken for a woman in years. Even his laugh had dropped out of its high range. He had a permanent rough layer of stubble. There was an angle to his jaw there hadn't been when he was younger and girlier. And he had liked the weight of his hair once, and how *different* it was. He had nice hair. He'd always had nice hair.

"Let's see what John thinks," he said. "And if I've not been limping more than usual before the wedding, we'll chop it off for the big day."

"That's the way to do it, honey."

BY THE TIME Chris was released—his hour session somehow having turned into two—the magic had been done. Bitter disappointment at his mother's lack of response had faded under Julian's chirpy attitude and brilliant hands. He nearly floated back into John's arms and laughed at his grumbled goodbye to Julian.

"Why are you so jealous of him?"

"Because he fancies you," John groused.

"He doesn't."

"Oh please. That flirting—"

"Is a show." Chris laughed. "It's you he's interested in."

John coughed awkwardly as they reached the car park. "I don't think so."

"He does!"

"Er. Well. Too late."

"Admit it. If you'd met him first, you'd have asked him out."

"Jesus. Fine. *Maybe*," John grumbled. "But I'd have dumped him when I met you anyway."

"Charmer."

The flirting paused until the car door, where great clumsy hands ruined Chris's carefully cultivated hair, and, by contrast, the kiss that captured his mouth was soft and sweet.

"Got to work to keep a man like you around," John murmured.

"Mm. You're onto something there."

"I'm glad you're feeling better, anyway."

"Much. And I've booked Julian for another session a couple of days before the wedding. I'm hoping it'll stop the nerves setting off the seizures."

"You reckon you'll be that nervous?"

"Even if Mum doesn't bother to come, have you ever talked to Caroline about weddings? I'll want to kill her by then. Blah blah blah, patriarchy, blah blah, oppressive systems of misogyny and property rights, blah blah blah."

"Property rights?"

"I don't know, dowries or swapping sheep for wives or something."

"What farmyard animal are you worth? A couple of cats?"

"Do you want to get married or not?" Chris asked as he let Poppy into the back seat.

"Depends if I get those sheep or not."

"I guess not."

John chuckled. The car dipped as he got into the driver's seat, the back door bucking in Chris's grip, and when Chris got in the front, his face was caught and kissed.

"Erm, I don't think so. No kisses for you, sheep-hoarder."

John snorted, then took his hand and kissed the back of it.

"Well, I just found out that days before our wedding, my fiancé is going to visit a man who endlessly flirts with him—"

"But fancies you."

"—so I think that's a sign I ought to take you home and remind you what a good thing you've got going here."

"Julian *worshipped* me in there," Chris taunted as the car creaked into gear.

"And I can worship you for the rest of our married lives, but I know you better than Julian. I don't think you want worshipping today."

"No?"

"Nope. How about I cancel those plans on refitting the banisters this afternoon, take you back to our borrowed campervan, and undo all of Julian's hard work with a long—"

Chris narrowed his eyes.

"—slow—"

He screwed up his nose.

"Fine."

His thigh was squeezed as the car bounced out of the final level of the multistorey and into the road.

"How about I throw you down on that mattress, open you up, and *break* you?"

Chris grinned and leaned back in his seat.

"Deal."

Chapter Seventeen

CHRIS STRETCHED. THERE were voices outside and the low rumble of a van or lorry. It didn't bother him. No doubt John had some of his mates round to help with something or other.

Chris turned over, dragging the duvet over his head. He chased sleep for a little while, but it was gone. A light rain pattered on the roof, distracting enough to prevent him sliding back into dreams.

"Fine," he muttered and pushed himself up. Poppy immediately nudged her bowl, the scrape of metal telling him it was offensively empty. "Oh, all right. I bet John's already fed you too."

He wondered what to do as he fed the dog and himself, then caught a quick shower. He ought to get Gina on board about decorations for the venue. John was all about interior design but was a typical bloody builder when it came to such concerns for anything else. He'd probably not even figured out they'd need flowers.

The voices had retreated indoors by the time he let Poppy out, and the lorry was gone. He padded through to the back door and into the kitchen, curious as to what they were doing. John hadn't mentioned any plans today, and having a whole crowd over said loud and clear that Chris was going to have to entertain himself for a little while.

Sure enough, he could hear banging and banter from upstairs. It sounded like they were in one of the bedrooms, and Chris wondered if the custom-made bed had arrived, or if John had decided on that built-in wardrobe he'd been on about. Resigning himself to a day of noise and chaos, Chris made for the kettle, intent on using the leftover water for a fancy coffee.

Only it was stone cold.

"Berk," he said and went to the foot of the stairs. "Oi! How many brews!"

One part of the banging stopped. Someone laughed and said something about Chris being a better host than John. Then footsteps stomped out onto the landing, and John's voice carried down with a distinctly bashful tone.

"Er, sorry. Morning. Uh, five if you can manage it?"

"Including you?" Chris asked sceptically.

"Oops. Six. Please."

"Coming right up."

He'd only just been introduced to the first floor, thanks to the replaced floorboards last week, and it was still new enough that a tray of six brews was a bit intimidating. He filled them deliberately a little low and rummaged for biscuits to sweeten the deal if he spilled any, then toed off his shoes to let his feet help with finding his way. One step at a time. If he had to shuffle like Jack on a bad day, so be it. He wasn't entirely relaxed about some of John's friends, and he'd like to not make an idiot of himself.

He'd just reached the last step, when the hubbub dissolved into comprehensible conversation, and paused, listening intently when he heard the words 'stag do'.

"No," John snapped.

"Darn't be such a farking pansy," Rhodri growled. His accent was a horrific, garbled mess, and Chris winced. "Yer 'avin' one. No arguments."

"I'm really not—"

"Sorted!" said one of the rugby lads. Something clanked. "Oi, Slag, get up there and give it your best humping."

"Fuck off," Slag replied easily. "And Rhodri's right, mate. You're having a stag do."

"But—" John tried.

"Missus has even made you a Tinker Bell costume."

Chris smirked. When they met, John had been firmly in the closet at his rugby club and played under the nickname of Shrek, for being big and ugly and the home kit being green. They all had equally unflattering aliases for the pitch. Slag. Gimli. Walkers, for his habit of constantly eating the popular brand of crisps. The new team captain was the only one who got to use his actual name because it was—unfortunately—Ponce. Once John came out, Shrek was abandoned for Tinker Bell. Chris had never met someone so pleased to be called a fairy and suddenly got the impression John was going to be spending his stag do in a skirt and a pair of glittery wings.

"I don't bloody think so!"

"It's not like we're going to let you go off the rails."

The sudden silence made Chris catch his breath. What did Slag mean, 'go off the rails'? He inched closer, straining his ears.

"Steve..."

John's voice was frighteningly quiet.

"We know you're worried, mate." Chris didn't recognise the new voice. "What better place to figure it out? Stag do with thirty big fucks who can handle you, and your Chris nowhere to be found."

John coughed a laugh. It sounded like he was trying not to cry.

"And then what? When I come home and you're not here to stop me if—"

"You won't be going home until the morning," Slag said. "We have it all figured out. You'll crash at mine and get a taxi home next day when you've sobered up. No harm, no foul. Hell, you could even time it right and send Chris off on his own do so he's not even home."

Chris cocked his head, trying to work it out. John hadn't said anything about a stag do. Chris had no doubt Luke and Gina would drag him out for something, and he was going to try for a spa day, but John hadn't mentioned anything. And sober? John didn't drink. He hadn't drunk since—

Oh.

Chris squared his shoulders and deliberately trod on a squeaky board.

"Tea!"

"Bloody mint!"

They cheered him as he shuffled into the room, and the cups vanished off the tray like they'd never existed.

"'Bout bloody time. More than this sack of shit does for us!"

"Oi, Chris, can the wedding with this twat and marry me instead."

"Fuck me, them's the good biscuits too!"

He pulled faces, slapped Slag's arm away from his waist, and told John to come and help with lunch as he'd obviously not fed anybody either. They whooped again, and he shuffled out with the familiar mix of feeling uncomfortably out of place and vaguely like he was being made fun of, and yet warmed by their relaxed nature with their mate's boyfriend.

John came down after about ten minutes and caught him with a kiss at the oven.

"Thanks for the tea," he said. "Sorry, the delivery company rang this morning before you were up, so I asked the lads to come and give me a hand."

"Is it the bed?"

"Yeah. Then we're going to put the dust sheets down and get the painting done. May as well make it into a proper room now the bed's here."

Chris turned in his arms and rubbed his fingers over bare, bulging biceps.

"So...stag do?"

John stiffened.

"You heard that?"

"Yeah. Sounds like they've planned a party for you."

"Apparently. I don't want to go."

"Why?"

"Being the sober guy at a piss-up is shit."

Chris licked his lips. "And why would you need to be sober?"

There was a long pause.

Then: "You know why."

He did. Or at least, he knew why John thought that way.

Chris's predecessor had fucked John up in the head until John became deeply depressed, convinced he was a dangerous thug and burning up from the inside with anger and unhappiness. He'd transformed from a happy, cuddly sort of drunk to a belligerent twat, and after nearly coming to blows with Slag on a rugby piss-up, had sworn off the booze. He'd been too scared of getting violent to risk it, and—rather than sort through his emotions—had stopped drinking to cope.

That had been four years ago.

Since, Chris had never seen John touch a drop. Not at Sunday dinners with Nan and Granddad, not at New Year's, not on their anniversary—not even a pint in front of the telly on long, lazy evenings. Nothing.

And since, Chris had seen John go from panic attacks if he left a bruise during sex to—well. Last night. Throwing him down and breaking him open, albeit the words had been much more daring than the actual act. But, still. Fucking him properly. Not taking seven hours to work him open enough for that truncheon of a dick. Screwing him so there was a bit of a sting the next morning.

"I know you were scared you'd get violent," Chris said softly.

John nudged his nose against Chris's forehead but said nothing.

"I also know you were miserable."

Still nothing.

"And I know before Daniel, you weren't like that with beer."

John let out a shaky breath.

"I think maybe Slag has a good idea."

"No," John retorted immediately. "I can't take the risk. If I came back here drunk and—"

"Hey, it's okay," Chris murmured, stroking his hands up to catch John around the nape of his neck. "It's all right. I won't make you do anything; you know that. But I think it's a good idea to figure out if that issue is still there, or if it's gone away again."

John dropped his face against Chris's hair. Broad hands slid around his chest and hung on. Chris squeaked as he was squeezed and waited for the pressure to go down again before carrying on.

"You were miserable and going through absolute hell," Chris said gently. "Of course that changed your behaviour when you were drunk. You were backed into a corner and defensive and *scared*. Don't you think I know what it feels like to be scared?"

John hugged him again but didn't reply.

"You couldn't so much as say hi to my stepmother without having a meltdown. You had a panic attack the first time you looked after me during a seizure, in case anyone thought you'd triggered it. You were *bad*, sweetheart. And now, here you are. Throwing me down on the bed and grabbing kisses like you're owed them and not letting my mum get to you. You wouldn't have been able to handle that back then."

"I know," John croaked. "I *know*. But—what if—"

"Okay," Chris said. "Let's say you go out with them, get smashed, and act like a complete arsehole. They can keep you in line. They did it then."

"Until I come home," John breathed. "And then you say the wrong thing, or I want to do something and you don't, and I—I—"

"And if I'm not here?" Chris said.

John shook his head. "I can't just chase you out of the house because I want a drink."

"If you go into dickhead mode at this stag do of yours, you're back on the wagon, and you're never having another drop," Chris retorted. "I'm not having a drunk knobhead for a husband. But this one time, why not do as your mates said? I'll go and have my own celebration with Gina and Luke, and we won't even tell you where. You won't know where to find me if you're being a prick, and by the time I come home, you'll have sobered up, and we know where we stand."

John pressed a kiss to his forehead, then stooped to kiss the bridge of his nose and cheekbones.

"I want to have a party," he admitted. "I—you know. I'm getting married. I want a big bash with the lads. If not for—if not for *that,* it would be fun."

Chris rose up onto his tiptoes to get a proper kiss. Gradually, John relaxed against him. Soon enough, his entire body weight was being held up by those ridiculous arms, and his feet were floating a good four inches off the floor.

"I think you'll be fine," he whispered. "Get your mates to pick a date, and I'll go and have a luxury stay somewhere well out of reach. I'll even switch my phone off so you can't ring me up and be a dick at a distance. How's that?"

John nodded.

"About farking time," said a thick voice from the door. "John, get yer fat arse up 'ere and give us an 'and wi' th' farking ladder."

CHRIS KICKED HIS feet up on the coffee table and dropped his head back.

"Bliss," he said and patted his gut. "Food baby."

"Food twins," Luke agreed.

Gina flopped back into her spot, leaving Chris bracketed by his two friends, and added her own appreciative groan to the collective.

"So, are we in agreement?" she asked. "Wong's is the new default takeaway?"

"Agreed."

"Agreed."

Chris groaned as his phone started ringing. "Bloody fuck. That'll be John."

"I'll get it."

Luke stretched, made a noise like he was dying, and the ringing stopped.

"Ey-up, John. Well, duh. Oi, Chris, it's your fiancé."

Chris flipped him off but took the phone. "Hey."

"We're done at the house," John told him. "Have you eaten?"

"Uh, *yeah*," Chris said heavily.

"Okay. Mind if I go get a curry with Rhodri, then?"

"Nah, go ahead."

"And, uh. When—when you coming home?"

"I dunno," Chris said. "Whenever Gina kicks us out, I guess."

It could be a while, though. Jemma had moved out, and Chris got the impression Gina felt a bit lonely. The flat certainly looked a bit lonely with all of the empty gaps where Jemma's stuff had been.

"Um. Do you—"

Chris raised his eyebrows. "John?"

John took a deep breath. "I'm going to have a pint *and* a curry with Rhodri."

"Ah."

"And...well, what with the kids and Amy and that sodding mastiff of his—"

Chris heard a faint "Oi! Farking twat!" in the background and laughed.

"I get it. You can't crash at his, so you want me to crash here."

Gina nudged his knee with her toes. "You can have my sofa if you want."

"Gina says I can stay over."

"Okay. I mean, you know, I just—it'll just be the one drink. Two, tops. But just in case—"

"For fark's sake, yer farking pansy..."

Chris laughed. "Go for your pint with Rhodri. You'll still be able to bloody drive, never mind be drunk, but if it'll make you feel better, I'll stay the night with Gina."

"Thank you," John burst out in a relieved rush. "Just—I won't make a habit of it; I promise. I just wanted to—"

"I get it," Chris said. "Can you bring my medication over, or do I need to come and get it?"

"I'll bring it now. Oh, and, uh, the boys chose a date for the stag do."

"Yeah?"

"Yeah. August bank holiday."

"Okay. I'll make some plans. Go enjoy your curry and a couple of cans, then. Love you."

"You too."

He rolled his eyes as he hung up, and Gina laughed.

"Guess you're up for a midnight movie marathon?"

"Better," he said. "John's stag do is going to be on the August bank holiday weekend."

"So when's yours?" Luke asked.

Chris leaned forward to drop his phone on the coffee table and collapsed back with a groan.

"Guess we better figure that out," he said.

Chapter Eighteen

A THUNDERSTORM WAS breaking when Chris got home the next day.

It was late in the evening. John had been called out to an emergency at six in the morning and texted hours later saying Chris had better get dinner for one. So when Gina had gone to her evening shift, Chris went to Dad's, stole food from the family table, and argued with Caroline about the symbolism of flowers until Lauren left work and could take him home.

But when she turned into the now-familiar cul-de-sac, she made a surprised sound and said, "Oh! John's home after all."

"He's probably only just got here," Chris said.

"He's in the house. Lights are on. You all right with the route now?"

"Yeah. Thanks for the ride."

The wind threatened to knock him off his feet. The campervan was horrible in a high wind, and Chris made straight for the back of the house, let himself in with a loud bang, and bolted it behind him. Poppy shook herself off, and Chris wished he could do the same.

"John!"

A muffled shout came from somewhere upstairs. Chris headed for the hall, was nudged around some kind of obstacle, and toed off his shoes before heading upstairs. The floor was smooth and clean, the new hardwood layer clearly polished properly, and the faint smell of paint rose from the radiators in waves.

"John?"

"Just finishing up here," came a distant reply. "The en suite is ready to use. Grab a shower or something, and I'll be with you in a bit."

Chris rolled his eyes and left him to whatever he was doing. No doubt another tiny job that could have waited. Like the radiators. Who painted the radiators when the roof hadn't been replaced and there was a hole in the living room floor?

The en suite was nice, though, and Chris stripped and got in the shower with a sigh of relief. He'd insisted on proper power showers, and it was like a mini-spa all on its own. The pressure was immense, and the pounding hot water released all the little knots and niggles he never quite realised he was carrying until they were removed. He tipped his head back under the spray and stood there for long minutes before reaching for the shower gel.

He took his time. John was quiet, Chris eventually losing track of him in the large house, and Poppy dozed on the mat. He liked the idea. He was getting tired of mattresses on the floor, and it was only a matter of time before he had a seizure in the narrow van and did himself an injury. God knew, he didn't need another broken bone.

The door cracked open as he rinsed the last of the conditioner out of his hair, and he stepped out into a warmed towel. John didn't say a word. He knotted the towel around Chris's chest, then locked those arms around Chris's hips and lifted until Chris perched on the counter, and his wall of a boyfriend slid closer between his knees. Dry hands raked through his drenched curls. Raw sensation crackled all along his scalp. His mouth sagged open in mute pleasure and was instantly captured.

For a long time, Chris simply drifted in the attention. There was a hungry demand, but gentleness too. John's sheer height and a hand on the back of his neck kept Chris trapped in the kisses, open and defenceless as if he'd been tied down. The hand at the small of his back and the wall of a body standing between his thighs prevented any escape or even much in the way of movement. He was held open by John's mere presence and trapped there by two hands and a height difference.

And somehow—forced open, wet and wearing nothing but a towel, pinned in place by a fully clothed man who weighed more than fifteen stone and could kill him with one punch—it was the safest Chris had ever felt in his life. He could have dissolved then and there, fallen apart, been scattered to the four winds, and none of it would have mattered. John would catch all the stray parts. John would hold him in.

He slid his hands up John's spine, bunching cotton in his fists before going back and starting again under the T-shirt. Muscles rippled under his fingers. Tattoos twisted and turned. He tugged at the top, and the kiss was broken just long enough for him to pull the T-shirt off and throw it aside. The moment the cloth left his fingertips, John's hands returned, and Chris was caught once more, a single bite on his lip serving as a silent reprimand for breaking away in the first place.

He sagged into John's chest, tracing his collarbone as though it were the first time. The tattoos were older and smoother over his pecs, blurring into nothing but skin. He covered both nipples with his palms and laughed breathlessly into that never-ending kiss as John's power and control were proven to be an illusion. His hips bucked involuntarily. Chris smiled. He shivered as a hand coursed up his spine and wound into his hair. His head was pulled further back. His mouth was explored, and he shivered helplessly under the assault, everything from the neck up paralysed and everything from the neck down ignored. It was a dizzying contrast, a single part of his soul anchored and everything else dissolving into the abyss, never to be recovered.

He felt—terrifyingly vulnerable, and overwhelmingly secure all at once. His heart beating like a rabbit's in his chest, far too hard and far too fast. And yet, he relaxed. He coasted in the instinctive fear like watching a horror movie from under a favourite blanket. He could hardly breathe, but who needed air? The vertigo dragged at his senses, but John would catch him. He could barely tell which way was up, but all of his senses were focused on John, and John never wavered.

But he wanted more.

He didn't want to float away. He wanted to be held. He wanted the weight of the wedding ring, the warm calluses of John's palms against his skin, the deep timbre of his voice radiating from the tips of Chris's toes to the top of his scalp. He wanted to be surrounded in that strength, not just his mind but his body as well.

He dragged his nails down that solid chest, so softly they barely moved the hairs on John's skin. The belt was thick leather, and he worked the buckle open with persistent hands. John's hips rocked forward as Chris slid the belt from the loops. The buttons strained and popped apart with groans of relief. Chris pushed until the denim fell away, and the jeans crashed to the floor in a jangle of change, keys, and heavy fabric. He stretched the waistband of useless boxers between finger and thumb before tugging those free as well.

Then John shifted, a jagged motion of stepping out of his discarded clothes. The hands in Chris's hair dropped to the knot of the towel. It was pulled apart and the rush of chilly air warded off by broad hands stroking down his spine. Fingers spread and covered the entire width of his back with ease. Then they hooked under his thighs, and he was lifted.

Chris usually didn't like being picked up. But coaxed into such a relaxed state, and with the low warmth of arousal slowly sinking from his chest into his stomach and soon to go lower, he looped his arms around John's neck and pressed his nose beneath John's left ear. Aftershave. Vanilla. The faintest traces of radiator paint. As John slowly paced from the en suite into the bedroom, Chris sunk his teeth into John's earlobe, and *sucked*.

It didn't work.

He meant to provoke a reaction. A slap on the backside. An instruction to behave. One of those growls that drove Chris crazy.

Instead, John jerked his head and shook him off. The world tipped. Chris yelped as John smashed them down into the new bed with an almighty thump. The mattress bowed. Pillows crowded in around him like mourners at the lip of a grave. He was buried under John's immense weight, driven down into the deep mattress like he would never be found.

Surrounded.

He was utterly trapped, and without a hand on him like before. John's body had come down between his legs and pinned them open. That barrel chest drove him down into the bed with an immense pressure. Shoulders flexed. The duvet settled over them, a cloud of softness cocooning their legs. How high it came, Chris didn't know. Everything else was blanketed in *John*.

And, suddenly, Chris didn't know what he wanted.

He hesitated, ghosting his fingers down John's face and carding them through shaggy hair desperately in need of cutting. He wanted—

He wanted to be *fucked*. He wanted teeth in his neck, power in the thrusts, to unleash a hurricane of passion and energy like the one still raging outside. He wanted to set off fireworks and revel in his power. He wanted to ride the storm and get drunk on being the one to cause it, the one to survive it, the one who controlled it even as he was subjected to it. He wanted to ache with it, feel it for days, be shattered apart and pieced back together like the fragments of a stained-glass window after the sacking of a church. Broken apart with the so-called sin and restored to ever-greater brilliance for it.

But—

He wanted to be the focal point too. He wanted to be the one that John lavished hours of attention on. He wanted to be utterly helpless and not care. He wanted to be touched like his body was utterly meaningless, and what mattered was who he was. He wanted to feel like it wasn't desire or lust or passion, no temporary flash of want, no brief burst of energy, but love. Something that was always there. He wanted to *feel*—not the physical burn, not the sexual release, but the emotion. He wanted to feel like it was their wedding day, and he was staring down the future.

Was it even possible to have—

"Fuck!"

Yes. Yes it was. He craned his neck, straining in a wordless blur of pain and pleasure as he was filled with a single, sharp jerk of the hips. John was far too large for that, yet one moment Chris was empty, and the next he was utterly full. *Completely.* John drove into him in a single thrust, relentless and overpowering, and Chris—shattered.

He was—

Gone.

Where he had gone? His veins hummed. His heart was so damn *loud.* The shaking faded, and for a wild moment, he wondered if it had been a seizure. A kiss nudged at his mouth, and he shook as he tried to accept it. The slow, rolling thrust inside him was not sharp pain but a slow and slick slide. He whimpered as every exhausted nerve sparked back into life, and then laughed, love-drunk, when he realised he'd just had the fastest, hardest orgasm of his life.

"Back?" John whispered against his ear.

"Mm."

He curled his fingers into John's arm and tracked the soft grip and release of his muscles. It was slow. The bed rocked gently, like a boat at sea, and Chris a gentle tide against a summer shore, infinitely relaxed and utterly helpless before the relentless tug of gravity. He could not have stopped even if he'd wanted to. John was everything. Everywhere. Inside, outside, all around. His hands tangled in Chris's hair, relaxed and gentle. His mouth massaged Chris's lips in kisses so sweet but so dirty it ached. His elbows bracketed Chris's shoulders, trapping him in a prison with a wide open door Chris never wanted to walk through. John's weight bore down on Chris's waist and hips, rendering him unable to pull away from that endless rhythm. Ebb and flow, ebb and flow, the tide on an endless loop, and Chris couldn't have cared less about escaping it.

"J'n—"

He never wanted it to end. He wanted to be here forever. Anchored. Adored. The kisses and the hands in his hair and the sex and the *power*. He had separated but never collapsed. He could end it all but never would.

"J'n."

He lifted an arm. Dropped it heavily over the back of John's neck. Caught him in a harder, darker, needier kiss. Not a clasping of lips or a messy slide, but a grip and a bite. The rhythm shivered. Gravity hesitated. Flexed. The universe was changing but staying just the same.

"I love you," he breathed, right there in the inseparable tangle they'd become, right here in the fortress they'd built around themselves, right there in the heat of a moment that had been going on for years.

The pull on his hair was a prickle of pain. The final thrust was a flood of pleasure. But Chris hardly noticed.

He just smiled, out of his mind with love yet stone-cold sober as John's deep voice rumbled an echo of his own words and said something Chris had always known.

Love.

Nothing else mattered.

Chapter Nineteen

"ALL DONE!" THE nurse said. "Let's pop a tiny bit of cotton wool on there so you don't get any blood on your boxers, love. *There* we go."

Chris pulled up his boxers and jeans, and buckled his belt. His arse, hip, and left thigh all ached right down to the bone, but the buzz of the shot was already kicking in.

"Thanks, Jodie. Is my next one booked in already?"

"It sure is, sweetie. I'll get them to send the text message again for you."

"Thanks. Come on, Poppy."

The doctor's surgery was quiet, and Chris breezed for the exit. He'd walk two stops up then catch the bus. It would give his arse time to get over its rude puncturing, and—

"Chris!"

He stopped dead just outside the door.

"Gina?"

Footsteps clapped on the flagstones, then an arm slid through his and the cane was jerked away.

"Come on!" she said. "My car's just here."

"Why? What are—"

"We're going wedding shopping."

"We are?"

"Yep. I called John this morning, and he said he wasn't going near a florist if you paid him, but you were at the doctor's for your shot."

"Traitorous c—"

"He even loaned us his younger sister and—" Gina's lips almost brushed his ear. "You're a right git! Why didn't you tell me about her? She's *cute!*"

"I hope you mean Fran, because Tasha's not…"

She *did* mean Fran. Who was in Gina's car, and bounced out to give Chris her customary shriek-and-hug greeting.

"Can't say I'm not surprised to see you," he admitted. "Why the sudden urge to go to a florist?"

"Um, because there's no way you two thought of it," Fran said. He was stuffed into the back seat with Poppy and the doors slammed. "And Gina and I put our heads together and came up with *amazing* centrepiece designs for the tables, and, hello, flowers have to be part of it!"

"They do?" Chris asked.

"Yep."

"What did John—"

Fran snorted. Gina called both Chris and aforementioned boyfriend unartistic. Chris gave up. He plugged his earphones into the phone handset and called up John's texts. He sent a single sadistic line—*you owe me*—and sat back to enjoy the ride.

Chris had never been to a florist in his life. John very rarely brought him flowers, and the ones that did occasionally materialise were from supermarkets or petrol stations. Chris liked flowers growing on plants just fine, but the idea of receiving a bunch of them made him squirm a little. It was just a bit—well. Men didn't really bring other men flowers. Not in Chris's experience. He felt weird when John did it.

So when they got there, the shop was both uncomfortable and pleasant.

It stank, for one. The mixture of artificial and natural perfume was overwhelming. It was even disorienting, and Chris had never smelled something so strong that he lost his sense of direction. He had to reach for Fran's arm to find his way again, and he had no hope of picking apart the various smells—aside from perhaps the particularly sickly stench of hyacinths.

"Okay," Gina said. "So what's your favourite flower?"

"Er...I don't have one?" Chris said.

"What's John's?"

"I don't know."

"How can you not know that?" Gina complained.

"We don't really do flowers."

"Okay, what's the colour scheme?"

"Um—" Chris thought. "Blue and silver? Blue and grey? There's definitely a dark blue theme."

"Wow, you are—you are just useless."

He flipped her off, pulling a face. "Why do I need to know about the colour scheme?"

"It's your wedding!"

"So? I'm not going to see it."

Then Fran started going on about the meanings of flowers, and Chris mentally checked out. They found an assistant. Chris ignored the lot of them and carefully meandered throughout the shop, prodding petals. The artificial ones felt revolting. The real ones spanned the full range between pleasant and soothing, to thick waxy petals like melting candles that he was only convinced were real by the stink they left on his fingers.

They should have gone abroad.

He shook himself. He was being uncharitable, and he knew it, but the itchy sensation of dysphoria was lurking just under the surface. Weddings were a landmine of triggers, Chris was discovering. The way people assumed he was the wife because he was slim and so much shorter than John. Picking flowers. Having to think about decorations—they weren't asking *John* about decorations. He was the husband. He was the wallet. He didn't have to actually come and decide these things.

"I just need a breather," he called and headed for the door, fumbling for his phone. Poppy seemed relieved to get out for five minutes, and he leaned against the glass to place the call.

"Reet Breet Electrics."

John sounded absent-minded, which probably explained the business greeting.

"It's me," Chris said. "You busy?"

"Ish. Let me put you on speaker."

Echoes started coming back to him, and then he heard John grunting as he wrestled with something.

"Well, that's ridiculously erotic," Chris said.

John laughed breathlessly.

"Gina kidnapped me from the doctor's."

"Sorry."

"You better be. Pick some flowers."

"What?"

"Pick some wedding flowers."

"We only need a bit for the main table and some buttonholes. What's there to pick?"

"Just pick some," Chris said. "I'm suffocating in there, and Fran's joined us—"

"*Fran?*"

"Yes, now help me escape!"

"Er." Something banged. "Right. Um. I mean, roses are pretty standard. You could always go for tulips, though."

"Tulips?"

"Yeah, they're nice. Remember, we were going to plant some in the front garden for next spring?"

"Done," Chris said. "What colours?"

"What?"

"What colours?"

"Wow, you are desperate to get out of there." John chuckled. "Mix up blue and white. Or white with something like forget-me-nots."

"Done," Chris said, and hung up. He steeled himself and rubbed Poppy's ears. "Sorry, sweetheart. Back into the perfume shop."

She huffed grumpily, and he completely agreed with her. He'd never suffered from hay fever in his life, but he could see why some people hated summer as he waded back into the stench and found the girls again, debating something that felt like a bee's arse.

"Tulips," he said.

"What?"

"White tulips with forget-me-nots."

"For the buttonhole?" Gina asked.

"And the rest. There. Flowers picked."

Obviously, it couldn't be *that* easy. The assistant twittered on about expensive and seasonal and blah blah blah. Fran flapped about meanings and the colour white not being appropriate and whatever. Gina just didn't like tulips.

"Groom picked them, they feel fine, let's go," Chris insisted. "And who cares about appropriate anyway? I'm not exactly the virgin bride in a white dress over here."

Gina snorted with laughter.

The assistant insisted on making up a sample buttonhole, though. Apparently tulips were tricky. Chris sighed but allowed it, mostly because Gina threatened to punch him if he didn't, but then—

Something happened when the little arrangement was pressed into his hand.

He paused.

It felt—

Delicate. The petals were soft and slightly waxy. The scent was incredibly understated, barely detectable over the melee of the rest of the shop. He stroked the small leaves and traced the cup shape of the tulip with the tips of his fingers until he ruffled the slightly feathery ends where they came together at the top, where the flower barely bloomed.

It was—

"I take it back," Gina murmured. "The look on your face right now..."

Chris handed over the piece without a word.

"It's perfect," Gina said.

Quietly, he agreed.

COMING HOME TO a campervan-sized space on the drive was strange.

Chris had walked home from the town centre after a late lunch with the girls, still rubbing his fingers together with the phantom memory of the flowers, but he stopped dead in the empty driveway for a long minute. The banging on John's phone call must have been the last of the new floorboards. The van was gone.

Chris paused and simply breathed.

The temperature was dropping, along with the sun. It had been clear and bright for days, and summer was starting to build up to a scorcher. It was promising for their big day, creeping ever closer, and Chris smiled to himself as he heard the distant sound of a drill whirring in the depths of the house.

With the house coming along fine, and John's business picking up now summer DIY projects were in full swing again, Chris had been left to wedding planning. The flowers had been a rude interruption to his day, but, ultimately, it was his job—dysphoria or no dysphoria.

And Chris had never been too much of a planner. His life had been spent coasting from one idea to the next. His only strict routines were walking the dog and taking his drugs. Everything else was flexible—no job, no college, and he'd quit football over a year ago. Having a self-employed partner hadn't changed things much, so Chris had gone years without being in the habit of planning anything.

But, weirdly, he kind of liked it.

The planning. Not the flowers or the feeling like a wife sometimes, but he liked having a checklist of things to do. He liked trying to figure out how not to spend a fortune on everything, despite John's insistence they could. And he especially liked roping people in to help test things out, like music and cakes, and discovering new favourites. Especially if he got to make fun of people while he did it, or act the Scrooge. What did he care if the flowers matched the colour scheme or not?

Seating plans, guest lists, collecting RSVPs—still minus Mum's, though he tried to forget it—arguing about renting a suit versus buying one, cars, talking Gina out of designing a bouquet, picking a band, finding good music, making sure John ordered some dress shoes in time for them to be custom-made for his feet which were the size of baby dolphins...

He should have hated it. It should have been stressful and horrible and causing rows.

But he liked it.

Except that flower shop, maybe.

He was starting to feel excited, and it was bubbling over into John as well. Like the day he brought home cake samples and tried to make John sample the coffee cake Chris wanted, and John just kissed him instead and said it tasted best that way. Like the day Chris tried on a silk tie Caroline had bought for him, saying it matched his eyes perfectly, and John just about went mad. *That* day was Chris's favourite.

Like today, if Chris was any judge.

"C'mon," he said, ruffling Poppy's ears. "Let's go see what Superman's been doing all day."

The kitchen-cum-lounge was warm and smelled of lasagne. Poppy snuffled about, and Chris figured John must have left his socks all over the floor again when he heard her drop things into the hamper. He locked up and followed the drilling into the living room, breathing in the smell of fresh paint and smiling widely when the whirring stopped.

"Hey."

"I didn't hear you come in. Stay right there. *Right* there!"

Chris raised his eyebrows and then laughed as a toolbox scraped and drill pieces were sprinkled back into their rightful place.

"Okay, c'mere."

John tasted like lasagne, too, and—to Chris's surprise—coffee. *Good* coffee. He chased it for a moment before letting John pull away.

"Why were you drinking coffee?"

"It was necessary to survive this morning's customer," John groaned.

"That bad?"

"He didn't need an electrician. He needed a social life."

"Aww, that's sad—"

"He wasn't some little old man. He wasn't even thirty, and he tried to talk me into staying and playing some video game with him. Kid needs to try a life."

"Who are you calling a kid? *I'm* not even thirty."

"And you have a life," John countered and rubbed his face into Chris's neck. "You have dinner with the girls?"

"Yeah. Well, dinner. KFC."

"Any needs tonight?"

"Hmm. Shower, text Julian for an appointment to sort out the blisters on my feet, maybe some sex."

"With Julian?"

"If he's up for it."

"Gobsod."

"Gob*shite*," Chris corrected primly but laughed as he was pulled in the rest of the way and stubble scraped against his shoulder. "Mm. I have a surprise for you."

"So do I," John replied. "Can I go first?"

"If you w— What are you doing?" Chris asked with a laugh as John slipped out of his grasp and darted across the room. He was in socks, and Chris toed off his own shoes hopefully. It was the first time he'd come into the living room since the new floor had gone down, and he buried his socked feet in the warm carpet. It was luxuriously thick.

"John?"

"One sec..."

"Can your surprise be on the floor?"

John laughed. "You wanna lie on the new carpet?"

"Yup."

"After. Can't have your surprise lying down."

Chris whined as the music started. It was some slow, smoochy song he didn't recognise—much more John's style than his—but he grinned hopefully when John returned. Chris spread his fingers along broad shoulders and turned his face up, but the hinted kiss never came. Instead, John planted one hand on the small of Chris's back and slid the other under his elbow, up his forearm, and into the soft curl of Chris's fingers.

"Step forward with your right foot."

"What?"

"Trust me."

Chris raised his eyebrows, but slid his right foot across the floor. John instantly nudged it back.

"*Step*," he insisted. "There's nothing in the way, promise."

"Except your great big feet."

"Let me worry about my feet."

Chris rolled his eyes.

"Go on. Step forward, right foot."

"Okay, okay..."

As he stepped forward, John stepped back. Chris chuckled as the arm around his waist drew him closer.

"Are we—?"

"Shh. Now step to the right. Just straight out to the side."

Chris did so, and once again was drawn by John's arm around his waist.

"Are we dancing?"

"We will be. Step back with your left foot..."

John coaxed him through a strange series of four steps—forward, right, backward, left—over and over again, until they were stepping together in an odd time with the cheesy song, and Chris's fit of mirth had subsided.

"Okay. Now I'm going to lead—"

"What?"

"I'll step first, you follow. Ready?"

"Um—"

That was harder, for a little while. Mostly, the point at which Chris had to step back. But in the end, he got the hang of that too. And when John began to gently turn them, Chris found himself oddly unsurprised. He relaxed into John's grip, leaning his head against John's chest as their dance gradually decreased, ever lazier, into a gentle hug-and-sway and little else.

"What was that?" he murmured as John's feet stilled entirely, and both hands slid down Chris's back to hold him close.

"Our first dance."

"We've danced plenty."

"Not a waltz. Nor for a wedding."

"You want to dance at the wedding?"

"Yep."

Chris hesitated. He wanted to, but worries had started to creep in. After all, it was a special occasion, and Chris didn't know how to dance. And dance in front of *everyone*? In front of the entire wedding party? He'd been practising for weeks to just sign the certificate at the ceremony without embarrassing himself, but dance in front of the whole wedding party? What if he got it wrong? What if he misstepped? What if—

He smiled, breathing in deeply as John's thumb stroked his back, and the swaying gently returned to turning in idle circles, although the steps were still gone. Fresh paint and orange juice. The deep humming like a rumble of far-off thunder, exciting and comforting all at once. Broad, warm palms holding him against the wall of love and security against his front.

So what if he did?

"We'll have to practice," Chris murmured. "Including at least once at the place."

"One last unmarried dance the night before?"

"Yeah."

"I can do that," John agreed. The dancing—or circling—stopped. Chris had his head gripped between both hands and the crown kissed and had to make an angry noise before his face was tilted up, and he managed to get that kiss on his mouth where it actually belonged. "Better?"

"Better."

"So—"

Chris laughed as he was pushed away slightly, his hand lifted in one paw, and he was twirled under John's arm. He grinned as he was pulled back in for another hug-and-sway and drummed his fists on John's chest.

"—what was your surprise, then?"

"I punished the girls for their florist trick and got them to run me down to the jewellers after lunch."

"Yeah?"

"I have two little boxes."

John stilled.

"You picked up the rings."

Chris grinned.

"Oh my God, you picked up the rings!"

Chris broke away to shove his hands into his front pockets and pull out the boxes. They were tiny, made of soft velvet, and he couldn't remember which one was which so held out both. John laughed and—instead of taking them—grabbed Chris around the waist and twirled him.

"Fuck!"

One of the boxes shot off into the room. Chris barely saved the other. John laughed like a drunkard, kissing Chris sharply as he was dropped to some point on the floor. Poppy nudged his side, and he decided to give up. He sat down with a bump on the fluffy carpet and hugged her as John hunted for the lost box.

"Okay. Okay. I got it. This one's yours—hand out. *Hand!*"

Chris cackled with laughter as John caught his left hand and spread out the fingers one at a time. Chris wiggled them just to earn himself a literal slap on the wrist, then bit his lip and grinned as cold metal slid into place. Snug, but not tight. Light, but overwhelmingly present. Chris clenched his fist, nudging the underside of the ring with his thumb, and opened his mouth.

And didn't say anything because John seized him in what was probably a kiss, but it happened so suddenly Chris wasn't entirely sure *what* had happened until it was over, he was flat on his back on the carpet, and John was toying with his belt.

"Oh my God," he said, laughing. "Seriously? On the new carpet?"

John clearly didn't much care for the potential problems on the new carpet, and Chris sniggered all the way through. Afterwards, he stroked John's slack hand resting on Chris's chest, turning John's plain engagement ring over and over until the metal was warm and familiar.

"Didn't know rings turned you on," he murmured.

"Don't ruin the moment with your dirty jokes."

"It was a serious comment!"

"Like heck it was..."

Chris smirked as he was bitten then sighed as John's hand drifted to rest on his nipple. He still hadn't regained much in the way of sensation, so it was like hot water covering only part of his chest. Odd, but pleasant. He ran his nails up the tattoos on John's arm and drifted for a while, half-asleep.

"Hey."

"W't?"

"Not to ruin the mood, but your mum called this morning."

"She rang?"

"Yeah."

"What about?"

"Said you weren't answering your phone."

"I was probably drowning in flowers."

"I figured. She says you've not been round for lunch lately."

Chris groaned.

"You avoiding her?"

"Honestly?" he asked. "Yeah. I was hoping once she got the invite, she'd get over herself, but...yeah. She must have it by now, and she's not said anything. She's not even tried to talk to me."

"Well, sounds like she was trying yesterday. You want to try back?"

Chris said nothing to that. He tried to drift again and, after a while, felt John settle down next to him and then eventually Poppy on his other side. It'd be murder on the back if they fell asleep, and he could do with a shower before packing it in for the night. But he decided to bask for a while longer and avoid thinking about an answer.

Partly because he wasn't sure what the answer would be.

Chapter Twenty

CHRIS WENT ROUND the following weekend, getting John to drop him off outside, but not letting him come to the door.

"I think this needs you out of the way," he'd said. "I'll ring when we're done."

Mum could be a touch unpredictable during the week. She'd retired from the university to look after Jack, but she'd kept a once-a-week position as a dinner lady at Chris's old primary school up the hill. Chris suspected it was to compensate for having no grandchildren and no prospect of getting any. But at weekends, she was always home. Usually cleaning, so Chris wasn't too surprised by the faint smell of bleach when she opened the door.

"Christian!"

"Hey, Mum."

"Mind your feet, I've been hoovering. No John?"

"Nah, he's going to run around a rugby pitch and get sweaty. I figured I could stop by and we could have lunch or something."

"That would be nice."

She sounded more normal too. Not happy or bright exactly, but less quiet and awkward than she had been for months. She flapped about the hoover cord and keeping his dirty shoes off her freshly mopped kitchen floor but told him to help himself to a cup of coffee while she finished the washing up.

"How've you been?" he asked as he balanced a spoon on the top of the mug and slowly filled it. He hadn't kept any of his kit at Mum's house since he and John had bought their first flat, and had to rely on the weight of the spoon suddenly rising against the coffee to avoid spilling any.

"Oh, I'm fine," Mum said. "Spring cleaning. Clearing some—some things out."

Jack's things. Chris winced as he took a seat at the kitchen table and elected not to ask.

"The house is very quiet," she continued. "I'm thinking of downsizing. Getting a little cottage out in the country. Maybe Derbyshire."

"John's grandparents live out at Hathersage. They've got a little cottage. It's nice."

She hummed, and he heard her pour out her own mug before joining him at the table.

"There's just too many memories of Jack here," she said quietly.

Chris turned his hand over and opened his fingers. After a short pause, she slipped her hand into his, and he squeezed.

"He'd understand if you needed to leave."

"I feel like I ought to stay," she admitted. "But it's just so quiet. I've had to move into the spare room to sleep. It's like I'm waiting for him to walk in the door."

"He'd understand," Chris repeated. "He knew what it was like to lose someone. And that it doesn't have to be the end of the world."

She didn't reply to that, but she didn't take her hand away either.

"You know what I miss?" Chris said. "The way he used to think he was being helpful by putting my shoes on the rack when I came round then trying to blame the cat when I shouted at him."

Mum's laugh was thin, but the most genuine one he'd heard from her since that awful day at the hospice when Jack had finally passed away.

"That was my fault, you know," she said. "I told him you could tell bright light from darkness still, and he took it to mean you just had terrible eyesight."

"Well, *technically—*"

"You know he was absolutely terrified of you?"

Chris blinked. "Sorry?"

"Do you remember Peter?"

"That dickhead ex you dumped because he called me a fucked up lesbian?"

"Oh good, you do," she said dryly. "I already knew Jack then, you know. I was—we were—well. Interested, I suppose. It wasn't right, not when Peter and I were engaged, but—"

"Oh my God," Chris said. "You were totally carrying on with Jack behind Peter's back!"

"It wasn't *that* far, but—well, I was already considering calling off the engagement before you broke your news."

Chris smirked.

"But, of course, I told Jack about what had happened. He was absolutely petrified of you."

"As he should have been," Chris said loftily.

"I think he was ready for another relationship, but he wasn't ready to be a father again," Mum said softly.

Chris tightened his hand on hers gently.

"He did fine."

"Yeah."

A soft silence fell. It was warmer than the ones that had occupied the space between them ever since the funeral, and that more than anything gave Chris the courage to break through into what had been bothering him, and what he'd really come round to say.

"I'm sorry I've not been round as much as I should have."

"Oh, don't be silly. You've had things going on."

"You had bigger things," Chris said. "Dad told me about—"

She huffed and took her hand back. "Oh, what does your father know? If you're staying for lunch, do you mind giving me a hand with—"

"He knows you."

She snorted. "Does he heck."

"He does," Chris repeated. "Said you get to know someone really well when you divorce them. Said I should be kinder about why you're opposed to the wedding—"

"I'm not *opposed*. I—"

"—and that it all goes back to when I had the accident."

And just like that, the barriers went up.

"I don't want to talk about that, Christian."

"He said you're feeling bad about how you were willing to let me go after the accident, and how you were relieved Jack is gone, and that you're projecting that feeling onto John and think he's bad too. Because anyone who feels like that might walk away when it gets too hard."

"Well he's bloody wrong," she snapped, her voice wobbling. "Tell him to mind his own f—his own business."

"Mum—"

"Now *drop it*."

"I'd do the same, Mum."

Chris wasn't used to being the calm one in a brewing row. Lauren had once called all three of them hot-headed, and it was true. Chris had grown up being talked down to and loathed it with a violent passion. The combination of blind, epileptic, and trans masculine made other people think of him as a child, and three times over. He'd had to drop a doctor last year for questioning whether he was 'really consenting' to his own relationship. And after more than twenty years of it, Chris operated on a hair trigger. He could—did—lose his temper too fast, and he suspected he always would.

But this wasn't about him. If he wasn't the way he was, it wouldn't be an issue—yet it wasn't *really* about him. It was about Mum. And how she thought.

The same way he thought.

"John and I made wills after we bought the flat," he said. "John's got power of attorney over me in case—well, in case. And I told him, I made him promise me, that if I couldn't do the things I love anymore, or recognise the people who love me, then he'd let me go."

Mum said nothing.

"I don't want to be here anymore if I can't enjoy my life. I like things the way they are now, but what if I'd never woken up again after the accident? What if I was on a tube in the hospital forever? What would be the point?"

"Chris—"

She almost never said that. She always called him Christian. It had been a deliberate choice between the two of them. Her clutch of much more religious friends, not to mention her parents, had been horrified at her pretty young lady turning out to not be much of a lady after all, and it was really down to them what Christian had chosen in the end.

"I like Christopher," he'd admitted. "But it's not very appropriate, is it?"

"If you want to be inappropriate, call yourself Christian," she'd said. "It's not up to anyone else, is it? Let them talk. What do we care?"

He was only Christian to anyone else when he was a complete stranger or in a lot of trouble. Even John had probably only called him that once. But Mum said it each and every time, like she was still taking jabs at the friends and family who'd abandoned them.

Yet, suddenly the end of his name fell off, and the little wobble made his breath pause.

"You didn't know."

She made a muted sound that might have been a sob.

"They told you I'd never get better. You made the right choice with what they told you."

"What mother—"

"You didn't want me to suffer. That's exactly what mums should be thinking."

She huffed a little laugh. "Oh, it's so easy when you haven't any yourself."

"That just means you and Dad raised me smarter than you two," Chris retorted and got his wrist smacked. "Hey!"

"Mind your tone."

He stuck out his lip in an exaggerated fashion, then sobered up.

"You didn't want me to hurt. The same as you wanted for Jack. The same as I wanted." He fidgeted, then decided to go for it and bare his own soul. "I was relieved when he died."

"What?"

"When he finally stopped breathing, I wasn't sad. I was happy. I was relieved. And—yeah, most of it was for him. You know how much it hurt him when he was still aware of everything. But there was a selfish part of it, too. No more confused phone calls at three in the morning, or being deadnamed because he'd forgotten and having to smile through it. No more—"

"No more answering to his dead wife's name."

Chris opened his hand again. Slowly, Mum's returned.

"I love him," Mum croaked. "I love you. I should never have wanted to let either of you go, but I did."

"You know what Dad said when we talked about it?"

"I don't want to—"

"He said you were stronger than he was."

Mum's teeth clicked as she snapped her mouth shut.

"He said he agreed with you, but he was too weak to let go. He called himself selfish for the way he reacted. Not you."

She took a hitching breath and started to cry. Chris hesitated, then decided to keep going.

"Thing is, I get that maybe you feel guilty and bad for the way you felt but—you stayed."

"What?"

"You didn't want to deal with any of it—nobody *wants* to deal with any of it—but you stayed. You didn't sign up for a kid with epilepsy and brain damage, but you stayed. You didn't sign up for a husband with Parkinson's, but you stayed. That's what matters, Mum. You loved us anyway. You stuck around. Like John will."

There was a long pause while she sniffled and, presumably, mopped herself up with the hanky perpetually shoved up her sleeve. Chris just waited. A strange sense crept over him that this was his only chance, and he wouldn't have another opportunity to break through to her.

"And you think he will?"

Chris shrugged. "He knew what he was in for."

"No, he didn't," Mum returned. "He still doesn't. He's seen your seizures and your stick, and he knows his way around the paperwork so your benefits don't get messed up for the thousandth time, but he's never seen you like *that*."

A flicker of impatience sparked in Chris's chest, but he tamped it down.

"Like what?"

"Like you were dying," she returned. "Like you were gone."

He exhaled heavily. That much was true. John had been there for his chest surgery, and he'd come to pick him up from hospital once or twice when Chris had had a seizure in public and some busybody had called an ambulance, but he'd never seen Chris dangerously ill or injured. As far as Chris knew, he'd never seen anyone like that.

"No, he hasn't. But he knows—"

"He can't know what to expect or what he'd do. Neither can you. It's—it's unimaginable."

The steel had returned to her voice, and Chris's back stiffened.

"I know you want me to be mindlessly excited about all this, and I *am* happy that you're happy, believe me—"

But he didn't believe her.

"—But I can't help but worry that John isn't strong enough to do what you might need him to in the end."

Chris snorted, shaking his head.

"Until it happens, you don't know *anyone* is that strong, Mum. I can't put my life on hold for that."

"I'm not saying you should—"

"But you are," he interrupted. His nerves were starting to fray around the edges. "That's exactly what you're saying. And you're right; I don't know if John's strong enough to keep his promise—but you're overthinking things."

"I'm being careful."

"Too careful," Chris retorted. "Nobody knows what's going to happen. It might not be me. John's granddad had a heart attack last year, and his mum's mum died of a massive stroke when she was in her fifties. His dad's had cancer twice. He might get smacked about one too many times at the rugby. There could be a billion things that happen. It might not be me that needs someone at the end."

"It's more likely to—"

"I know it is, but it's not a guarantee. Someone's going to die someday. One of us will go first. It doesn't mean giving up everything else in case John doesn't handle it quite the way I want. And let's say he does leave me one day—so what? I can get divorced, like you and Dad did. And I've rinsed him, Mum. Jack's rinsed him. That house is mine. John's name is nowhere near it—it's mine. If he leaves me, I'm the one left holding the keys to an expensive house. I'm the one with half a million sunk into that property. All he gets is the car and half the contents of our joint bills account."

He expected her to laugh. John had whined about being the trophy boyfriend when Chris had figured that part out the other day, but Mum remained grimly silent.

"I'm not *not* getting married because the future is a bit unpredictable. If you'd known I would recover, you would never have suggested letting me go. If I knew John was going to leave me, I wouldn't be marrying him. But you didn't, and I don't. I love him. I intend to be with him for the rest of my life. Whether that works out in the end or not, I'm getting married in September, and we're going to give it our best shot."

He pulled his fingers out from under hers and curled them into loose fists. His temper was starting to boil over at her shutdown. It had been going so *well*, and then she'd retreated to the same dogged refusal. He took a soothing breath and tried to dispel it.

"When I'm with John, nothing else matters," Chris said softly. "Nothing at all. Everything just gets smoothed away, and I'm home. Some people never find that. Can't you be happy for me that I did?"

Her hand grazed his own. He felt her wedding ring. It was very cool, and he tapped it lightly with his index finger.

"Do you regret getting married to Dad or Jack, even though they ended?"

She coughed a laugh. "If not for you, Christian, I would regret ever meeting your father."

"Okay, bad example. What about Jack?"

She sighed. For a long while, they sat in a silence that was half-awkward, half-peaceful. The clock ticked gently on the wall. The cat was scarfing its food from the bowl by the fridge. Next door's two-year-old was throwing a tantrum about the colour blue, or maybe needing glue. A car trundled past in the road outside—and Mum seemed to shake herself. She straightened, and her hand slid away again.

"No," she said. "No, I don't regret that. Not for a moment."

"Then can you see why I'm doing this?"

She didn't answer. Chris tapped the ring one last time and pulled back.

"I want everyone at our wedding to think we're making the right choice," he said. "If you don't, don't come. But please tell me, so I can stop worrying about it."

She caught his arm as he turned towards the kettle, intent on another coffee and a change of subject.

"I'll be there," she said.

But it lacked the conviction Chris needed.

Chapter Twenty-One

CHRIS WAS WOKEN by the low sound of canned laughter.

He was warm, and there was a strong smell of cologne. The front of the seat was dipped slightly forward, and when he investigated with his fingertips, he ran into the back of John's neck.

"Hey, beautiful."

The deep, hoarse rumble made Chris sink further into the blissful warmth under the blanket. He wriggled forward to press his nose into the back of John's shoulder and inhale deeply. Soap. Cologne. Homemade chilli. A hand scratched at his hair before dropping again, and Chris slung an arm over John's other shoulder and hugged him messily from his nest.

"Seizure?"

"No," Chris mumbled. "Just tired and had a nap. S'my drugs. G'd session?"

"Yep. There's some chilli in the microwave if you want it."

"Later."

"Not too late. It's already six."

"M'kay..."

He dozed there for a while longer. John's shoulder was red hot through his thin cotton T-shirt, the wash of canned laughter from the telly a soothing counterpoint. Some old BBC comedy or other. Chris half listened and half drifted, until the smell of the chilli became too tempting.

At which point, because he was comfortable, he shoved John in the back.

"Hey!"

"Feed me."

"All right, all right…"

Chris turned himself into a blanket burrito as John messed around at the counter, but untangled himself again when John came back. He ended up seated between John's thighs, working his way steadily through the chilli as John watched his TV show and finger-combed Chris's messy curls.

"So how did lunch with your mum go?"

"I don't know. She seemed to soften up a bit, but then the barriers went back up. She's adamant that I can't rely on you because you don't know what you're in for, and how do I know you're strong enough to let go if the worst happens?"

"Jesus, you know how to go for the heavy topics," John groused.

"So, I don't know. She said she's coming, but I want her to be happy, not be grim throughout the whole thing."

"When did you come home?" John asked.

"Eh?"

"When did you come home?"

"Two-ish?"

"She rang me about quarter past two."

"Mum *rang* you?"

Everyone in Chris's family had John's phone number—and even if they didn't, one Google search for John's name brought back his contact details for anyone requiring an electrician, no job too big or small. But only Lauren called him with anything like regularity.

"Yep."

"What did she say?"

"Er. Well. She invited me round for lunch next weekend."

"What?"

"Yeah. Said we needed to talk. And that was about it."

"Oh my God. I'm going to ring—"

John's hands locked around Chris's waist and held him fast.

"Relax. I'll go."

"It's been nearly four years! If she wanted to do a whole interrogate the boyfriend schtick, she should have started ages ago!"

"And if she had started when we'd met, she'd have scared me off," John pointed out.

Chris swore anyway. It was true, but he was still pissy.

"Now—who cares?" John murmured. "She can't scare me away now. I've laid Daniel's ghosts to rest, and it's not like I don't know what might be in store for us later down the line. Let her interrogate me. Maybe I can do a bit of work towards talking her round."

"I wouldn't bet on it," Chris said sourly. He twisted over to put the empty bowl on the floor and settled down with one ear over John's heart. He simmered while John channel-surfed, surfacing from his sulking only once to veto the news, and stewed when John settled on some match of the day bollocks.

"Hey."

A heavy hand smoothed down Chris's curls before they sprang free again, and he grumbled.

"It'll be all right," John coaxed. "She'll come around. And she'll come."

"What if she doesn't?"

It had been bugging Chris ever since her first muted response. What if she didn't come to the wedding? What if his own mother was so upset that she stayed away? He didn't want her to be a wet weekend at the event, but what if she didn't want to come at all?

Immediately, his response was much like John's. So what? He'd still love his big day. He'd still get married to the most incredible guy in the world and have to listen to John debating which photo to put up in the hall for the next month.

But what about after?

When Mum hadn't come to his wedding, and he had a whole lifetime to remember that, beyond the excitement of planning for it in the first place? When the happiness of getting married in the first place wasn't enough to override just how much it would hurt?

"I think she will," John murmured. "She's upset and she's grieving, but she loves you more than any of that. She'll come through."

"And if not?"

"If not, me and Rhodri will park up outside in his van with some loud tunes, onion sandwiches, and not a belt in sight. His builder's crack is like the Grand Canyon—she won't like her neighbours seeing any of that outside her front door."

Chris smirked but didn't quite laugh.

"Don't worry about it," John insisted, finger-combing Chris's hair absently. "There's plenty more to get stressed about. You know Nora's furious we're not having bridesmaids?"

"Why would we? No bride," Chris said.

"We've done her out of coordinated ballgowns or whatever."

"That's your problem. I wouldn't know how to coordinate a dress if you paid me."

"I think the idea was we ought to pay her..."

"I'm not getting your sister a free dress," Chris said and pushed himself up. "I'm going to wash up."

John followed him to the counter, though didn't do much for a while but dry dishes and put them away. Chris stewed anyway. He was tired. Just *tired*. He'd turned her resistance over and over in his head, again and again, and he was no closer to a solution. He was just going in circles.

"John?"

"Mm?"

"When you talk to Mum, I want to know what she says."

"I can te—"

"I want to hear it. Invite her over. Tell her I'm out; I don't care. I want to hear it for myself."

"You want to eavesdrop?" John asked in a surprised tone.

"Yeah." Chris hunched his shoulders. "She won't— I don't know. She put the barriers up with me. She's careful. I want to hear what she actually says to you."

"Ba—"

"And I swear if you call me babe right now, I will gut you!" Chris snapped.

There was a sharp pause, and John exhaled heavily.

"Chris—"

"I'm sorry," he muttered. "I'm just—sorry. I'm sorry."

To his embarrassment, tears prickled in the corners of his eyes. A heavy hand rubbed up his spine, and he was tugged under John's arm. He shook the suds off his fingers and curled them into John's shirt instead.

"Why can't she be *happy* for me?"

CHRIS WOKE TO heavy rain in the morning.

He'd been unable to sleep and gone downstairs to listen to one of his audiobooks and let John sleep in peace, but he must have dozed off on the sofa. The thunderous noise was alien in the new house, and he lay for some time just figuring it out. The soothing pattern on the kitchen window helped him along, and he eventually pushed back the blanket John had draped over him and groped for socks and underwear in the hamper of clean laundry waiting by the dryer.

John's voice stopped him.

It was raised. Indistinct—he sounded like he was right at the front of the house—but loud and stern. Not quite shouting, but Chris instinctively paused anyway. John had a gorgeous voice, and he was about as frightening as a kitten, but when he yelled anything, there was a momentary flash of danger that would make anybody pause. Chris had to unstick himself again and inched across to the kitchen door with a mixture of trepidation and curiosity.

"—lose both."

John was in the hall. Chris cracked the kitchen door open but paused until a faint murmuring said he wouldn't be seen. They were upstairs, probably at the top of the stairs. Chris tiptoed towards the downstairs bathroom and slipped inside, closing the door so softly it slid into the frame without a sound.

"It's nothing to do with me. I just don't want him upset about this."

Chris clenched his jaw as footsteps came down the stairs. Heavy boots in a long, stomping stride, as familiar as his own. And a lighter tread in shallow heels. A short but firm walk. Even more familiar, in a way. Chris slid the bolt across and locked the door.

"I think you're lying to yourself," John snapped.

"How *dare* you."

Mum. She was using her icy tone, the one that made people shrink. Even behind a locked door, Chris withered a little. But John's voice didn't change. He was too big to shrink. There wasn't anywhere else for his bulk to go. Chris squared his shoulders and reached for the bolt again. Like hell he was going to let Mum just chew John out when—

"I know what it's like. You and me, we're the same."

Chris hesitated. John's voice had dropped out of the steely resolve that had startled Chris in the kitchen and sunk into a soft, almost coaxing murmur Chris had to strain to catch.

"When I met Chris, I was lying to myself as well. I had all this fear inside, and I kept telling myself that other people were the problem. They looked at me funny, they wouldn't trust me, and they thought I was dangerous. It wasn't that part of me believed it— It was just them. There wasn't anything to fix in my head, just in everybody else's."

Chris bit down on his knuckle, his heart a solid ball of aching muscle in his chest. He sat down on the closed toilet and gulped a shaky breath.

"That's what you're doing, Ruth. It's easier to avoid the wedding than to ask yourself why it hurts. It's easier to try and fix what's on the outside than what's on the inside."

There was a strangely quiet sound, as if Mum had coughed or choked.

"I know this counsellor," John murmured. "They helped me. Maybe they can help you."

"Help me with what?" Mum asked, her voice cracked all down the middle.

"With the guilt."

Chris covered his mouth with his hand and screwed his eyes shut as John walked past the bathroom door and into the kitchen. A fridge magnet scraped. He passed back along the hall again, the boards bouncing gently under his weight.

"Just give them a call, and try one session with them. It could really help."

"How do you know what I feel?" Mum asked hoarsely.

"I don't. I just know that ever since you lost Jack, you've been losing Chris too. And you don't deserve that. Either of you. But whatever's going on, if you miss his wedding, you'll lose him. He won't forgive you, and I don't want him to lose his mum as well as his stepdad."

Chris leaned back against the wall and tuned the conversation out. He'd obviously missed the better part of a brewing row, and now he just wanted to hug John for the way he'd handled it. Nadia had been great for John, and maybe they'd be great for Mum too. Why hadn't Chris thought of that? He'd pushed and pushed, but it had never occurred to him to ask her to get some help. After all of John's sessions with Nadia, after all those sessions Chris had been forced through to be allowed to transition, and he hadn't thought once of suggesting that Mum try counselling?

"He'll still be in bed," John rumbled, not five feet from the bathroom door. "I can tell him you came over, or—"

"No," Mum interrupted. "No, I'll—I'll call him."

"You better."

The hard edge was back. Mum's shoes clicked softly on the mahogany floor that supposedly matched the old banisters. A door closed softly, and then John sighed gustily—and knocked on the bathroom door.

"Hey."

Chris pushed himself up enough to slide back the bolt, then sat down with a thump. The door opened and closed. Denim creaked, and warm hands rubbed over his knees.

"How much of that did you hear, then?" John asked gently.

"Why was she here?"

John squeezed his calf. "I called and asked her to come round. Made some excuse about work being too busy for another day."

"Why?"

"I want to say because of how upset you were last night, but honestly? I wanted to get it out of the way too. You're not the only one who finds her difficult." He rapped Chris's kneecap. "So? How much did you hear?"

"You telling her it wasn't anything to do with you."

Arms slid around his hips. Chris bowed to lean against John's neck and shoulders.

"You okay?" John murmured.

"I didn't even think of telling her to go to a counsellor," Chris mumbled.

"Yeah, well, you and I have slightly different experiences with them," John remarked dryly. One hand rubbed up Chris's back, dragging him further into the hug. "She was all right. I think she expected me to get annoyed."

"What did she say?"

But Chris already knew. The same things she'd been saying from the beginning. That John didn't get it, that Chris was too difficult, that getting married was a bad idea. And underneath it all, that she had never seen Chris the way he thought she did. That she never really believed he could have a life of his own with someone who loved him.

"About what you'd expect."

Chris grimaced.

"I don't know what I'm letting myself in for, blah blah blah," John continued in an easy tone. "Almost like we get married now, or I walk out. Wasn't like I was going anywhere, wedding or no wedding."

"I don't know," Chris mumbled, scrounging for some humour to paper over the cracks in his armour. "I'm hoping once we're married, you'll learn to stop leaving your socks everywhere."

"Er..."

Chris pushed up, bracing his weight by his hands on John's shoulders. His elbows were tickled until he buckled back down into a brief, warm kiss, and then John staggered upright with a groan.

"Old man."

"Watch it!"

Chris was tugged up into a proper hug and turned towards the door.

"Come on. Breakfast for you. It's nearly ten, and I've got an appointment this afternoon. So if you still want a lift to Gina's, you need to start getting your stuff together."

"Shit together."

"Whatever."

Chris whined for a bacon sandwich and made his way to the desk that had been wedged between the fridge and the back door while John was bullied into cooking. The seating plan had been taped to the surface with little Braille labels stuck on for everyone's place in the conservatory once they were married and sitting down to dinner. Chris refused to call it a wedding breakfast.

He ran his fingers over the labels and paused on hers.

Ten, eleven weeks to go, and she was still digging her heels in. He peeled Mum's label off the seating plan and threw it away.

Chapter Twenty-Two

CHRIS GAVE UP.

He deleted her texts, he ignored her calls, and he gave up on his mother with a sharp absolution that was like ripping off a plaster. Painful, but brief. All too soon, she stopped calling, and the agony receded under the building pressure. The mixture of nerves and excitement kept him too busy to bother with her, yet the lingering ache injected a steeliness he'd been sorely lacking.

Weirdly, he felt more like himself in the aftermath.

Chris didn't do second chances and dithering. He cut people off and that was the end of it. He wasn't forgiving by nature and was oddly more comfortable to cut his mother out than to keep trying. And that comfort bled over into all the other plans. He wrenched them together while John worked, until—by the end of July—he met John at the new front door with a kiss and a command.

"Jump in the shower and put some clean clothes on. Everyone's coming over for six."

"What? Who?"

"Dad, Lauren, Caroline, your nan and granddad, Fran, Nora, maybe Raj—he said he was going to try and get Aadit to cover the shop—and Tash didn't really give an answer, but Fran said she'll drag her by the ear if she has to, so maybe Tash and Daisy."

"You're *kidding*."

"Nope. Shower."

John grumbled, but stomped off upstairs obediently. The house was livable, and even nice in the hot, dry summer. The back garden was still a jungle, and none of the spare rooms had been finished, but they had moved into the main rooms, and John had finished the plumbing for the utility room. A new dryer was a matter of days away, and Chris was looking forward to fluffy towels again.

He padded into the kitchen in his slippers. Poppy was lurking hopefully, the smell of homemade stew taunting them both. The table had already been set, and by the time he heard the crunch of tyres outside, the stew was on a low simmer to keep it warm, and the garlic bread toasting lightly in the oven.

"Door's open!" he bellowed.

The latch clicked, and little feet pounded down the hall.

"Uncle Chris, Uncle Chris!"

"Hi, Suresh."

Suresh was Nora and Raj's toddler, and Chris raised suspicious eyebrows when Nora hugged him. She'd denied anything going on, but Chris couldn't quite believe the growing bump between them was entirely teacakes and Prosecco.

"Don't say a word," Nora warned, and Chris mimed zipping his lips.

"Raj with you?"

"Where do shoes go?" the aforementioned husband shouted from the hall.

"Under the hall table!"

Dad and his bookends were hot on their heels, then Fran barrelled in—alone, but noisy enough to cover for the missing Tasha and her kid. She brought wine, which

Dad cracked open at once, and the families mingled until Nan and Granddad arrived, both dressed up like they were going to the theatre.

It was the first time the house had felt full, and Chris enjoyed the warmth and the hubbub. It was like Sunday dinners at Hathersage. Not everyone could fit. Dad and Caroline had to sit on towering bar stools borrowed from next door. John's sisters migrated to the little footstools dragged in from the living room so Nan and Granddad could have proper chairs. Lauren perched gingerly on a camping stool. Raj held Suresh on one knee. Plates jostled for room, and once everything was eaten and the dessert had been dished up, Chris kicked his chair out of the way, rescued the seating plan from the desk, and sat in John's lap.

"Right," he said and dropped the plan on the table. "We made a seating plan for dinner. We have a plan for our ceremony. And I swear to God, if anybody argues, you can leave. This is our wedding, not yours, so think before you open your gob."

John pressed his face to the back of Chris's shoulder, and Chris felt the smirk.

"Quite right," Nan said. "Let's see it, then."

The seating plan was remarkably uncontroversial—or Chris's warning had been good enough to silence any dissent. But he'd laboured over it painstakingly. Their friends were easy—they didn't overlap much, so they'd just been grouped together at various tables scattered throughout the room—but family was trickier. Caroline had to be kept away from John's rather more traditional grandparents. Chris's future mother-in-law loathed babies, despite having had four of them, and would spend the whole evening in a foul mood if she was anywhere near

Suresh, grandson or not. It had taken a lot of shuffling, and would probably take another helping of luck to make it through.

But, naturally, proximity wasn't what got their attention.

"We're not on the high table?" Nan asked, peering down her nose through her little glasses at the plan.

"No," John replied. "That's just going to be us. Family on the nearest tables and friends further out."

"Not even your best man?"

John coughed. "Ah. Well. Yes. About that."

"We're having a small ceremony," Chris interrupted. "Just us and our two witnesses in a private room, and then we'll come out into the garden to meet everyone else once it's over. We don't really have best men, per se."

There was a short, sharp pause.

"Like I said," Chris said. "Our wedding. Our choice."

To be fair, Nan agreed with him once more, and Granddad simply muttered about the family church being plenty small enough for that kind of thing. But Lauren made an annoyed noise and said, "Alone?" like it was a dirty word.

"Yes."

"As in, we all stay in the gardens?" Caroline asked.

"Yes."

"Why?" Lauren pressed.

"Because John wants a big wedding, and I want a small one, and this is our compromise. I want a small, intimate ceremony—then we come out, newly married, for a big celebration."

Fran cooed. Nan made a little squeaking sound. But Lauren wasn't swayed.

"I see," she said. "So your family aren't invited."

"If you weren't invited, you wouldn't be here," Chris said. "That's what we want. Our wedding, our rules."

"Your family should be at your ceremony."

"And I should be in a bloody dress, but we're not getting married by the 'should' rulebook, so this is how *we* want to do it," Chris retorted.

"It sounds nice," Dad interrupted in a loud voice.

"*Anyway*," John declared before it could get going, "afterwards, we'll come out to the garden—just like coming out of the church—and there'll be confetti and photos. *Lots* of photos. And then we're having dinner in the conservatory, with all the speeches. After that, your usual party."

"What if the weather's bad?" Nan asked.

"Then same plan but the party in the conservatory instead. The pub's really nice inside, so it wouldn't really matter too much."

"I still say your family ought to be there," Lauren sniffed.

"Nobody but me and John *ought* to be there," Chris returned flatly. "The decision's final."

"So who are your witnesses?" Fran asked.

"Well, if they'd agree to it, we were hoping Ted and Granddad would step up," John half asked, half replied.

Dad coughed. Granddad dropped his spoon.

Chris just waited, smirking. It had been John's idea. Both of them were ex-servicemen, and Granddad didn't even own a suit. His dress uniform *was* his formalwear, and when Dad had let slip about getting his own dusted off for the wedding, John suggested having them as witnesses. John and Chris in their wedding suits, flanked by Dad and Granddad in their brass. It would make for an amazing photograph, John had said.

Chris didn't know about photographs, but he knew the gruff coughing fit that swept over Dad.

"Well," he ground out eventually, once Lauren thumped him on the back. "You know. Of course. Be—" Another gruff rumble. "Be my honour."

"I'm not wearing no penguin suit," Granddad groused. "I don't bloody care what you've decided. I'm wearing my uniform and my brass and like hell I'm doing otherwise!"

"Be a bit offended if you didn't, Granddad."

"Dad'll be in his as well," Chris added.

Instantly, the two men turned on each other with interest and began swapping regiment details. Nan sighed gustily.

"Honestly," she said. "He's been polishing those medals for weeks; they'll be all worn away!"

"It'll look great," John gushed. His arms tightened around Chris's waist. "We're more or less ready."

"Says the man who's funding it instead of organising it," Chris sniped.

A snigger washed round the table, but it was broken by thick knuckles rapping the wood.

"Where's Ruth on this here seating plan?" Dad asked.

Chris clenched his jaw. John's hand stiffened on his waist.

"She's still—having some issues," John replied diplomatically.

There was an odd stillness. Chris patted John's arm and got up when he was released. "Bathroom," he muttered to the question written in John's lingering touch and heard another chair scrape as he reached the hall.

"Kid."

Dad. Chris swallowed thickly, hand on the bathroom door.

"I just need to go—"

"I'll talk to Ruth."

"Don't," Chris said. "I've talked to her. John's talked to her. I'm— If she wants to come, then there'll be room for her. But I'm not going to persuade her any more."

"I could—"

"You could leave it," Chris said. "I shouldn't need everyone telling my mum to show up to my own wedding. If she doesn't come, that's on her."

He opened the door. Dad's boot stopped it.

"Dad—"

A meaty hand squeezed his shoulder.

"She loves you, kid."

"Sure," Chris said. "But she doesn't respect me."

"WELL, I THINK Lauren's going to sulk for a few weeks at not getting to hear our vows, but otherwise—" John squeezed Chris's shoulders until something popped. "Oof. You need a massage?"

Chris sighed, gripping the counter and arching into John's hands. Thumbs dug into his shoulder blades, barely shy of the spine. He groaned as something creaked.

"I'll take that as a yes," John muttered. "C'mon. Leave the dishes and come to bed."

"I have to—"

"Do as you're told?"

"Arsehole," Chris muttered, but it was half-hearted at best. It didn't take much more effort from John to bully him up to their room. He'd planned the attack too. The duvet was turned down, and the window let in a light breeze from the garden. A candle burned, the soft vanilla scent sweet but understated.

"Give me this."

Chris usually hated being dressed or undressed, but he decided to just roll with John's obvious plans. He let himself be stripped and poured onto the bed, settling on his front and curling both arms around the pillow under his cheek. The massage oil was a pool of liquid heat against his skin, the first pass of John's palms so heavy that bones groaned. The second was whisper soft, the contact barely there, and the third somewhere between them. Chris relaxed into the pattern—a long, wide stroke from shoulder to the small of his back and then the heavy press of individual fingers walking their way up, pressing into knots and nerves until they dissolved, one by one.

"Better?" John murmured.

Chris hummed.

"Want a head massage as well?"

"Y'r not as good as Julian..."

"Bollocks I'm not."

Chris smirked as his ploy worked, and the massage migrated to his neck and scalp. His hair would be revolting in the morning from the oil, but it was worth it for the shiver that sank into his spine. There was something about a head massage. Especially as John's fingers stroked his ears and rubbed the spaces behind. Even as the rest of Chris's body relaxed, he got hard from the heavy pleasure radiating from his mind. He drifted in it, almost asleep yet passionately awake. He barely registered being turned over, and only curled his fingers into John's hair as kisses were pressed to Chris's neck, his chest, his stomach, and lower. It never built into anything more than a gentle, almost sweet climax, and then the duvet was flipped up, and he was dragged backwards to John's chest. No doubt he'd cook to death somewhere around two in the morning, but he was too relaxed to care.

"Better?"

"Much…"

"Drifting off?"

"Mm."

"Good time to mention it, then."

Chris prodded John's arm.

"I finished my vows."

"Oh my Christ. I was hoping you'd give up on that one."

The arm tightened. Chris grumbled as the air was squeezed out of him.

"No chance," John replied.

"Go on, then."

"What?"

"Tell me what you've written."

"That'll spoil the surprise," John complained, kissing his neck. "You know what I'll say anyway. About how you're—"

"No."

"—and—"

"*No.*"

"—and when you—"

Chris pulled the duvet over his head. John's laugh was warm and all-encompassing, and the whole world seemed to curl as the hug enveloped him. Knees tucked up behind his. From shoulder to hip, he was locked inside enormous arms. Chris just smirked and sagged into it.

"Tell you the truth, it was hard," John continued.

"Well, it was earlier…"

"Tit. The *vows*. Writing the *vows* was hard."

"Oh, right—"

"I mean, what am I supposed to promise, eh?"

Chris was meant to laugh. He opened his mouth to crack some line—another blowjob, dirty socks to go in the hamper where they belonged, riches and servants, something daft. But the words morphed between brain and mouth, and what he actually said was...sincere. Horribly, offensively sincere.

"This."

John's voice dropped too.

"What?"

"This." Chris tightened his grip on John's wrist.

"What, a massage, a blowjob, and a goodnight cuddle?"

"Love." A short pause. Then the bed moved. A hand wedged itself firmly under Chris's armpit, and a bristly kiss nudged at his cheek.

"Love you too, beautiful."

Chris smiled.

Chapter Twenty-Three

TIME STARTED TO bleed away.

Chris had always thought summers went on forever. John worked for most of the time, and Gina usually got dragged on some family holiday, so the sensation of the weeks dissolving in front of him was strange. One minute, the kitchen table was covered in wedding decorations, the next, he was renting a suit, the next, it was August and the usual humid heatwave had landed. If John was home, they worked on the garden; if he wasn't, Chris basked in the cool shade of the kitchen and worried about the seating plan, Aunt Glynis's booze-fuelled homophobia, and the empty space where Mum's name should be.

Before he knew it, John's birthday—and thus a month until the wedding—was on top of them, and Chris woke to early morning birdsong and a mixture of dread and excitement in the pit of his stomach that had nothing to do with his medication.

"Holy hell," he whispered.

John was snoring lightly on the other side of the bed, and Poppy slept across their feet. But Chris knew he wasn't going to be drifting off again. One month to go. *One.*

"Fuck."

He threw back the covers and got up, sneaking downstairs with Poppy on his heels to start breakfast. Before getting out the pans, he opened the kitchen door for her and threw some seed into the jungle of a garden for the noisy birds. If he was up, he might as well take his mind off the sensation in his gut.

John's birthdays were a thing of routine, and the routine always started with breakfast in bed. Sausages, bacon, mushrooms, tomato, hash browns, eggs, baked beans, fried bread, and even four rounds of toast. And, of course, bloody tea.

John was turning forty.

Chris knew there were plans. Nan and Granddad had been very firm about dinner at theirs, and Fran had come round a few weeks ago to rummage through his stuff. Chris preferred to be left out of the surprises that John's sisters arranged on his birthdays. Then he had the get-out-of-jail-free card of not having the first clue about what was going on.

Chris kept his celebrations on the quieter side. John was shy. It seemed a bit of an odd thing to say about such a giant of a man, but he was really quite shy. He didn't like his birthday because he didn't like being the centre of attention. He'd go wild on Chris's birthday if left to his own devices, but he always tried to sneak his own past without anybody noticing.

And, of course, it never worked.

So Chris opted to let him start a milestone birthday with a smaller sort of celebrating. He fried away, letting Poppy have the odd malformed sausage, and by the time the bacon was just the right level of crispy, heavy footsteps were moving around upstairs.

"Chris!"

"Kitchen!"

Stairs creaked. They paused halfway, then sped up, and Chris laughed as John stopped dead in the doorway with an incredulous, *"Are you frying bread?"*

"Yes, and I'm not touching it once it gets on your plate, so I hope you're hungry."

"You're the best fiancé ever."

Fiancé.

One month.

"I should bloody well hope so."

He wasn't all that hungry himself, so he made a sandwich with spare bacon once the platter had been delivered and then leaned up against the counter to eat it while John decimated his breakfast and answered various birthday texts.

"Do you know what Nora has planned?" John asked. "She told me to make sure I wasn't working today."

"No idea."

"Damn."

"All I got told was we need to be at your nan and granddad's for five."

"That's early. Double damn."

"No demands to go out on the piss with your rugby mates?"

"Nah. Apparently we can pour it into the stag do. I'm getting a bit nervous about that, to be honest. I think Gimli's going to drink himself to death."

"Eh, he survived the World Cup."

"Good point."

Chris polished off the sandwich and dumped the pan in to soak before wandering over to the table. He stopped behind John's chair and pressed a kiss to the back of his head.

"I'm going for a shower," he said. "Put that in the sink when you're done with it, then come and get your birthday present."

"What's my birthday present?" John asked, tipping his back.

Chris smiled and kissed the end of his nose. "It'll be in the shower."

He could almost feel John staring at his arse as he walked out, and why wouldn't he? Chris was only wearing one of John's T-shirts, after all. And John was a bit of an arse man.

Chris had just washed the shampoo out of his hair and was reaching for the shower gel when the bathroom door opened and closed again. The sound of the lock turning over was excitingly loud, and Chris grinned when John said nothing at all. He leaned against the tiles, tipping his head back, and very deliberately spread his legs.

"Coming or going?"

"That depends."

John's voice was impossibly deep. From another man, it might even have sounded threatening. Chris shivered, despite the hot water.

"On?"

"On what a guy like you is doing all alone in here."

Chris bit his lip, and let it go again deliberately slowly.

"I'm not alone," he said. "My boyfriend is downstairs having breakfast."

"Well then—"

The shower door opened.

"—we'd better be quick."

Chris had never had shower sex before. And to be honest, he'd probably not bother again if not for how downright selfish it was. Maybe it was the shower or maybe it was the birthday, but John's usual worship and insistence on getting Chris off first went out the window. And best of all, so did the gentleness. Cold tiles? To hell with it. Not enough room? Tough. John just shut the shower door, grabbed Chris by the knees, and hefted him up the tiles like he was utterly meaningless. He did get a brief finger-fuck with some soap, but after that, all bets were off. In a matter of minutes, Chris was being fucked like it was a one-night stand in a nightclub toilet. No kisses, no endearments, just powerful thrusts that were like being punched from the inside. He couldn't do anything but yell, hang on for dear life, and relax everything between his cervix and his labia.

And holy *fuck*, it was fantastic.

And after, when John had fucked his brains out and shot off inside him, Chris was taken to bed and eaten out until he came twice just on John's mouth.

Then they had one of their more usual screws. Slow, worshipful, and leaving Chris feeling like every inch of him had been doused in pure pleasure then set on fire. He was drunk on the exhaustion and the ecstasy by the time John stiffened and groaned for the second time that morning, and Chris sighed at the hollow emptiness when John slipped out of him in a messy rush.

"Wow," John breathed, cupping his face.

"What?"

"You."

"What about me?" Chris murmured.

He didn't bother to kiss back. John wet his lips gently, then pulled the sheets up and folded Chris over into his arms. Chris snuggled in, utterly unashamed. 'Making love' was never a phrase he was going to accept, but he *had* come around to the idea of snuggling a little bit.

"You're beautiful," John whispered and kissed the top of his head. "That was amazing. *You're* amazing."

"Happy birthday."

"Thank you."

Chris basked. John gently fingered the cum out of him, but it was oddly non-sexual. It simply *was*. A pleasant feeling, but no thrill or excitement. Chris relaxed, let it happen, and hummed with every idle kiss that touched his scalp as John worked.

"We should get up."

"Nah," John drawled.

"Your sisters will want to steal you."

"Tough."

Chris chuckled, stretching his arm over that powerful chest. It rose, and he went with it.

"Four weeks."

Chris smiled.

"I found us a place for our honeymoon."

"Where?"

"Not telling."

Chris huffed. "If you don't tell me, I'll get out of this bed."

Arms locked around his back.

"Go ahead."

"Urgh. Too lazy."

"Called it."

"Dick."

"You've had that."

"And very nicely." Chris brushed a thumb over a nearby nipple, but John was clearly fucked out, too, and there was no real response. "You haven't fucked me like that in more than a year. What set that off?"

"Dunno," John admitted. "Just—I don't know. You were being all sexy and sly, and I—"

He trailed off, but Chris sensed more, and waited. He patiently explored the blurry tattoos that time was slowly erasing from John's skin. Oh, he had no doubt the colours were still there, but the grooves and gouges of fresh ink were easy to see. Old tattoos became steadily more and more invisible to him. He couldn't even remember what they were supposed to be.

"I don't know," John finished finally. "Usually I want to love you. Or make you feel like you're worth the world to me. But that was just pure lust. You looked hot, and I wanted you, and that was it."

Chris squeezed.

"It was amazing," he said.

"Yeah?"

"Yep."

"Maybe I should do it more often, then."

"Oh, *fuck* yes! Yes, please. Literally, whenever you feel like drilling me like that again, go right ahead. I'll even drop my jeans for you on command."

John cracked up laughing. Chris slid off to the side, grinning widely, and was soon buried in chortling boyfriend, all arms and legs and ink.

"Don't get ahead of yourself," John growled, gnawing on his ear. "You're much more beautiful when you're spread out and making those little breathy noises under me."

"I can do those while you plough me."

"Oh, grim. Ploughing? Come on..."

"Drilling me."

"Urgh—"

"It's big enough. How about pounding? Not my word of choice, but—"

"If you don't knock it off, I'll hold you down and make love to you for hours."

"Eurrrrgh..."

Chris lost the word war by being kissed into a daze, and that cleansing touch down below turning dirty and distracting again. He wasn't going to get another fucking, slow or otherwise, because John was a superman in bed, but he was also forty years old.

Chris didn't care. He spread his knees and encouraged that adventurous hand with one of his, and if he couldn't win his word war because there was constantly someone else's tongue in the way, then what did he care?

"Happy birthday," he whispered when he finally could, and earned himself a smile.

"Tell you what. For your birthday, let me catch you in the shower."

"Deal."

THEY WENT UP to Nan and Granddad's for five, as per orders.

John's sisters had never materialised to kidnap him, and it made Chris intensely suspicious. He wasn't the only one either. Turning up at Hathersage to find all three sisters in attendance, plus Raj and the kids, was in itself suspicious. One hundred percent attendance was just...odd. And John's response was entirely predictable.

"What are you lot up to?"

"Never you mind," Nan said. "Come here and give me a hug. Hello, Chris, darling. I've got some new treats for Poppy once you're settled. John, don't stand there like a lout; go and sit down. Dinner's nearly ready."

It was a complete lie. Chris knew the smell of Yorkshire puddings when they were done to perfection, and they weren't yet. They were gearing up for gift giving at the table, and he took his seat with no small amount of trepidation.

"Come on, then," John challenged them. "Out with it."

"You're so impatient," Fran said.

"And you're a dick."

"Naaaaan!"

"Shut it, the pair of you. Here you go, darling."

Chris cocked his head at the quiet. No crinkling of wrapping paper. Nothing being set on the table. The soft ripping sound was of an envelope, and he frowned. Tickets? A card?

"Oh my God—"

John's voice was choked up. Chris frowned, reaching for his arm.

"What did they get you?"

"Jesus Christ—"

"Happy birthday!" the table chorused, and then Chris grimaced as John took his hand and almost broke his fingers with the sudden squeeze.

"Hey!"

"Sorry, sorry."

"What did they get you?"

"Us."

"What?"

"They got us a—how could you guys even afford—"

"Oh, John, for God's sake," Nora said. "We all chipped in and bought you guys a proper honeymoon, Chris."

Chris's jaw sagged.

"We *had* a proper honeymoon," John whispered. "A week by the sea in Brittany. This is—holy hell."

"What is it?"

"It's a cruise," John blurted out. "Two weeks from Portsmouth."

Chris had to cover his mouth. A—

"Seriously?"

"Yeah."

"Holy fuck," he blurted out, then flushed. "Er. Sorry, Nan."

She hmphed at him, but Granddad chuckled hoarsely.

"All-inclusive, down the coast of Spain and Portugal to Gibraltar, two nights in Gibraltar, then back. Holy—"

John's chair scraped and his hand fell away. Chris sat in mute, stunned silence as John presumably delivered hugs around the table. A cruise to Spain and Portugal? Chris had never been farther than Paris. He couldn't fly. He'd never even dreamed of going somewhere like Gibraltar. And a *cruise*? Weren't they insanely expensive? How had they all—

He swallowed his astonishment as John came back and smiled into the kiss planted on his mouth.

"Thank you," John croaked. "All of you. That's—that's the second-best birthday present ever."

"What was—"

"I *don't* think so," Nan interrupted sharply, cutting Fran's rather naïve question off in the middle. She pushed up from the table. "It's time for dinner. Nora, come and help me with the dishes."

Chris relaxed into John's side, taking the email receipt from his hands as if he could read it. He smiled.

"You'll have to get me a Braille version," he murmured, and John laughed. "I won't believe it otherwise."

"I will then. Because one of us needs to believe it, and I sure as shit don't."

A wedding in four weeks, then two weeks in Europe.

That panicky feeling in his stomach was back.

Chapter Twenty-Four

CHRIS SLAMMED THE boot and held out his arms.

"Have a good time," John whispered and hugged him until Chris's back creaked in warning.

"Kiss me," Chris said imperiously.

John laughed but did so. Chris hung on after it broke and nudged his nose against John's, enjoying the powerful rise and fall of John's breathing against his own. As John slowly straightened, Chris's feet drifted up from the drive.

"Have a good evening out with your lout mates," Chris murmured. "Don't worry about anything, all right?"

John's arms shifted around his waist, hoisting him a little higher.

"I'll try."

"There is no try."

"Fine, fine. I'll do my best."

"What's to worry about?" Chris pushed.

The answer, of course, was 'nothing'. If John was right and he turned into a twat when he was drunk, then— big and brutish as he was—he'd be surrounded by thirty-odd other big twats to knock him into line, and Chris would be a hundred miles away getting his arse waxed, or whatever else Gina had signed him up for.

And if Chris was right—

"You'll have a good time," Chris promised and tightened his arms around John's shoulders. "Have fun.

Don't fuss. Call me in the morning when you've stopped throwing up."

"Come on!" Gina shouted from the car.

John chuckled and set him down.

"G'wan," he said and kissed Chris's temple. "Have a good time, and I'll see you when you get back."

"If you need me, ring Gina. I've left my phone in the house."

"Will do."

Thankfully, Luke had won the argument about whose car to take. Chris stretched out in the middle of the back seat, one footwell per leg, and they argued about the radio all the way to the motorway. Then Luke put his foot down, and they shot north.

And Chris had no idea where they were going.

Gina had booked a spa weekend for his stag do. It was better than Chris had hoped. He didn't drink often, and a boozy evening at the pub hadn't been a promising thought. But one last dirty KFC en route to a luxury spa was much more appealing—even if he was curious about how Luke had been talked into going along with it.

It was a fairly long journey, and Chris guessed they came off the motorway just shy of County Durham. Then they dived into the countryside, with hedges scraping the windows and Luke's usual method of driving—at speed— giving way to rocking over bumpy tracks and long-since eroded roads. At least Poppy was enjoying herself. Gina sounded like she was going to be sick.

Then the car swerved violently to the left, and the crash of branches vanished. The tyres surged over smooth gravel and coasted to a gentle stop in the shadow of a building.

"Luke, what colour's your car?" Chris asked as they got out.

"Red."

"And what colour is it now?"

"Piss off."

Chris smirked as he opened the boot and hefted his bag over his shoulder. Thank God he'd folded the cane up and tied it to the bottle netting. He shook it out and explored a little until the boot slammed, and Luke fell into step alongside him.

"C'mon, then."

The spa was in some kind of manor house. Huge stone steps swept up to a lobby with a squeaky marble floor, and meditation music drifted around them like steam. A sunny girl with a broad Geordie accent checked them in, and Chris was ushered into an enormous lift, complete with bellboy. He hadn't realised bellboys were still a thing.

They were sharing a hotel room. Chris had no qualms about bunking down with either of them—hell, they'd gone camping once and had to all squeeze into one sleeping bag after an unfortunate accident involving a cow. But the hotel room was more like a flat, with a living area surrounded by three bedrooms—complete with four-poster double beds—and an enormous wet room.

"Is this the accessible room?" Chris asked as he touched the light cords and found an emergency bell, the distinctive plastic tab knocking against his knuckles.

"Yep."

"I wish they were all like this."

"They've even put down a dog bed for Poppy!" Gina gushed.

"Like she's going to use it," Chris snorted. "She got used to sleeping on our feet when we were in the campervan, and now she whines if I try and make her get down at night."

"Pushover," Gina said.

"Heartless."

There was even a balcony. Chris opened the French doors to step out into the blazing sun. Birds chittered somewhere below, and a piano played faintly. He trailed his hand around the wall, the smell of flowers powerful, until he came across some climbing plant covered in huge, waxy trumpets.

"What's this?"

"Purple," Luke said.

"Helpful. What type of flower, arsehole?"

"How should I know, gay-boy?"

Chris flipped him off, plucked one of the purple trumpets off the vine, and stuck his nose in it. He usually didn't like strong-smelling flowers, but this was nice.

"Gina, take a picture and send it to John. I want some for the garden."

He held out the flower, but the shutter on her phone went off without her coming anywhere near him, and he rolled his eyes.

"Of the *flower*, idiot."

"He'll like this one more."

"Tart."

"Grump."

Chris rolled his eyes, stuck the flower in his hair, and retreated to his bag. He unzipped it and produced his trunks with a flourish.

"Sod the pair of you," he said. "I'm getting changed. Then I'm going to see if anyone around here can do a head massage even half as good as Julian's."

THEY DID.

In fact, by the time Chris had put proper clothes on for dinner at the hotel's terrace restaurant, he felt like he had no bones left in his entire body. Everything was just— mush. Content, placid mush.

He'd worried that the aromatherapy might set off a seizure. He'd fretted about his surgery scars being too obvious. He'd been anxious that some of the treatments might want him naked, which just wasn't going to happen. And every single worry had been smoothed away between the masseuse, the reflexologist, and the constant supply of hot towel presses.

He was going to have to get more into spa treatments. And maybe persuade John to like them too.

Even his usual caution had been sapped away. Normally, Chris would never dream of a mud bath or a steam room, much less a Jacuzzi. He didn't fancy drowning if he had a seizure, or setting one off with the heat. But he succumbed and nearly floated to the restaurant afterwards, wondering if this was how everyone without epilepsy felt all the time.

"I wish," Gina sighed when he voiced the idle thought. "Can we persuade you into one flute of champagne?"

Chris laughed. "Go on, then. Just one."

She whooped.

"A toast," Luke said.

The clink of glasses was satisfying. Champagne really didn't taste very good, but Chris downed it anyway and sat back in his chair.

"So we got you a wedding present," Luke said, and something rustled. "Here. Open it before they pounce with the starters."

He handed over an envelope. It was flimsy rather than a card, so Chris opened it carefully with the edge of his nail—and rolled his eyes when there was just a piece of paper inside.

"Gee," he drawled. "I wonder what that could say."

"It's a ticket," Gina chirped.

"For *what*?"

"For tomorrow," Luke said. "Owl and falconry experience day at a bird of prey centre."

Chris's jaw sagged. "You're shitting me."

"Nope."

He could *hear* the shit-eating grin on Luke's face. He must have been wearing a similar expression because Gina went off into a fit of giggles and rocked into his side to hug him.

"Oh my God," Chris said, beaming from ear to ear.

It was no secret he liked birds, but owls were his absolute favourite. One of his earliest memories was when he was four years old, and Mum and Dad had taken him camping. He'd heard owls hooting in the nearby woods all night and dragged Dad out at three in the morning to go and look for them. Mum was annoyed, but Chris hadn't cared. The trees were full of magical midnight birds, and he wanted to see some.

He didn't, of course, but Dad took him to a bird show for his fifth birthday, and he got to hold a kestrel. Tiny and delicate on the end of his gloved fist. She was the most beautiful thing he'd ever seen, and he hadn't dared to breathe the whole time, terrified she'd vanish.

"We called them up weeks and weeks ago," Gina said. "Obviously, the flying demonstration won't mean much now, but you get to hold some of the birds, and they said they'd do a special handling session with some of them for you, 'cause of how you can't see them in their aviaries."

A lump swelled in his throat.

"Oh shit. C'mere."

He crushed them both up into a hug to avoid making a spectacle of himself by crying. But it was like getting to go back in time right before he got married. He could feel the weight of that little kestrel on his hand again. He'd get to touch an owl. He might not be able to see one again, but he'd never touched one before either.

"You're both fuckers," he mumbled.

"Yeah, yeah." Luke thumped him on the back.

"You deserve it," Gina said, squeezing him tight. "And you deserve this, and the best wedding ever. John doesn't know how lucky he is."

"Nah, he does," Luke interrupted, much to Chris's surprise. "That's why you should marry him. 'Cause he treats you right. Or we'd kill him."

"Oh, good luck," Chris said, letting go with a shaky laugh. "One punch and he'd kill you stone dead."

"He can't throw a punch, though."

"Good point."

Chris put the ticket and envelope down on the table. "Jesus. This is all starting to feel a bit real, now."

"What is?"

"Getting married."

"Hey, you voted for it," Luke drawled.

Chris smirked but didn't reply.

"It'll go great," Gina said. "How can it not? You'll be marrying *John*. That'll be amazing no matter what happens."

Even if he had a seizure that called the whole thing off? Even if he embarrassed himself at the reception? Even if Mum didn't come?

He curled his fingers into the tablecloth and imagined John's wide, rough hand in his own. John's whisky voice reading those mysterious vows. John kissing him in that private room for the first time as his husband.

"Yeah," Chris said, and his grip loosened. "It will be."

Chapter Twenty-Five

"HELLO!" CHRIS SHOUTED as he opened the front door.

Silence.

"Guess John crashed at Slag's for the night," he said.

"Slag's?" Gina asked.

"Steve Slaggern. One of his rugby mates."

"*Slaggern?*"

He told her all the nicknames he knew as he threw his clothes in the washing machine, and Gina separated their respective things from the messy tangle of packing up to leave the spa. They'd taken the longest route back to Sheffield possible, stopping off for lunch in some isolated pub near Wetherby that Luke knew, then spending a couple of hours at a bird of prey centre. The flying demonstration was rather lost on Chris, but he'd got to hold some owls. They were much...fluffier than he'd imagined.

"Are you and John getting dinner, or d'you want to go and get Mexican?" Gina asked once the washer was up and running, and Chris sat back on his heels.

"No idea," he admitted. "We didn't make any plans about afterwards. I'll give him a ring."

He wasn't especially worried. Even without drinking, John sometimes stayed the night with Slag or Gimli after an away match with the team. If so, John usually wouldn't show up until the following evening. Chris found his phone where he'd left it on the side table in their bedroom and sat on the bed as he switched it on.

And was immediately flooded with notifications.

"What the—"

Chris headed for the texts first, starting at the bottom of the list and working his way up. One from Caroline—who always sounded angry by text, though he suspected that was the text-to-speech function on his phone—and a couple of automatic ones about his next doctor's appointment.

Then John.

"Hey, beautiful," the app said. "Hope you have a good time at the spa, and I'll see you tomorrow. Love you."

Chris shrugged, deleted it, and moved on.

"Going to be late home tomorrow. Slag keeps buying me shots. Love you."

He smirked. John hadn't had a drop in years, and Slag had him on shots? He was going to be fragile when he came home.

"Hey I know you're away and you won't get this for a bit but I just wanted to say you're the best thing that ever happened to me and you'd laugh at me and call me a soft git but sod you, you'll have to listen to it now, so yeah."

Chris snorted with laughter. The next one was even better, and he started just—giggling.

"Apparently, we're going to a gay bar. I think it might be a strip joint. Whatever they tell you later is lies."

"Gina!" Chris yelled. "Come and listen to John's drunk texts!"

He pulled up the next one as her footsteps padded up the stairs.

"Yo Chris, it's Rhodri."

Chris raised his eyebrows. Half of the surprise was simply that it was Rhodri. The other half was that he could understand something Rhodri was trying to communicate.

"John's off his fucking tits, so Steve's taking him home. Don't expect him back too soon. Cheers."

Chris laughed. He'd run out of messages, so pulled up his voicemail in the hope of a drunk message and was rewarded by John's absolutely hammered voice. He still had the phone on speaker, and for a split second, it felt like John was in the room.

"*Heeeey*, gorgeous."

"Oh my God," Gina said as she bounced down onto the bed next to him. "How smashed is he?"

"Absolutely wankered." Chris replayed the message, which had been lost under their sniggering.

"—gorgeous. Think I've been texting you. Sorry f'r anything I said unless it was about how amazing y'are in which case—"

He trailed off. Someone shouted in the background. Then Chris and Gina collapsed into laughter when John took a very deep, very loud breath, and *bellowed* his reply.

"Go jump off a fucking bridge, y'wanker!"

It took some time to recover. People were laughing in the background of the message, but it was nothing to the mirth in the bedroom. Gina and Chris ended up tangled together in a giggly hug against the pillows. Chris buried his face in his hands, sniggering helplessly, as Gina took the phone and replayed the message for the third time.

"—wanker! Sorry. Sorry. Not you. Obviously. Slag's being a *bellend*!" John yelled, causing a second eruption of giggles. "Keeps calling me sappy. An' you know what, I am, yeah, an' I don't care, 'cause I've got every reason 'cause I've got you an' you're perfect. Y'are. Y'fucking perfect."

"Aww," Gina cooed.

Chris smiled, dropping his head into her shoulder.

"An' none of them knows what that's like 'cause they're all heartless shits," John finished triumphantly. "I love you. I really, really love you. More'n anything. An' I don't care what anyone else, not *anyone*—you're it. You're th' only one I ever wanted an' I'll tell you e'ry day forever."

"Give it 'ere, you wet fuck!"

There was the sound of a scuffle, and then some extremely drunk voices cheered.

"Oi!" shouted whoever had the phone. "Oi, Chris, you're a fucking saint for 'aving him, and if you fuck 'im up, we'll break your legs, you slag!"

And with that, the message ended. No goodbyes, no more noise, nothing. Gina dropped the phone and curled around Chris's upper body, giggling helplessly.

"Oh my God," she said. "That was amazing. He's going to be so *bad* later!"

"I'm going to be winding him up for the next thousand years," Chris said, grinning.

But under the amusement, he felt warm. Not only had the messages been sweet, but they were proof of what he'd suspected. John's shitty attitude when he was drunk *had* been all about his miserable state of mind. He'd spent his stag do wasted and happy. The last ghost had been laid to rest.

"What's going on in there?" Gina asked softly, prodding Chris in the temple.

He smiled. "Just thinking I'm lucky."

"Yeah?"

"And he *does* swear."

She laughed again, and Chris found the phone to replay it one last time.

THE FRONT DOOR banged, jerking Chris out of his doze.

He blinked muzzily and rubbed a hand over his eyes. He was far too hot, and something was scratching his face. He shook his chin to dislodge it and realised it was Gina's hair.

Huh.

They must have dozed off. Boots were clomping about downstairs, so he slid his shoulder out from under Gina and got up. Poppy pushed against his calves before he reached the bedroom door and followed him downstairs with an eagerness that said loud and clear he was a shitty charge and should be giving her the good treats for waiting so long for dinner.

"Hey," he said when he shuffled into the kitchen. He lifted his arms. "C'mere."

John's jaw felt like being rubbed with some unholy cross between a pumice stone and a power saw. Chris grimaced and retreated hastily, earning himself a croaky laugh.

"Sorry. Slag and his lass share a razor, so I didn't dare touch it."

"Good plan." Chris put down some fresh food for Poppy, then pushed up on his tiptoes for a careful kiss from his suffering boyfriend. He looped his arms around John's neck and swayed gently. "Good night?"

"I think so?"

Chris smirked. "You think?"

"Well—" John dropped out of the hug by collapsing onto the sofa with a groan. The sofa was still their old one from the flat, and it groaned too. Chris grinned and added to the pile by sitting in John's lap, tucking his bare feet under the spare cushion and settling with one arm over John's shoulders. "Hello."

Chris accepted the kiss and the light slap on the arse but then tugged the collar of John's shirt.

"There was a story there. You thought you enjoyed it?"

"I enjoyed what I remember," John replied with a chuckle. "Even when I was an apprentice, I didn't drink that much on a night out. Bit surprised I didn't wake up having my stomach pumped."

Chris wrinkled his nose at the thought.

"We kept losing lads until it was just me, Slag, Gimli, and Rhodri, so we ended up in that old gay club down the bottom of the Moor. I don't really remember much after that. Slag pulled, I think. And a drag queen kept giving me shots, and there was glitter *everywhere* when we woke up at Slag's this morning."

Chris had to admit he wasn't entirely surprised Slag had pulled in a gay bar. Most of John's mates were friendly but a bit awkward about Chris's existence, and Chris didn't particularly want to know what they'd think if they found out he was trans. They were already all about the "no homo" remarks and all that macho bollocks. By contrast, Slag would openly flirt with him and had threatened to steal him more than once. Very technically, Slag had proposed first.

"So he'll be in trouble with his missus?"

John laughed. "Probably, but she pulled the same stunt you did. Didn't fancy dealing with him pissed so took the kids to see their nan for the weekend in Wales."

"Rough morning, was it?"

"Little bit." The hand resting on Chris's bum patted it, and John slid down on the sofa a little. Chris didn't bother to climb off. "How was the spa?"

"Great. You can take me again sometime. And we had lunch today and went to this falconry place. I got to hold owls."

"Owls aren't falcons."

"Bird of prey place, then. Jesus." Chris pinched an earlobe for the sass. "Git. Anyway, thank you for all the texts."

John coughed. "Erm—"

"Do you remember them?"

"Not really," he admitted. "I remember sending you some, but I don't know what I said. I'm guessing by the hug I'm not in the doghouse?"

"Nope. They were very sweet. And you swore."

"I did not."

"You did, I have the voicemail to prove it," Chris retorted. "I'm going to save it and keep it for the next time you tell me off for my bad language."

John groaned.

"Oh, and someone threatened to break my legs if I fuck you up."

"Probably Gimli," John admitted. "I wouldn't worry about it. You could take him."

"I would have said that I shouldn't worry about it because I won't fuck you up, but okay," Chris said, tracing the shell of John's ear with his finger before kissing it. "Gina and I were going to get Mexican before we dozed off. You want in?"

"Jesus, no. Puking guacamole is not my idea of fun."

"You gonna stay home and rest your aching head?" Chris teased.

"Nah, I'll come. I just won't eat anything."

Chris rolled his eyes. That was John's code for not *buying* anything. Chris would have to order a full three-course meal to cover for John stealing off his plate.

"Thanks."

Chris raised his eyebrows. "For what?"

"Pushing me to go. I mean, don't get me wrong, I'm not going to get back into the habit or anything. I'm too bloody old for hangovers now. Felt like I was going to die this morning. But—thanks."

Chris raked a hand over the fluff starting to turn into hair on John's scalp.

"You know you can go for a pint or two with the lads after a rugby match, though," he said. "And have a glass at Sunday dinner with Granddad. I don't really want you going out on binges either, but you don't have to be resolutely teetotal anymore if you don't want."

"To be honest, I will be." John shrugged. "Most of the time, anyway. I didn't miss it much. But—thanks. I like having the option back, even if I'll still not bother more often than not."

"So champagne at the wedding?"

John laughed. "Oh God. I didn't tell you. The lads got me a wedding present."

"Oh?"

"Free bar."

"Holy fuck," Chris said and started laughing.

"Yeah. I told them the venue after we booked it 'cause some of them live out near Barnsley and need to sort out travel and hotels and whathaveyou. And when I got the first round in last night, they told me they'd rung the place up and added a free bar, and they'd foot the bill."

"Christ."

"Most of the bill will be them, mind."

"That's what you think," Chris said. "Dad will get absolutely arseholed so he won't cry. And all his family are boozers. And Luke and Gina will probably decide to split mine between them."

"You going to drink?" John asked.

"Am I heck."

Technically, Chris could drink. The medication he'd been switched onto last year didn't interact badly with alcohol like the previous stuff—but it did stop it from working so well. Ninety-nine percent of the time, a bad day with heavy auras and repeated seizures wasn't worth a night before with alcohol. And the first day of being married didn't make the leftover one percent.

"I'm not risking it," Chris said. "Everyone else can get wasted, and we'll laugh at them."

"Deal," John agreed and clapped a hand down on Chris's thigh. "C'mon. I need watering, and you and Gina must want something to eat by now. Go and wake the tart up."

"I'll tell her you said that," Chris said as he climbed off John's lap and made for the door.

"What if I buy dinner?" John shouted after him, and Chris grinned as he reached the bottom of the stairs.

"I'll still tell her!"

Chapter Twenty-Six

SEPTEMBER ARRIVED WITH a roaring thunderstorm.

In the midst of the woods, it sounded beautiful, and Chris appreciated the outlet for his nervous energy. After all, there was nothing else to take up his attention anymore. Various relatives had started travelling to Derbyshire. The suits had been picked up. The flowers and decorations were all at the inn. Even John's car had been for its service and valet job, and was sitting pretty in the drive, ready to go.

The only thing left to do was wait. And Chris wasn't so good at waiting.

The storm crackled around the house, thunder slamming through the trees like a giant on the prowl, and Chris pulled himself away from the window to find John. Faint flickers outside suggested lightning, but they could have been car headlights or even an incoming seizure for all Chris knew. Poppy followed him to the utility room, tail waving like a flag and bouncing off the doorframe. His first guide dog had been terrified of thunderstorms, but Poppy seemed to like them. Maybe he was just easier to look after when he wasn't going outside in the lashing rain.

"John?" he called, pushing the door open. "You in here?"

"Yeah. Mind your feet; I'm doing the tiles."

The utility room was off the kitchen. John said it was probably a former outhouse, and the cold suggested he was right. It was narrow and permanently freezing. There was no radiator, and a series of large windows were set high in the walls to let the steam and water out. The ceiling was also pretty high, making heating the place impossible, even given how much a dryer alone could throw off. The walls weren't so thick as the main house either, and the thunder clapped deafeningly overhead.

"Mind if I sit here?" Chris asked, sinking down in the doorway.

"Knock yourself out," John replied easily. "Storm got you worked up?"

"Wedding has me worked up."

"Anything in particular?"

"Just nerves now, I think." Chris took off his sock, wound it into a ball, and tossed it for Poppy. "Fetch!"

"Well, everything's done," John commented. "Vows memorised, decorations sent, Mum and Dad en route, rings ready, your appointment with Julian tomorrow morning. You keeping the longer hair?"

Chris fluffed it out. It was chin-length, and he'd started to pull it back with a rubber band occasionally.

"What do you reckon?" he asked.

"I think it's bloody gorgeous."

"Then I'll keep it."

John chuckled. "Oh, I see. A ploy to get my attention, was it?"

"A ploy to get fucked raw on my wedding night, more like."

A snort. "Oh, right, because anything but the longest—"

"If you say lovemaking, I'm calling it off."

John snorted again, but he notably didn't utter the word. Chris smirked as he shook slobber off the sockball and threw it again.

"To be honest, I probably won't be up for it on our wedding night itself," John admitted.

"Oh? Too tired?"

"Too...in awe."

"What?"

Boots creaked. Chris guessed that John had abandoned the tiling and sat back on his heels.

"It's going to take my breath away. You'll have never looked so stunning, and you'll be wearing your happiness on your sleeve. And it's happiness that I've given you. There's still days that I wake up and just lie there in bed next to you, because I still can't believe I'm this lucky. So getting to actually marry you—and you *asking* me to—"

Chris flushed.

"I won't be able to breathe throughout the whole thing, and there's no way I can ever make love to you well enough to live up to a day like that."

For a moment, Chris considered letting the spell woven by John's burning voice linger in the dusty, cold air.

Then he decided to hell with it and called him cheesier than a margarita pizza.

"Oh, shove it." John laughed. "Nearly four years and you'd think you'd learn how to take a compliment."

"Nearly four years, you'd have thought you'd stop trying to chat me up," he retorted, wrestling Poppy for the sockball.

"I have the most amazing, capable, brilliant bloke in the world. Why would I stop trying to chat that up?"

Chris reddened. "You're a sleazy, slimy little charmer," he accused, and John abandoned his laying to crawl across the packed floor and kiss him, bracing his hands either side of Chris's denim-clad hips.

"And you love it," he said.

"You're mocking me."

"Nope." John nosed at the spot where Chris's jaw met his ear. "Someone as stunning as you can't be mocked."

Chris pushed him. He was seized instead. John twisted them and landed Chris flat on his back on the fresh tiles.

"Blue on blue. They bring out your eyes," John mused.

"Yeah? So I'm caught between the devil and the deep blue sea?"

John groaned dramatically and kissed him. Possibly to prevent another bad joke. Chris didn't care.

"I thought you were working," Chris murmured once it broke.

"Taking a break."

"If you keep taking all these breaks, you'll never get anything done."

"I can live with that," John returned, shifting to prop himself up on his elbows, bracing his arms either side of Chris's shoulders.

"What are you up to?" Chris asked, brushing his fingers lightly over John's face. John's skin was rough even on his face. He'd never exfoliated in his life, and he'd not shaved in a while. The beard was impressive, but Chris just stroked it, letting his hands relax. He felt serene here, under John's weight, but buoyed by his good mood, the anxious press of nerves in his stomach easing.

"Just looking," John replied.

"Why? You get plenty of chances to look."

"Mm, not enough," John countered, pushing his curls away with both hands until they all made a bid for the tiles, not one of them twisting back to touch his skin. "I could look at you all day and it wouldn't be enough."

"Now you're being daft."

"Nope, just honest," John retorted. "I saw you in that coffee shop and knew I wanted to spend the rest of my life looking at you."

"You could have just stalked me, you know. It would have been easier. And cheaper."

John chuckled, pushing Chris's face to the side to kiss behind his ear. "One look and I knew."

"You couldn't have."

"I did," John insisted. "One look, and I was done for. That was all it took. I was in love with you from the minute I saw you."

Chris flushed. "You didn't even know me."

"I didn't need to," John countered, tugging on his hair lightly and stroking it out until the curls made looping patterns. "I didn't believe in love at first sight until you, but that's the truth."

"Weirdo."

"Maybe," John allowed, running his lips in a line from Chris's temple to his chin without quite kissing him. "But you didn't see yourself, sat there with your spilled coffee in a shirt that was two sizes too big..."

"You fell in love with a caffeine-addicted mess, then?"

"Oh, I know that."

Chris laughed, tracking his fingers over John's mouth as though touching his words as they escaped.

"Chris? I love you."

Chris smiled widely. "What's gotten you in this funny mood?"

John shrugged.

"You're a strange man sometimes, John Halliday."

John snorted with laughter. "You can't ever just tell me sweet nothings, can you?"

"You wouldn't love me if I was nice to you *all* the time."

"Maybe," John allowed, nudging Chris's cheek with his own, "but you could still try it once in a while."

"Yeah, well, it's not your birthday, don't get cocky."

"You're only going to be nice to me in August?"

"On one day in August, don't get your hopes up," Chris said, but then his face softened again, and he drew a clumsy heart with his fingertip in John's shirt, close to the breastbone. "Love you too."

He was kissed once more. Open and lax, although remarkably chaste. Warm like evening cuddles in bed when John was torn between sex and a hug. Chris relaxed into it and figured he'd go wherever John's mood took them.

"Let me show you how to lay tiles."

Eh?

Chris hadn't been expecting that, and said nothing for a moment, blinking stupidly. He didn't get involved in John's DIY nonsense. Didn't like it, and why bother when he was engaged to an electrician?

"Think I can?"

"Sure. You can feel your way around tiles. C'mon."

The work was slow, and hesitant, and the most pleasant afternoon Chris had wasted in a good couple of weeks. And it felt like wasting time, but in a good way.

They would be married in a few days. So what if the house wasn't perfect? So what if the decorations were lopsided? So what if Mum didn't show?

Chris carefully nudged a tile into perfect place, and figured that none of it—absolutely none of it—mattered.

"WE'RE HERE."

John hadn't said a word for the whole drive. Neither had Chris, really. The nerves were building up again, his stomach a ball of knots, and he was *definitely* going to have a seizure tonight. No two ways about it.

"You okay?"

The car dipped slightly as John put the handbrake on, and Chris let out a wobbly breath.

"Yeah. Just getting nervous now."

"Me too."

Chris smirked. John had been nervous all day. The suits were hanging from the hooks in the back, after three goes at being taken out, checked, and rechecked. The ring boxes were in Chris's first aid kit so they wouldn't accidentally get lost. They had a spare satnav, just in case they took a wrong turn, despite it being an easy route and the invention of smartphones. If Chris felt a bit sick with anxiety, John was probably ready to puke.

"Come on," John coaxed. "Nobody else has arrived yet, so we can take a few minutes."

It turned into a couple of hours, but Chris refused to feel guilty. The building seizure struck as they were unpacking in the honeymoon suite, and he slept it off while John showered and checked the suits for the fourth time. By the time Chris had stablised enough to have his own shower and change, the birds were settling down for the night, and a steady trickle of cars were pulling into the car park below the window.

"Are they here?"

"Can't see out of the window. Skylight job," John replied. "I think I heard Caroline, though."

Chris swallowed as he buttoned his shirt. The last meal before the big day felt more like the Last Supper. His fingers were shaking, and he wasn't surprised when John caught him by the hips and towed him to the bed.

"C'mere..."

Chris kicked up his legs and curled up in John's lap. John slumped back into the pillows so they were tangled in a comfortable cuddle, and Chris took a deep, calming breath. His ear pressed to John's chest, he heard a dull thumping, and when John covered the other ear with the palm of his hand, Chris felt utterly surrounded.

"I love you."

Chris found a wrist and squeezed it.

"Tomorrow will be the second-best day of my life," John whispered.

"What if—"

"No matter what. The only way it won't be is if you refuse to marry me."

Chris laughed.

"Any chance of that happening?"

"No."

"Then it'll be the second-best day of my life," John repeated.

"Thank you."

John kissed the top of his head.

"Hey."

"What?"

"What was the best day?"

John groaned. "I was banned from cheesy lines!"

"It's a cheesy story. I'll make an exception."

"Fine. Jesus."

"Go on…"

John sighed dramatically. "The first day in our flat. That Sunday, when there were just boxes everywhere and you were swearing at the oven because you couldn't figure it out, and we couldn't find the bedding so we ended up cuddling up in that sleeping bag from your camping trip with Luke and Gina, and it was the worst sex we ever had."

Chris laughed. "*That* was the best day?"

"Yeah."

"How?"

"Because it was the day I knew you were the one."

Chris groaned. "*Jeeeeesus.*"

"Hey, I *warned* you about the cheese!" John retorted. "I *told* you, but did you listen? Did you heck."

"Just once can you say fuck? Just once before we get married?"

"No."

"Please?"

"No. I'm classy."

"Like fuck you are…"

It turned into a wrestling match and some banter, and then John won by pinning Chris down by the hands and leaning in to kiss his hair.

"Fu—"

Chris inhaled sharply.

"—dge."

"Oh, you utter cunt."

"Language," John scolded and let go.

"I'll clearly have to use enough for the both of us," Chris retorted and then grinned as he was dragged up into a hug and kissed like they were running out of air. "Mm. Er. You were saying?"

"You feeling better?"

"Uh-huh. Even better if—"

John smacked his hand away from his belt and chuckled. "Later, beautiful. Let's go and have dinner. Everyone will be really excited, neither of us will eat a damn thing, we can come back up here, and I'll make love to my boyfriend one last time."

"Fuck."

"Make love."

"Have sex with."

"Make love."

"Sleep with."

"Make love."

"How about shag?"

He attempted to wring anything but that godawful phrase out of John all the way downstairs, but—as usual—failed utterly. By the time they stepped into the conservatory, turned into a cool and airy dining room in the long summer twilight, Chris's smile felt natural, and the ball of terror in his gut had shrunk to something a bit more manageable. No doubt it would be back soon, but he'd take what he could get.

His family and John's didn't get together often, but a bubbling enthusiasm had broken any ice long before they'd arrived. Dad and John's granddad were well into a bottle of port, swapping literal war stories from their respective services with the armed forces and laughing like drains. Fran and Gina were chattering away nineteen to the dozen about the big day. Even Luke, who could be an antisocial git, was being surprisingly patient and entertaining Suresh. John's mum and dad had arrived from France, and he was treated to a rare hug from his even more rarely seen future mother-in-law.

It was warm. Noisy. *Busy.* The terror eased as Chris was passed around for hugs before being allowed to take his place at the table, surrounded by family irrespective of their actual relationship to him. Then he jumped when someone clinked a glass and cleared their throat.

"Bit of attention, please!"

"Dad?" Chris said and had his knuckles rapped by Lauren. "Ow!"

"Shh. Listen."

The table fell quiet, and a chair scraped as Dad got to his feet.

"I'd just like to say a couple of words," he said.

To Chris's surprise, Dad's voice was clear and sober. He usually didn't want to toast jack shit unless he was three sheets to the wind. Chris curled his fingers around the stem of his lemonade-filled wine glass and waited with trepidation.

"Last night, John rang me up and asked me a question."

Chris cocked his head. John's hand came to rest on Chris's wrist, but there was no hint in the easy touch.

"He asked to take Chris's last name."

The breath stopped in Chris's lungs. He froze solid, from head to toe, and for a wild second wondered if he hadn't seized out of nowhere. But then the warmth flooded outwards from his stomach, like sinking into a hot bath, and stunned tears prickled at the backs of his eyes.

"I didn't answer him. I said to do what he wants. But I'm answering him now."

John's fingers tightened minutely on Chris's wrist.

"I'm proud of my son," Dad said. "I'm proud of who he is, who he's become, and who he's going to be. He's gone out into the world and found himself a home, a family, and a life. He doesn't need me anymore, and I'm proud of him for it. And John, you've been part and parcel of Chris's life for the last four years. And I'm right proud of how you've done that too."

Chris ducked his chin into his chest, swallowing against the scratchy lump in his throat. A single tear escaped, and he scrubbed it away hastily. He wasn't going to cry. *He wasn't going to cry.*

"I stand by what I said last night—do what you want. But I'm proud of my son and my son-in-law. You're part of the family, and I'd be honoured if you had our name."

John was bawling. Chris could hear it in the way he sniffed and the hoarse rasp of his thanks. The table jumped as his knee hit it, but he stood to shake Dad's hand with a noisy clap of connecting palms in mid-air.

"A toast, if you don't mind, ladies and gents. To family—"

"To family!"

"—and to John and Christian Bannerman."

Chris lifted his glass for the second one but barely heard the reply, his mind buzzing. *John Bannerman. John Bannerman. John and Christian Bannerman.* He'd laughingly refused to change his surname, but he'd never thought John would do it instead. Yet here he was, adhering to one final daft tradition.

Chris tugged on his wrist. John laughed wetly and kissed him as if they were just married, not having dinner the night before.

"You're a tit," Chris whispered.

"Yeah, well, you're stuck with me."

"Not yet. Don't get cocky."

The second laugh was less shaky. Chris tucked one of those massive arms around his own waist and settled into John's shoulder.

"Is everything sorted for tomorrow, then?" Lauren asked as the starters were served. Tomato soup had never smelled so good, yet Chris was disinclined to move.

"Yep," John replied.

Chris chewed on the corner of his lip. Nope. Oh, they'd done all the confirmation calls with the various firms. The band had dropped off their kit already. The suits were hanging up. The flowers were scheduled to arrive first thing in the morning. Julian had texted saying he'd arrive at nine to start the pampering session. The one seizure had already been and gone, and there were no threatening auras lurking around the edges of the world.

But—

"Phone."

Chris jumped as John rolled the shoulder under his ear.

"What?"

"Your mobile's ringing."

"Oh. Oh, shit—"

He got up from the table, fumbling with his pocket. John rescued the chair before it could crash over, and Chris ducked into the main section of the pub with the demanding phone—which immediately stopped.

"Oh, for fuck's—"

"Hello."

The voice came from mere feet away. He jumped violently, and then his brain caught up with instincts, and his heart leapt.

"Mum."

"I didn't want to just interrupt," she said.

His heart was in his throat and climbing higher. He stuttered out a couple of random letters. She'd thrown him. Utterly thrown him. He stood like a blithering idiot in the middle of the pub and couldn't form a single word.

"I hope I'm not too late for dinner."

He heard the tiny pause before the last two words. He felt the hesitation in the soft touch of her fingers on his forearm. A faint, almost imperceptible tremor in her palm.

Chris closed the gap and enveloped her in a hug.

She smelled of her posh perfume and a hint of hairspray. Her curls were delicate and stiff against his cheek. She was wearing short heels and her expensive department store coat. He felt the cool metal of a drop earring against his cheek and the faint powder of carefully applied makeup.

"You're not too late."

She gripped back, her hands tiny against his crisp shirt. For a moment, he just clung to her. She'd come. She'd finally come.

It felt like she'd come *home*.

"I'm sorry."

"What?"

"I'm sorry," she repeated softly. "I never meant to make you feel like you weren't enough, or that John wasn't."

"I—"

"I love you, and you're so happy with John and so much better, but all I could see was him feeling the relief I felt when Jack passed away. But you were right. I'm relieved because I didn't want to see him suffering, and I stayed even when I didn't want to see him go through it.

If it comes to it, John would do the same for you. He'd stay. He loves you just as much as Jack and I."

Chris squeezed her arms.

"Thank you. Come and sit down with us. Did you book a room?"

"Oh, in Bakewell. It's only fifteen minutes away. I'll—"

"You'll come and have dinner with us," Chris said. "There's always room for my mum."

It was exactly what he wanted. What he needed. No huge dramatic apology, or some grovelling, begging, or even another tense argument to clear the air. He wanted a hug. He wanted her to just be Mum again. To put on her best dress and her fancy earrings for the pre-wedding dinner. To wear one of those horrible wedding hats and squeeze herself into some crushed velvet suit in a lurid colour that was two sizes too small, because that was what mothers of grooms all over the country were supposed to do. To fuss over everything in the morning, then sit and bawl during the actual event. He just wanted her to show up and be happy for him.

They could argue more when it was all over, but right now—

Chris hooked her arm into the crook of his elbow and drew her into the conservatory. For a split second, he sensed a quiet from his own family, but John's—either unaware of the tension or uncaring—noisily welcomed her, rustled another chair from somewhere, and summoned the waitress back. The happy bustle and her mere presence soothed Chris's fears, and he sank into his chair without a trace of nerves.

"Better?" John whispered under the pretence of kissing his cheek.

"Better."

Chapter Twenty-Seven

KNUCKLES BANGED ON the door, and Chris turned as it opened.

"Ready?"

He spread his arms. "How do I look?"

"Like you're about to get married," Dad said gruffly—then to Chris's surprise, he closed the door.

"Dad?"

"C'mere, kid."

The hug was suffocatingly hard, and the thump on the back made Chris cough. Released only to be gripped by the shoulders, he had the distinct impression he was being looked up and down.

"You'll do."

"Thanks."

"Got your ring?"

"Yep."

"Got your vows memorised?"

"Yep."

"What's the happiest moment of your life?"

Chris blinked. "I—what?"

"What's the happiest moment of your life?" Dad repeated.

Chris opened his mouth, about to say, "About ten minutes in front of me." Then he closed it again. And thought.

"John's thirty-ninth birthday," he said.

They'd had a weekend at the beach in Cornwall. It was hot and windy, and they'd gone wading in the surf. Some lonely little cove John knew about. It took Chris and Poppy half an hour to get down the cliff to the sand, then thirty seconds to get in the water. The sea was cold, and Chris laughed at some bad joke John had told, and then—

John had just taken him by the waist and kissed him. Out of nowhere, in the middle of some terrible banter, he'd stopped and kissed Chris as though Chris were the entire universe. Chris had dissolved in his arms, then and there. He'd hung on and kissed back as if nothing else in the world existed but them in their cove, Poppy chasing waves, and Chris being kissed as though he was the sun in someone else's universe. As though there would never be anything else, and as though it was plenty enough for the both of them.

"It was the perfect moment," Chris murmured. "No planning. No pretences. Just the way he kissed me. Like he didn't even mean to, it was just the best way to express himself in that second."

After the kiss had broken, he'd slung Chris over his shoulder and dumped him in the sand, and Chris had kicked him and called him a bastard before they'd wrestled for a while like bloody idiots. The kiss was gone as quickly as it had appeared, yet Chris had always remembered it.

"It was like after all that time, he still looked at me like I was the most amazing thing he'd ever seen."

Like he still did. And like Chris did sometimes, when he just paused in the middle of what he was doing to rediscover the way John made a mug of tea, the way he kissed the crown of Chris's head in passing, the way he cuddled when he slept, the way he huffed and refused to swear no matter what Chris tried, the way he laughed at Chris's shitty jokes, the way he *was*.

Dad squeezed his shoulders and said, "Good."

"W-what?"

"Weddings are artificial. Your happiest moment with someone should always be something natural. Spontaneous. A moment when you knew how much you loved them without having to dress up and say some bloody promises to prove it."

Chris nodded.

"That said, this is your day. And I couldn't be prouder."

"D-Dad—"

"Can it, kid. He's a good man. So are you. And there's nothing you can do to make me stop supporting you, but I'd back this bet even without that. You've been better since you met him, and he's not the nervous lad your stepmother conned into coming round to meet us that first time."

Chris coughed a weak laugh. "He's still not forgiven her for that."

"Neither have I, bloody woman," Dad grumbled. His hands dropped. One briefly returned to clap Chris on the shoulder. "I'm proud of the pair of you. And I'm honoured that I get to hear those vows today."

Chris reached out.

He hadn't really hugged his father in years. Mum hugged. Caroline and Lauren hugged. But Dad was more hands off. Stiff upper lip, be a man type. Chris had only been hugged by his father a handful of times since he'd come out. As a daughter, he'd been hugged almost daily; as a son, he was the recipient of back thumps and handshakes.

But he reached, and the returning grip was hard and solid like he'd known it would be.

"Thank you," he croaked.

"Knock it off, you little shit," Dad grumbled. "Can't go bawling before you even get there. C'mon. Let's get you married off so I can have a bloody beer and call this fatherhood lark a day, huh?"

Chris coughed a wet laugh, scrubbed at his face, and nodded at the door.

"Go on then," he said. "Time to give me away."

Dad did lead him. He did rest a hand in the crook of his father's elbow. Poppy padded along peacefully at his side, and they descended the stairs into the silent corridor in unison. Chris heard the gentle intake of breath as they passed into the private room, then Dad stepped aside, and John's presence loomed in his place.

Chris slid his fingers through John's and squeezed.

"Shall we?" the registrar asked.

"Yes."

Chris could hear the smile in John's voice. He could hear the soft clink of medals both behind him and in front as his ex-Marine father and his ex-RAF soon-to-be grandfather-in-law breathed. The reverent hush was oddly peaceful, rather than stressful as he'd feared. The rest of the world clamoured outside, but it died away as the registrar began to speak.

"There is little need for me to carry on," she said in her soft, amused voice. "It is plain as day the love that is shared between you. So let us simply begin."

Chris didn't hear the rest of her little speech at all. He squeezed John's fingers in his own as Dad and Granddad stated their names as witnesses to the marriage and their support for it. He touched the titanium ring lightly as the registrar said a brief prayer—John's one concession to Nan and Granddad's beliefs—and took a deep breath as the moment came when he'd start crying.

"I believe the happy couple have written their own vows. Christian, would you like to begin?"

He wasn't much of a writer. He didn't like to talk about his feelings much. He hid behind humour and touch, trusting John would understand what he couldn't quite say. But the vows were different. He'd spent weeks and weeks working on them, all on his own and in complete secrecy. And if they weren't poetry, so what? They were his. They were what he needed John to know.

"John."

The hands in his own tightened.

"Almost four years ago, you threw a coffee in my lap."

John coughed a hoarse laugh.

"That was the best coffee I never drank. You came into my life out of nowhere, and you said you loved me from the start. You were shy and infatuated, and I was doubtful and a little bit distant. I didn't believe in anything but passion at first sight, but you were convinced. So I guess you win."

John laughed softly, the sound thick and creaking. He was going to cry. Chris knew it.

"Now here we are. And after almost four years, you still take my breath away when you kiss me. You still make my heart flutter when you laugh. You'll still be talking about nothing at all, and I'll pause in the middle of my thoughts and be hit with just how much I love you, like it's the very first time. You can still do that to me, and you don't even know you're doing it."

He swallowed as he heard a deep sniffle. John had started bawling, and if Chris didn't hurry up, he'd be next.

"I could make a thousand promises, but there's only one that really matters when everything's said and done. I promise to be there. For your greatest accomplishments and your worst failures. For your boring days and your wild adventures. For the moment you need to be brought back into line, and the days you need to be pushed out of your comfort zone. Whether you're fine or not, whether you need me or you don't—I will be there. Forever."

His heart leapt as he made it to the end of his little speech without crying or cracking, and he took a deep breath. His lungs shook, but he made it.

And lost it when John's deep, whisky voice breathed into the room.

"Christian Bannerman, you are the greatest man I've ever known."

Chris laughed, and a rogue tear escaped.

"I was a mess when I met you. I was scared of what we could be. I had been convinced that I was somebody I'm not. And you took my hand. You helped me find the path when I was lost in the dark, and you've walked beside me all this time."

John's hands shifted around his own, until Chris's lay atop John's open palms, resting rather than holding on.

"You are the sun. All the warmth and light in my life comes from you. I know exactly how I felt the day I fell in love with you, because it never left me. I don't have to remember, because it's right here. And the most incredible part is that *you don't need me*. You never have. You were a force to be reckoned with before I ever spilled your coffee, and you still fight your battles just fine without my interference."

His thumbs circled Chris's wrists. His fingers curled closed. Chris's hands were encased and held once more, and the gentle grip was the softest squeeze in the world.

"I love you. With every part of my heart and soul, I love you. And I promise to tell you. To never let you forget. To never let you doubt it. To remind you, from this day until your last, that you are utterly, completely, eternally loved."

Chris's lip wobbled dangerously.

"Can we hurry this up? Because I want a kiss now," he whispered, and a soft ripple of damp laughter swept through the little room.

"We certainly can," the registrar said gently. "Do you have the rings?"

It felt like moving through water. The cool metal in his fingers. The weight of Jack's scratched ring, with the inscription that they'd added in his memory. *No matter what happens, love remains.* The loud noise of Granddad blowing his nose like a foghorn as their adorned hands gripped each other once more and they recited the proper words. They felt thick and foreign on Chris's tongue, as though he was just going through the motions until the right moment arrived.

Then the registrar said, "I now pronounce you—" and everything vanished but John's neck against his palms and the kiss that tasted of spearmint and coffee. Strong hands caught him by the waist. Dad's laugh sounded somewhere, far away and insignificant. John's smile twisted their kiss into a messy, happy thing that probably looked ridiculous but felt perfect.

They weren't married when Chris kissed him.

But they were when it broke.

About the Author

Matthew J. Metzger is an ace, trans author posing as a functional human being in the wilds of Yorkshire, England. Although mainly a writer of contemporary, working-class romance, he also strays into fantasy when the mood strikes. Whatever the genre, the focus is inevitably on queer characters and their relationships, be they familial, platonic, sexual, or romantic.

When not crunching numbers at his day job, or writing books by night, Matthew can be found tweeting from the gym, being used as a pillow by his cat, or trying to keep his website in some semblance of order.

Email: mattmetzger@hotmail.co.uk

Facebook: www.facebook.com/mattjmetzger

Twitter: @MatthewJMetzger

Website: www.matthewjmetzger.com

Other books by this author

Walking on Water

Big Man

Bump

Tea (A Cup of John, book 1)

Coming Soon from
Matthew J. Metzger

Like the First Moon Landing

Excerpt

Pain.

It was the first thing Maggie knew. A dull throbbing, starting in the fat weight of her brain at the base of her skull, and rippling outwards like stones into still water. There was a stabbing sensation in her shoulder, and when she opened up her lungs to breathe, they spasmed and she choked.

Everything *hurt*.

But pain was good, as Ma used to say. Pain was proof of life.

"You and me, we're like the first moon landing."

Gradually, Maggie ran through the rest of Ma's wisdom. She flexed her toes in her boots. Fingers in her gloves. Gingerly tensed her neck, and roll—

She stopped dead at the wave of intense nausea and took a moment to just breathe through her nose. Don't be sick. Don't be sick. When her stomach eased from a violent jerking to a slow, sinister churn, she carefully eased her hips and chest over, perfectly in line with each other, and eased into a recovery position on the metal grating.

The grating.

Urgh, no wonder she hurt. She'd been in the pilot's seat when the asteroid—or whatever it was—hit. And belted in too.

"You'll touch down to feel a little rough ground..."

Her lungs still didn't want to breathe. The band around her diaphragm was only getting tighter. There was nothing else for it—she needed the drugs. And her medical kit was in the top drawer under the console, so she'd have to get up. Sooner rather than later.

Maggie reached up with her left arm. It was like moving through water or sludge, her body almost drunk on the chaos of clamouring nerves all bidding for her attention first. She didn't dare open her eyes just yet, so groped blindly above her head. She found the bunk frame. Hell. She'd been thrown from the pilot's chair to the gap under the bunk, and she was still alive to know it. Suddenly, the pain didn't seem so bad. Better than a broken neck.

"Pain is proof of life," she grunted to herself and turned her boots towards the wall. Braced her feet there and swallowed against the vomit rising up through her chest and neck. "Pain. Proof."

She pushed.

The sound of her body sliding out from under the bunk was like a landslide off Mount Olympus. The nausea won out, and Maggie shoved herself up on shaking hands just in time to throw up a gutful of stringy, pink-tinged bile onto the grating. Her stomach punched into her diaphragm like a living thing, furious and intent on revenge, and her head burst like a firework.

"—I'm...here..."

The next thing she knew, the smell of sick was in her hair and nose, and a damp patch covered her cheek.

"Fuck," Maggie hissed and pushed herself up from the pool.

The blackout must have been for a little while. The pain was worse, but the sick was cold and the fog in her head had eased a little. She could think better. And breathe better too—mostly.

"Get it together," she told herself and cracked open her eyes.

Blissful, soothing darkness. The emergency lighting was a low blur of soft blue, almost comforting, like a hot water bottle on cold winter nights. Painfully, Maggie heaved herself up on quivering limbs and sat down on the bunk with a thump. It jarred, a shock of pain bouncing up her spine, and she leaned forward, opening her mouth, and spat another mouthful of pink vomit onto the floor between her boots.

"And you're out looking for worlds unseen."

First things first.

She was injured. That much was obvious. But no broken limbs or ribs. There might be an internal bleed in her stomach, but there wasn't anything Maggie could do about it. Her head throbbed, though. Gingerly, she reached up and patted down her hair. She'd shaved her head when she'd gotten her first shutter job, and never grown it out to more than an inch or two of tight, springy curls since. Which made it easy to find the savage cut, the knotted wad of wet hair keeping a lid on it, and the near-dry fountain of blood that had gushed down the back of her neck and shoulders.

"Great," she muttered, but at least it explained the pain. Her skull felt intact. Lucky, if she'd met the wall head first.

Her neck was stiffening rapidly. Whiplash. A starburst of pain kept reappearing in her shoulder joint—she'd probably briefly dislocated it when the belt snapped and flung her across the cockpit. Even if she couldn't see it, the violent bruising all down her right side made itself known. But just bruises. A bit of bleeding. Nothing that wouldn't fix itself, given enough time.

All in all, she'd live. Probably.

"You and me, we're like the first moon landing."

So, onto the second point. Would her ship live?

Maggie was a shutter. The space equivalent to long-haul truck drivers. She piloted single-crewed transport and haulage ships between stations and colonies, on the move for weeks at a time. But the antisocial lifestyle at least attracted good pay, especially for someone without the proper papers like Maggie. She only had a B license, so she wasn't qualified to land on moons and planets yet, but she'd done her theory and was booked in for her tests on Barrane when she got back from this run. It all added up to a lonely but very well-paid job—and lonely and well-paid was just what Maggie had wanted when she applied in the first place.

But lonely in space could be fatal.

Especially lonely in space on a shortcut.

If the ship was damaged beyond her ability to repair, or she couldn't get back to the proper trade route, then she would die out here. The delivery wasn't due for another two months. And she'd been taking a shortcut through uncharted territory to make it on time after having to replace two of the solar batteries at Barrane. One more late delivery, and Maggie was fired. And she was a good pilot. She'd been flying for years on her own without any incidents at all. She could handle a measly shortcut, right?

Apparently not.

Right now, going on the credit seemed like a much better idea than this stupid shortcut. Maggie had been regretting it from that first crackling comms call.

"You'll touch down to feel a little rough ground..."

She squinted across the cockpit at her pilot's chair. The top half of the belt was still attached, the bottom half missing. The chair was crooked, but still upright. All the lights on the console flashed in random patterns, and the viewscreen was out. The comms system blinked, waiting for her reply.

Most insultingly, the fluffy dice that Sam had bought her as a joke when she'd gotten her license were gone.

"Fix it," Maggie told herself. "Fix it, then find the dice."

She lurched up from the bed.

The grating spun beneath her. The cockpit was barely ten feet of space between bunk and chair, but she fell most of it. She caught at the chair with both hands, and her knees collapsed as the whiplash reminded her that falling, in any way, was an intolerably bad idea.

When she managed to open her eyes again, a red mist clouded her vision and iron tainted her tongue. Her chest was getting tighter, and the black spots of panic and oxygen deprivation clustered around the edges of her eyes.

The drawer was right there.

"...but I'm right here where I've always been..."

She dropped into the chair just as her fingers closed around the plastic tube on top of her medical kit, and that first spray in her mouth and throat tasted like foul ambrosia. At the second, she aspirated it properly, and her chest began to open up again.

"...and you're out looking for—"

With a smirk, Maggie cancelled the stereo. The silence swept in, as soothing as the low light. Trust that damn stereo to keep playing even through—whatever that had been.

She took another hit off the inhaler and set it on top of the console. The burst blood vessel in her eyes made the lights appear blurry and pinked. Maggie was grateful she'd paid extra to do the disaster simulations when she'd gotten her license. The transport companies didn't give a shit if the pilots died—if the cargo was damaged or lost, who cared about the pilot too stupid to do their damn job? But Maggie had wanted to give herself a shot at living, back then. She had a plan.

The plan had fallen by the wayside some time ago, but at least the simulations were about to pay off.

Maggie wasn't a navigator or an engineer. Transport ships were fitted with the most basic of navigational computers, amounting to little more than the devices in a personal car, and trade routes were long series of beacons. The computers kept the ships following the right beacons. That was all they were designed to do.

Follow the lights, Sam had always said. Just follow the lights, and they'll take you home.

But Maggie had been running late. And the lights had taken her in a great curve around this section of space. Why not go through it, she'd thought. Calculate the line between the two ends of the curve that cupped this territory, and keep the ship flying straight. Any idiot could do it, and it would shave five weeks off the trip

"Should have just followed the fucking lights," Maggie muttered.

She couldn't tell exactly what had happened. Out of the endless silence, her comms channel had come to life. A tinny voice had said something, maybe several somethings, and then gone quiet. It had happened again, and then again.

And then—

It had felt like an asteroid had hit her, but that would have completely destroyed the ship. Even a sideswipe from a passing object would have ripped the cargo from its holdings and breached the hull. But if Maggie was breathing, the hull wasn't breached.

Had something fired on her? She'd never been in a war, but she'd done plenty of military simulations in her time. It had felt a little like those. A heavy punch to the ship and system-wide destruction, but no loss of hull integrity.

But what was out here to attack her?

Nothing, that was what. A big fat nothing. No moons, no planets, no passing military vessels. Just...deep space. Nobody's territory. She'd crossed nobody's border. There was nothing here to attack her—yet it was the only thing Maggie could think of.

"Right," she muttered. "Right. Okay. Whatever."

Whatever. Whatever had happened didn't matter. She needed to find her bearings and get back to the trade route. She could figure out what had hit her, attacked her, exploded, whatever, once she was safe.

The navigation sensors were fried and telling her nothing. The black box tried to respond, but the readers were bust. The atmospheric sensors in the hold promised a quick and painless death if she left the cockpit without a mask. The engines were out, only two thrusters running on batteries, and the fuel pressure seemed abnormally low. She'd sprung a leak.

Holding her head in her hands, Maggie realised the awful truth.

The only thing still working was the hull. There had been no hull breach, and that was the only reason she was still alive.

Everything she needed to *stay* alive? The oxygen recyclers, the engines, sufficient fuel to get back to the trade route, the navigation computers needed to avoid another hit that would finish her off? All gone. The only electrical systems were running off the emergency batteries, which weren't designed to last long. If she'd been attacked, maybe that was why she hadn't been destroyed. From the outside looking in, the ship was gone. She was floating in a husk, in deep space, and alone.

For a brief moment, despair eclipsed her. Why not just open the cockpit airlock and walk out into the toxic air fouling her cargo hold? Hell, why not open the external airlocks and let the vacuum of space crumple her and her ship like snotty tissues in a fevered fist? There was no way out. She didn't have the skills, the knowledge, or the equipment, to make any of these lights stop flashing. She was dead.

Slowly, Maggie drew her boot back—and savagely kicked the console.

A crackle of new pain, hot and indignant, flashed up her foot.

"Get it together," she told herself and turned the stereo back on. She skipped past *Moon Landing* and settled on Rixi's less popular, but far better song, *Get A Move On*. Maggie wasn't some damsel in distress. Nobody was going to ride in on a white horse to save her. She needed to save herself, or die trying.

Also Available from NineStar Press

Connect with NineStar Press

www.ninestarpress.com

www.facebook.com/ninestarpress

www.facebook.com/groups/NineStarNiche

www.twitter.com/ninestarpress

www.tumblr.com/blog/ninestarpress

9 781951 057275